Also by Micheal Maxwell

Cole Sage Mysteries
Diamonds and Cole
Cellar of Cole
Helix of Cole
Cole Dust
Cole Shoot
Cole Fire
Heart of Cole
Cole Mine
Soul of Cole
Cole Cuts

Logan Connor Thrillers
Clean Cut Kid
East of the Jordan

Adam Dupree Mysteries
Dupree's Rebirth
Dupree's Reward
Dupree's Resolve

Flynt and Steele Mysteries (Written with Warren Keith)
Dead Beat
Dead Duck
Dead on Arrival
Dead Hand
Dead Ringer

Copyright © 2020 by Micheal Maxwell

All rights reserved. No part of this book may be reproduced in any form or by any means, electronic or mechanical, including photocopying, recording, or by any information storage and retrieval system, without permission in writing from the publisher.

ISBN: 9781099763311

HEART OF COLE

MICHEAL MAXWELL

"If what I live for and value most dies when I do, then I've wasted my life."

Chapter One

"All my friends are dead or have moved away," the old lady said mournfully into her flip phone.

There were only a scattering of people in the park. A man in a pale green warm-up suit was walking a dachshund that insisted on stopping at every tree for a sniff. The old lady frowned as the dog relieved himself against a Poplar.

"I know Atlanta's a long way from San Francisco."

The bench down the walk was occupied by a sleeping homeless man, wrapped, mummy-like, in black plastic garbage bags. His gravely snoring was punctuated by gasps and sputters.

"It has been nearly three years, sweetheart."

Since the old lady arrived in the park, only the occasional bicyclist interrupted the otherwise slow pastoral setting. This was her park. Every morning and sometimes afternoon, she strolled the narrow walkways. It was her habit for over sixty years. As a young woman, she brought her children to run and play. For two brief years, she brought her granddaughter to the park while her daughter finished her graduate degree at the University of San Francisco.

"I know, I know, soccer, ballet, I know. If it's important to her, I know, your yoga classes help pay the bills."

Over the years, she saw the park's landscape change. Trees that were old friends, grew sick or tired and broken and were removed. The carefree dancing, singing, hippies of the sixties were replaced by the junkies of the seventies. The emptiness of the eighties brought the death of her husband, her children moving to the far corners of America, and a lot of the people she knew moved to the Central Valley. During the nineties, a flood of "people of color", as they liked to be called, invaded her park. They too have grown old like her, and like her, their children disappeared in the new millennium.

"No, my," the old lady paused, "my money is tied up in CDs, and it is all I have to pay my bills. Social Security is nice, but things are expensive here."

As she approached her eighty-second birthday, she ached for the days gone by. Sometimes she would look across the grass and see her children running, chasing a ball, or making bubbles with dish soap and plastic hoops—a good life. Now, it seemed a slowly repeating cycle of morning coffee, dressing, not remembering what she wore the day before, walking to the park, soup and half a sandwich for lunch, a nap, the five o'clock news, toast and a bit of jam and a hot cup of cocoa in the evening, an old movie on TV, waking to find the movie over, and going to bed, only to repeat the process the next day.

"What if I came to Atlanta? Are things cheaper there? No, I know you don't have room for me, I know your house only has five bedrooms."

The weekly call from her son in Atlanta was more drudgery than pleasure. She tired quickly of his litany of complaints about his, job, wife and kids. Too little money, too much work, too many demands, and she rarely got a word in. *Perhaps she coddled him*, she wonders. *At least he calls. Something his sister hasn't done in two years.*

"Uh huh," the old woman responded but no longer listening.

Across the park, a black dog attempted to join the dachshund, but was met with snarls and barks from the dachshund, and a series of yelling curses from the dog's owner. The old woman was so distracted by the dogs she didn't notice the person who approached the bench.

"Mind if I sit down?"

The old lady smiled and motioned to the stranger to be seated on her right. She wasn't afraid of people; she loved to talk. The bum in the plastic ensemble, on the other hand, should have been shooed away.

"Alright, I've got to run, too." The old woman snapped her phone shut.

"I haven't seen one of those in a while," the visitor said, pointing at the flip phone.

"I take a lot of ribbing about it." The old woman held up the phone. "But if it ain't broke…"

"…why fix it." Her guest finished her sentence.

The two strangers sat on the bench and watched the man with the dachshund leave the park. No words were exchanged for a long time; they just sat in the morning sun.

The silence was broken when the stranger spoke. "What's your greatest regret?"

The old woman turned and looked at the stranger for a long moment. "Having children. Shocking thing for a mother to say, isn't it? But, I must have done something wrong somewhere. They turned out totally self-absorbed, selfish shits." The old woman chuckled.

"I've heard that before. So what's your greatest joy?" the visitor asked.

"You're a funny one," she said. "Let's see. I would have to say marrying my husband. We had a wonderful life. He's been gone almost forty years now and I still miss him. It hurts like a toothache in my soul."

The new friend looked at the old woman for a long moment, and then asked, "Are you a religious woman?"

"I like to think I know where I'm going when I die."

"So…you're ready to go?"

"You know the old story about the bus to heaven?" The old woman smiled with the anticipation of telling a story to a good listener.

"No, I don't think so."

"I'm not really good with stories but, a preacher once gave a rousing sermon and as he closed, he said with real dramatic flair, 'The bus to heaven is waiting at the front door!' But, nobody went to get on."

"I don't get it." The stranger frowned.

"Nobody is really ever ready to die, are they?"

"I guess not."

"So, what is *your* greatest regret?" the old lady said cheerfully, fully enjoying the conversation.

"That you have to die."

At that moment the stranger's left arm flew across at the old woman. A faint flash of metal glimmered a second before an ice pick was driven deep into her heart.

The old woman's last act on earth was a disgusted humph, and a sneer. Her chin went down and gently rested on her chest. The stranger withdrew the five-inch spike and wiped the small amount of blood on the old woman's coat, where it covered her thin thigh.

"I guess you missed the bus," the stranger said.

The stranger reached the sidewalk that ran in front of the park and turned to look back to where the old woman sat. The late morning sun cast a broad swath of light on the bench. The old woman looked as if she were napping in the warmth of the light.

The stranger's blank stare showed no emotion, no sign of satisfaction, no remorse, or conscience at all. The park was the same idyllic scene; there was just one less soul inhabiting it.

Across town in Golden Gate Park, the sun was just as bright, but the atmosphere was completely different. Families picnicked, kids played, lovers strolled, and bicyclist of all styles cruised in the sunshine. The air was clean and the magic that was San Francisco was in full display.

"What a beautiful day."

"What a beautiful girl." Cole Sage replied rolling on his side to face Kelly Mitchell.

A few yards away, their granddaughter Jenny did somersaults down a small grassy knoll. She surrounded herself with a group of children that looked like the cover of a UN pamphlet. Cole watched as Jenny showed and coaxed the other kids into rolling and tumbling down the hill. How could a seven-year-old have leadership skills? He thought. She must get it from her grandmothers.

"Those chocolate chip cookies taste like more."

"Too bad you already ate the last one!"

"Really?"

"About a half hour ago."

"You should have told me."

"Why?"

"So I wouldn't live in anticipation of having another."

"Poor baby," Kelly sympathized.

"You know, we have a pretty wonderful life. I feel such peace. It is all because of you."

"That's sweet, but I think it is the life we have been given. We are so blessed that Erin and Ben found each other. Then *we* found each other. It is pretty amazing when you map it all out."

"Kind of like that old song. Up from the ashes, up from the ashes, grow the roses of success!" Cole sang.

Cole rolled back and looked up at a big polar bear of a white cloud crawling slowly across the sky. So many things in their life could have gone so wrong. Tragedy was averted time and again. Kelly's houseboat burning, Cole being thrown into harm's way too many times—they truly were blessed. Because here they lay, in the soothing spring sun, on a blanket in one of the most beautiful places on earth without a care in the world.

Gratitude was an attribute Cole Sage began to embrace far too late in life. Now it was something to share, encourage, and offer thanks for. The sermon he heard the previous Sunday came to Cole's mind.

"I am not a Bible scholar."

"Where did that come from?" Kelly sat up.

"I was just thinking about the Sunday sermon."

"And?"

"Well, the pastor said Satan accused God of building a wall of blessing around Job so that Job couldn't help but be thankful to God. The devil said God spoiled Job, so of course, he loves God."

"But it wasn't true. God blessed Job because he loved Him and lived a righteous life. A bit different, don't you think?" Kelly studied Cole trying to figure out where this conversation was leading.

"I don't think that spoiling a person necessarily brings gratitude. It's more likely that people who are given everything become self-centered, selfish jerks."

"OK, I guess that's true for the most part."

"I just hope we're not spoiling Jenny." Cole watched the little golden-haired girl leading the play on the hill.

"Wow! Sometimes your thought connections amaze me. No, I don't think we spoil her that way. We don't bury her in gifts. We *do* give her a lot of love and attention. Not the same thing."

"We are pretty blessed. I hope I am not guilty of just thanking God for what He does for me. I wasn't brought up in a church like yours."

"I think you have a huge heart and are seeing God's blessings in your life and you appreciate them."

"You lost your houseboat and everything in it. You didn't complain once. You just went on with life."

"Well, I was plenty angry. I prayed some pretty angry prayers. But, in the end, I was grateful I didn't end up barbecued." Kelly laughed and slapped Cole on the leg. "Come on, that was a good one.

"Did you ever wonder what you would do if you had lost everything like Job?"

"*Though he slay me, yet will I trust in Him.* I think that's the lesson to be learned from Job.

"I wonder if I lost you, or Jenny, or Erin, if I would be able to still love God?" Cole lay back and gazed up at the clouds.

"I hope you never have to find out."

Chapter Two

Cole Sage looked around the third floor of the Chronicle building and took in the exodus toward the elevator. Like a zombie march, fifteen to twenty men and women, with boxes of pictures, plants, and mementos in their arms, silently joined the group huddled at the shiny, reflective doors of the elevator.

Hanna Day looked up at her boss. "Good Morning. Quite a sight, huh?"

"It looks like the Israelites fleeing Egypt. What's going on around here?"

"A blood bath. Pink slips taped to their monitors when they arrived."

"And you?" Cole asked.

"Safe so far," Hanna replied.

Cole leaned back against his secretary's desk to watch the occupants of the third-floor cry, laugh half-heartedly, and chat around their cubicles. These were the lucky ones. The bomb dropped on the house next door. They were safe, but they lost friends, co-workers, and the familiar faces they saw every day.

In the early seventies, Cole worked briefly for a newspaper that went under. He was among the displaced and unemployed. He was young, however, and got another job within a month. That new job set the course for the rest of his life. Many of the people at that bankrupt paper ended up as clerks in department stores, or tried their luck as realtors, or became insurance salesmen. Most never worked in their first love again.

The guys gathered at the elevator were lifers. More salt than pepper. They gave their youth, and life, to the newspaper that had now crumpled them up and tossed them aside. The purge couldn't have come as a complete shock to anyone. Revenues were down. Advertising took a body blow that it still hadn't recovered from. Craig's List, eBay, and Facebook, garage sales—these all but replace the classifieds.

The Internet was an enemy to print that Gutenberg could never have begun to imagine. A world of information was a few keystrokes away, and news reports were instantaneous. No matter how up-to-the-minute the newspaper was, it was always hours, sometimes a day, behind online news sources.

Sheltered behind the buffer of opinion and editorial journalism, Cole Sage walked a thin line between relevance and obsolescence. He maintained a strong following in print, and to his surprise, when the number of hits was reported from the webpage, he topped most of the other columnists and certainly the world and national news sections.

As he watched another elevator full of the redundants leave their home away from home, he couldn't help but wonder why no one looked out on the room. Was it embarrassment, anger, or fear of making eye contact with the survivors?

Because of his unique position with the paper, Cole was isolated from the fact checkers, proofreaders, and copywriters with no bylines. He sat day after day in his corner office, secretary at the ready, and did what he did best: telling the stories of the city. Feature articles splashed across the Sunday editions about people wronged by a system from which they had no protection, officials trying to pull a fast one on the people they were supposed to represent, and the well placed, powerful, and connected who abused that privileged place in the food chain.

Group by group, the cogs that had made the machine work were loading into the elevator and exiting the floors below into a world with no demand for their talents. Cole turned and went into his office. Before he could be seated the phone on his desk rang. He turned and looked at Hanna. She shrugged and shook her head. The desk phone almost never rang on its own.

"Hello?" Cole said.

"I need to see you." Before Cole could answer the line went dead.

"That was Waddell. Be back in a bit. Maybe." Cole didn't like the feeling of being summoned in five curt words.

"You don't think…." Hanna's voice trailed off, not wanting to finish the sentence.

The air on the top floor was thick with grief. The past was dead and the future seemed to be on life support. Stunned people sat at desks, in cubicles, and could be seen staring into empty offices. The heavy sword of termination cut a wide swath through the executive floor as well.

"What's going on in here?"

Chuck Waddell looked up and gave Cole an insincere smile.

"Chuck?" Cole pressed.

"It seems my services are no longer needed." Waddell picked up a small, hand-carved, ebony dolphin. "This was the first thing Chris ever bought me." He gently placed the dolphin in the file box sitting in his office chair.

Cole was not sure how he wanted to proceed. He was expecting his pink slip to be personally delivered by his old friend. It was not to be the case.

Chuck spoke first so he didn't have to decide. "You need to think about your future, Cole. The Internet has changed the news business. We're dinosaurs, old friend. Print is dead and the bottom line is blood red around here.

"Is that what this is about?" Cole moved toward the desk.

"I make too much money. God knows you make way too much." Waddell laughed and put a small model of a rider and motorcycle in the box.

"This is so sudden. Have you even had time to think? What's your plan?"

"Costa Rica. Chris and I always planned to retire in Costa Rica. We would have if…." Waddell stopped short.

"He would have liked that." Cole felt a wave of emotion come over him. He felt a lump lodge in his throat, and he moved to the bookcase against the wall.

"Maybe I'll write a book," he said, running his fingers over the titles. "Seems everybody I know has."

"You need to write a book, Cole. It would sell. I think you've lived three lives." Chuck nodded as if thinking that he should try writing. "Get out of here before some smartass little punk from HR puts a pink slip in your pay envelope."

"Instant deposit."

"What?"

"I don't get checks anymore. It's an instant deposit."

"I *am* a dinosaur." Waddell looked up at Cole for the first time. "Marry the girl, ride off into the sunset, live happily ever after—all that crap. I got nothing but memories. So this is where I get off."

"It's been a good ride. You got the brass ring."

"It was gold, and Chris was buried with it." Waddell slapped the side of the box. "You're a good friend, Cole Sage, maybe my best. I wanted to be the one to tell you I was leaving. I kind of figured we would go out of here together. Changing of the guard and all that."

"Still might." Cole shrugged and picked up an autographed baseball and placed it in the box.

"If you don't mind, I would kind of like to do this by myself. It's a kind of rite of passage, you know?"

"No problem." Cole started for the door. "I'm sorry it ended this way."

"Doesn't matter," Waddell said with a shrug. "Cole, watch your back, this new guy Faraday is a shark. He has no feeling for anyone, or anything, just the bottom line."

As Cole walked down the hall to the elevator his mind went back to a cold February afternoon when he watched Mick Brennan being lowered into the ground. The man who taught him most of what he knew about being a newspaperman had been reduced to nothing more than a minor player on the newspaper he loved so much. Journalists never get to stand in Yankee Stadium and say, "Today I consider myself the luckiest man on the face of this earth." For the most part, they are burned out, used up, and tossed out like yesterday's early edition.

Sure, once in a while there is a Tony Snow who is given a platform to go out with grace, dignity, and a smile. Cole thought of something he once heard Snow say, about his job: "You're blessed... Leave no room for regrets." Cole was beginning to regret what he saw as the beginning of the end for him.

It was Chuck Waddell who brought him to San Francisco. It was Waddell who fought the big boys upstairs for Cole's freedom to be Cole. Without Chuck as a buffer, Cole's days were numbered.

As the door closed on the elevator, Cole decided he would leave on his own terms, before that pink slip was faxed, e-mailed, posted on his door, or something worse. It was time for him to go. On his own terms, in his time.

"You're back!" Hanna smiled and gave Cole a double thumbs up.

"Waddell wanted me to know he'd been let go," he offered without irony.

Cole closed the door behind him, as he went into his desk. He sat down, slapped the desk hard, and picked up the phone.

"Randy, can you come up and see me when you get the chance?"

"How 'bout after lunch?"

"That would be fine." Cole set the handset in the cradle.

He pulled out the drawer of the credenza behind him. The last time it was opened was his first day at the *Chronicle*. Cole turned over several small white notebooks, a folder with a welcome letter and map of the building, and found what he was looking for: the *Employee Benefits* binder. He turned and set the binder on his desk. The guacamole green binder seemed to glow against the scattered mess of white paper and yellow legal pads. He flipped several pages until he found it: "Contract of Employment".

"Two years to go." Cole ran his finger over the date on his contract. 'Termination of this agreement by the employer requires a thirty-day notice. A severance package to include one year's salary and, one year's medical insurance coverage shall be paid beginning with the date of termination of this contract.'

"Thank you, Chuck."

Cole closed the binder and leaned back in his chair. He closed his eyes and weighed several options, two of which were completely impossible. Kelly would never agree to open a peanut butter and jelly sandwich shop in Tahiti or a writing school in Costa Rica. That one might actually work. Cole's future would fly or flounder, in the next few hours.

"Ms. Day?"

A broad-shouldered man, with an equally broad belly, stood a few feet from Hanna's desk. His light blue shirt was pressed with perfectly straight creases, sleeve, and chest. The dark navy trousers he wore were starched stiff enough to stand by themselves, and the creases may have been sharp enough to cut your finger.

"Good morning, Craig," Hanna greeted the front lobby security officer.

"I caught this one wandering around on the second floor. With all the comings and goings this morning, the entry door was propped open, and the buzzer was shut off. She claims she's Mr. Sage's niece, and just got off on the wrong floor. I thought I would escort her if you know what I mean." The security guard turned slightly to look at a girl of about sixteen standing behind him.

"Hi, I'm Hanna."

"I'm Lindsey, is my uncle in?" The girl's tone and demeanor were bright, sharp, and matter of fact. Yet there was a major problem with the story: Cole Sage was an only child. He never married, so there was no possibility of "in-law" relatives.

"He's on the phone at the moment," Hanna lied. "Thanks, Craig, I got this." She redirected her attention to the girl: "Have a seat, he won't be a minute."

Lindsey made her way to one of the two chairs that backed against the wall to Cole's office. She popped in her earbuds and reached in the pocket of her hoodie to click on her iPod. The Queen of England couldn't have looked more in control. She crossed her legs at the ankles and silently tapped her foot to the beat of whatever she was listening to.

Hanna let her wait for nearly five minutes and then got up and tapped gently on Cole's door. "There's someone out here I think you'd like to meet." Hanna closed the door and returned to her desk.

Cole appeared in his doorway and smiled at Hanna and then at the girl sitting outside his office. A blind man could have seen there was absolutely no recognition in his eyes. He looked at Hanna for some help and guidance, and she just grinned at him.

"Lindsey is here to see you," Hanna finally offered.

"Lindsey." Cole nodded. He knew he was about to be the butt of a prank of some kind. Hanna was enjoying this all too much.

"Lindsey," Hanna replied.

"Lindsey?" Cole questioned.

"Lindsey," Hanna said with a big grin. "Your niece? Lindsey?"

Cole looked down at the girl who was now peering up at him, earbuds still firmly planted. Cole reached down and tapped the girl on the shoulder with the back of his hand. He motioned for her to remove the obstacle to their conversation.

"Hi, I'm Lindsey, remember me?"

"Can't say I do."

"It's been a long time."

"Could be more than what fifteen or sixteen years?" Cole fished.

"Six actually. I was nine the last time we were all together. Yeah, mom, grandma, me and you. At grandma's house after my dad's funeral."

Cole took the seat next to Lindsey and looked over at Hanna. She was still grinning from ear to ear and thoroughly enjoying the scene playing out in front of her. He stretched out his legs in front of him and crossed his ankles. Lindsey left her ankles crossed and stretched her long legs out just like Cole.

"You know, Lindsey is it?"

"Yes, sir."

"I'm a tad bit confused here. You're going to have to help me out."

"OK," Lindsey offered.

"Tell me about your grandmother. Where does she live?"

"Here in San Francisco."

"Your mother?"

"With my grandma."

There's no phasing this kid, Cole thought. "This will sound kind of dumb, but what's your last name?"

"Frost. Lindsey Frost. My mom's Natalie and my grandma is Marie."

"So your dad was Jack?" Cole decided to see just where this all would go.

"No, Curtis," Lindsey said emphatically.

"OK, I give up, Lindsey Frost. Who are you, really? I have no nieces, nephews or anybody else except my daughter and her family. I'm an orphan and only child. So you want to tell me who you really are, and what you are doing here?"

"I *am* Lindsey Frost. My mom's Natalie and my grandma's Marie. I'm a writer. I'm one of the best. I go undercover a lot and usually can bluff my way into people's confidence. How'd I do?"

"Except for the part about being my niece, and the funeral? Almost perfect."

"That bad?" Lindsey asked.

"Yeah."

Lindsey stood and faced Cole. She put out her hand and offered it to Cole. "I'm Lindsey Frost and I want to be a writer."

"I'm Cole Sage. Nice to meet you. What brings you here today?"

"I asked Tico at the newsstand on 24th who was the best writer in the city. He said you. So, here I am. I've come to go to work for you."

"How old are you, Lindsey?" Hanna asked.

"Sixteen, well, fifteen if you want to be technical. But I'm closer to sixteen than fifteen. My birthday is next month."

Cole took the opportunity of the female exchange to give Lindsey a once over. She was tall and lanky, and a little grimy. Not filthy, just grungy, and in need of a good scrubbing behind the ears. Her clothes were both too big and too small. Her hair was cropped short, and not by a professional. But, she was kind of cute, in a Huck Finn kind of way.

"Do you know what time it is?" Cole asked.

"No idea." Lindsey smiled looking around for a wall clock.

"It's nine-thirty. Now, I haven't been to school in a while, but as I recall, school should be in full swing about now. Why aren't you there?"

"I believe education is where you find it. In a city like San Francisco, there are opportunities to learn something everywhere you look."

"That is very true, but a writer needs a good strong education to open the doors so they can show what they can do. I went to school a lot longer than I wanted to. I had to…to get anyone to take me seriously when I applied for a job. Know what I mean?"

"I know but it is so boring."

"You miss a lot of school?" Hanna asked.

"My grandma thinks so. The teachers keep calling her."

"Tell me something," Cole said and patted the chair next to him inviting Lindsey to sit back down. "Where does a fifteen, excuse me, almost sixteen-year-old go when they're not in school?"

"All over. I chase down stories. I interview people. I get a feel for the color and heartbeat of the city. There are so many things to see, and do, and people to meet."

"You sure sound like a writer." Cole smiled broadly.

"Look, I brought my stuff," Lindsey said excitedly. She took off her backpack and unzipped it, revealing several spiral notebooks of various colors. "This is my *Story of San Francisco*. I'm almost finished." She began pulling out the notebooks and handing them to Cole.

She hopped up from her chair and handed two notebooks to Hanna. Cole grabbed the first one on the stack and flipped it open. The handwriting was the first thing that struck him. It was perfect, almost machine-like in its form and clarity. He thumbed through the entire notebook before reading a word. The penmanship was consistent back to front. When Cole looked up at Hanna she was staring at him with her eyebrows raised high in amazement.

Then he began to read. Her prose was crisp and insightful. By the bottom of the first page, he was hooked. Cole continued to read in silence, page after page. The descriptions of commonplace things elevated them to treasured pieces of the multi-layered city that the young girl obviously adored.

When Cole turned to look at Lindsey she was watching him read. Hanna, as she read, sat with a charming smile of enchantment across her face.

"This is all yours?" Cole asked.

"No, I have more at home," Lindsey replied.

"No, what I mean is, you wrote this?" Cole asked gently.

"Yes, sir. Is it OK?"

Cole laughed heartily and put his arm around the girl's shoulders. "Lindsey Frost, I think we are going to be great friends. What do you think, Hanna?"

"I think we already are."

"Look, here's the deal," Cole said as he stood. "This is a working newspaper. At least for a while longer. You saw all the people carrying boxes out of here? They are out of a job. So, this is not the best day for a visit."

The phone on Hanna's desk rang. "Cole Sage's office. Yes, sir, I will give him the message. Yes, sir. I will, sir." Hanna put the phone down. "That was the new Editor-in-Chief, Mr. Faraday. He wants you in his office. Now. Right now."

"I tell you what, Miss Frost, how about my very capable secretary, slash, assistant, Hanna here, takes you on a tour of the paper? Depending on when I return, what do you say the three of us have lunch and talk about what it takes to be a writer in the digital age?" Cole hesitated. "And getting you to go to school?"

"That sounds really good. Except for the school part," Lindsey said, shaking her head with a coy smile.

Cole dipped his head half an inch. "Then we will all meet back here."

"Just let me turn the voicemail on and we'll get started," Hanna said, smiling at Lindsey.

Somehow, Joseph P. Faraday managed to move into Chuck Waddell's office before Chuck got to his car. At the desk outside the door a woman with the face of a pit bull, and a temperament to match sat guard.

"Cole Sage, to see Mr. Faraday."

"Wait your turn." The woman jerked her head in the direction of a row of office chairs all currently occupied except one."

"Nice to meet you as well," Cole said with a big, fake smile.

Cole made his way to the empty chair and was greeted by Tucker Locklear, a sports writer. "You, too?" Locklear whispered.

"Rain falls on the just and the unjust alike."

"What?"

"Nothing. Just a quote. How long have you been sitting here?" Cole queried.

"Long enough to hear Franklin from Circulation go ape and start screaming at the new boss. This is really bad, Sage." Locklear glared at the woman at the desk. "Isn't she a peach? What a bee-auch."

"He must have brought her with him. Anybody know where this guy's from?"

"Not sure. Someone said Baltimore. Who knows?" The man in the third seat injected.

Cole wished he was alone. Locklear's questions began to grate on his nerves.

The door of the Editor's office opened, a woman that Cole recognized, but didn't know, walked past the group without looking up.

"This is taking forever." The man speaking was short, expensively dressed, and looked nothing like any newspaperman Cole ever met. Faraday was close-shaven, but the blue-black of a dense beard gave his face the look of an old Warner Brothers cartoon gangster. His hair was equally thick and freshly trimmed. From head to foot he was immaculate. Cole looked down and picked at the small food stain on his thigh.

"So, what have we got here?" Faraday's eyes passed over the group of five waiting to see him. He turned his back to the group and said something inaudible to his secretary. She handed him three envelopes.

"Alright, Carrack, Zepeda, and Turner." Faraday slapped his leg with the envelopes. "Thank you for your service, due to the restructuring, you won't be part of the new staff. Good luck with your future endeavors."

Three men stood and took an envelope from Faraday. No one spoke and none of them looked at Faraday. Locklear nudged Cole with his knee. They didn't make eye contact.

"So which one of you is Sage?" Faraday asked.

Cole began to stand but stopped short when Faraday pointed at Locklear. "You. Come with me. You're the sports guy, right?"

"Tucker Locklear."

"Yeah, whatever."

The two men entered the office and Locklear turned and closed the door. He looked at Cole and raised his eyebrows and smiled. It was a smile of resolve. The clock was running down and the game was lost. Cole grimaced.

Tucker Locklear was in the editor's office less than five minutes. He walked out with a bewildered look and nodded as he passed Cole and simply said, "See ya."

"Sage!" The voice from inside the office conveyed the tone of one who was used to having people jump to his every command. Cole didn't move. "Sage!" Faraday bellowed again. Cole stayed as he was.

Cole thought: *the first one who blinks loses.*

Faraday appeared at the door of his office. "Are you deaf?"

"No," Cole said, devoid of any emotion.

"Didn't you hear me call you?"

"I heard my name."

Faraday stared into Cole's eyes. Cole repeated in his head: *First one who blinks loses.* Faraday blinked.

"Come in, come in. I haven't got all day."

Cole stood and walked passed the editor and into his office. Two chairs sat in front of the desk Chuck Waddell occupied for so long. Cole moved to the one on the right and stood behind it.

"Have a seat."

Before he sat, Cole glanced around the room. All traces of Waddell were gone. His essence was gone as well. All in less than an hour. Cole did not like Joseph P. Faraday or his bronze embossed nameplate. He was a nasty little man, with a nasty attitude. Cole couldn't abide the I-am-the-god-of-all-you-see attitude of a lot of executives. Faraday was beyond that. He possessed a mean spirit and an aura of evil. He was a high-priced punk. Cole hated punks.

"So, Mr. Sage."

Cole noted that Faraday began every sentence with *so*. This was either an affectation, in which case another item to add to the ever-growing list of things he disliked about this man, or it was just a bad habit. In either case, Cole didn't respond.

"Is there a reason you don't answer me?" Faraday seemed annoyed.

"I'm not sure how to respond to 'Mr. Sage,'" Cole replied.

" 'Yes, sir,' would be appropriate."

Cole didn't respond.

"You seem to be a money maker for this paper. Your column is popular, as are your reruns on the blog. You are an award-winning journalist, which gives the paper credibility. Is that about right?"

"I suppose so," Cole answered.

"None of which means a damn to me. This paper is an albatross around the neck of the corporation. My job is to cut the fat, turn a profit, and bring this dinosaur into the twenty-first century. According to HR, you have two years to go on a bloated, overpaid, unjustified, iron-clad contract. You make too much, and you work too little. I can't fire you because your contract has an air-tight severance package, thanks to my predecessor who, I understand, is an old friend of yours."

"So, Mr. Faraday?" Cole said, loving the ironic tone.

"So, Mr. Sage, I am stuck with you."

"It would seem we are stuck with each other." Cole was beginning to feel his anger rising up.

"That is the case."

"Let me ask you something," Cole began.

"I don't think…" Faraday interrupted.

Cole pressed on, and a bit louder than the editor, "What paper did you come from?"

"I didn't. I come from finance and acquisitions."

"That explains your total lack of understanding of the history, tradition, and value of the press."

"Like that overpaid jock that was in here before you? Sports should be a list of scores like the Dow. Pages of retelling accounts of silly games are a waste of paper. But, there is an element of society that must relive the thrill of victory and the agony of defeat. I prefer my news online, and capsulized, so I don't waste time being bothered with things I don't like. Which brings us back to you, Mr. Sage."

"You should have been a writer, you have such a way of turning a phrase," Cole said, confident that Faraday didn't know he was being insulted.

"I can't be flattered, Mr. Sage, nor can I be swayed from my course. Your column needs to be more focused. Who gives you your assignments?"

"No one."

"It shows. There is no pattern, no continuity, and no consistent political ideology. From now on I will assign the topic, and the final approval will come through me. You are an expensive racehorse, Mr. Sage. I am here to see you hit home runs and convey the agenda of this organization."

I just hope they don't put all their eggs in one basket, and it misfires. Cole fought to keep the smile from his face. You want to mix metaphors? Never tell a writer he doesn't know how to paint! Cole nearly giggled at his own thoughts.

"So, Mr. Sage here is your first assignment. Father Thomas Melo is leading the fight to keep San Francisco a sanctuary city. Frankly, I don't care one way or the other, but this is a liberal city and we need to back the play of our movers and shakers. I want a piece done on Melo that makes him out to be the next Mother Teresa. We run it this weekend." Faraday stood and began walking to the door. "Understood?"

Cole didn't move. He didn't turn his head. He spoke as if Faraday was still sitting at his desk. "That's not what I do."

"How's that?" Faraday fairly choked on the words. It was apparent he was not used to having his order questioned.

"I don't write puff pieces to reinforce someone's public image. That's what PR firms are for."

"So, I'll order a new sign for your door. Now, if you don't mind, I have more weeds to pull."

Cole didn't move for a long moment. Then, he stood with his back still to Faraday. He took a deep breath and exhaled slowly. Turning, he walked toward the editor pausing for a moment in front of him. The height difference was substantial. Cole was standing close enough to smell the splash of his three hundred dollar a bottle Clive Christian cologne, and sensed he was seriously invading the new editor's personal space. There was a battle of wills playing out. Cole understood the dynamic: Faraday couldn't step back without showing what he perceived as weakness. Cole had no intention of moving for a while longer. He was enjoying the thought that this little bully was getting a taste of his own medicine. Unspoken, non-threatening, Cole wasn't angry or hostile, but he was making Faraday extremely uncomfortable, and it showed.

Cole smiled broadly and said, "I think we understand each other quite well."

Faraday didn't respond, but Cole heard the new editor let his breath out as he walked through the doorway.

A door just opened, and there was no question as to *if* Cole would go through it, just *when*. Faraday was just a minor player in life's plan. People come and go in life, and Cole knew in the end, Joseph Faraday would be nothing more than a footnote.

Hanna and Lindsey, the aspiring writer, had not returned when Cole reached his office. He flipped through the mail but didn't bother to open any letters. He wasn't mad. He wasn't frustrated. He was done. He neatly stacked the mail in a tight pile and set an old bronze "S" paperweight on the pile.

"We're back!" Hanna called from her desk.

Cole walked out and joined Hanna and Lindsey. "Well, young lady, do you still want to work in a newspaper?"

"It seems a bit confining. But if it's what I need to do to be a real writer, I guess so."

"All the walking around must have made you two hungry. Ready for lunch?" Cole glanced over at Hanna.

"Sounds good to me," Hanna said.

"Me, too," Lindsey agreed.

"Then we're off!" Cole raised his pointed index finger to the sky.

Chapter Three

Lunch consisted of chicken strips and fries for Lindsey, and a salad with oil and vinegar for Hanna. Cole ordered two brownies and a café mocha. The conversation was light and hit on a dozen non-threatening subjects before Cole got down to what he really wanted to know.

"Tell me something, Lindsey, what part of the city do you live in?"

"Near the Tenderloin. On Eddy Street above a gay Karaoke bar."

"Kind of a tough neighborhood, huh?" Cole took a sip of his mocha.

"Can be. I've been there since I was six, so some of the old guys look out for me. It can get scary 'specially when it's late. I try to get home before two."

"What time is school out?" Hanna asked.

Lindsey laughed and replied, "Not in the afternoon, at night."

"You're out of school at two in the morning?" Hanna was trying not to seem as shocked.

"I'm not trying to be nosey, just trying to get acquainted." Cole broke off a piece of brownie and watched Lindsey dip another French fry in the mayonnaise she had squeezed onto her plate. "What's your mom do?"

"Meth," Lindsey said as nonchalant as if she were telling the time.

"No, I meant for work."

"Whore sometimes, panhandles at the Wharf, mostly lives off my grandma's Social Security and guys she brings home."

"You seem pretty relaxed with the life." Cole smiled.

"I suppose if I walked into it today I might find it off-putting, but after a lifetime of it you tend to become desensitized." Lindsey didn't look up.

"You're a pretty smart kid. Do you read a lot?"

"I like to surf the net at the library. Did you know that Barack Obama never had a real job? I was reading the other day that he went to college, did community organizing in Chicago, whatever that is, and *then* went into politics. Is that crazy or what? Oh, and I read that Hitler wanted to be an artist, but they wouldn't let him into art school. Man, that must have really pissed him off. You know what I think? I think the head guy at the school was a Jew. Think about it. That could be why Hitler hated the Jews so much." Lindsey reached in her pocket and took out a palm-sized notebook and a pen. She flipped back several pages and began writing feverishly.

"Notes?" Hanna asked.

"Yeah, I'm going to do some research on that Hitler idea." Lindsey stared down at her notes and nodded her head.

"You know, I have carried a notepad in my pocket since I was in college. All of us geniuses do." Cole winked at Lindsey.

"If I don't, I forget things. I get a lot of ideas and I don't want to lose them."

"How old are you again? I have the same problem! But mine is old age."

Lindsey looked up at Cole and giggled. "This is nice."

"What's that?" Hanna asked.

"Sitting and talking to real adults who aren't high on something, who actually listen to me. Ask me questions about me. It's nice. Almost never happens."

"I like it too," Cole nodded. "Say, if we were to figure out a way to get you to school on a more regular basis, and a way for you to spend some time here at the paper, who do we get permission from? Mom or grandma?"

"I don't need permission. I do what I want. Nobody cares."

"I care, and I'm pretty sure the paper will care. For insurance and stuff, you know?" Cole tried to play down any impression of responsibility in hopes of getting Lindsey to agree to more structure in her life.

"In that case, grandma. She is my guardian really."

"OK, when we finish we'll go back to my office, make a few calls, and see what we can come up with. Whaddaya say?"

"You know something, Mr. Sage?"

"What's that?"

"You always say 'we' not 'I'. I think that's cool."

"It's *your* life. We're trying to get *you* on track to be a *real writer* like you said."

"I think *we* are going to be friends. Are you what normal is like?"

"Oh, hell no!" Hanna blurted out. "I'm normal. He's a writer!"

Lindsey smiled broadly and looked at Cole with pure admiration. "Then I'm not going to be normal either."

Cole worked the phone for nearly an hour before he got what he wanted. He tried hard to not let the bureaucrats at Lindsey's school, and paper shufflers in HR, hear his frustration with their lack of imagination.

Finally, he was able to get a young sounding woman at the San Francisco Unified School District on the speakerphone who agreed with Cole that a work experience internship at the paper could be the carrot dangling in front of Lindsey that just might keep her on the road to success. The woman was willing to fax Cole the necessary paperwork, and he promised to get all the required signatures.

"I think we're set. Be on the lookout for a fax."

"Here it comes," Hanna replied.

Lindsey was writing in her notebook when Cole exited his office. She was so focused she didn't look up.

"She's been at it since we got back," Hanna said.

* * *

The stairwell was gloomy, and dark green paint chips from the wall covered the stairs. The hollow, unpainted door was missing a long, thick section of the veneer. Lindsey grabbed the doorknob, gave it a quick hard jerk upward, a stiff shove, and the door opened.

"Nice lock, huh?" Lindsey stuck her head in the partially opened door and yelled, "Grandma, I'm home! Got company!"

The door opened to a view of a large wall, badly in need of paint, and the windows at the front of the apartment. The floor was cluttered with beer cans, paper, Styrofoam take-out boxes, and clothes.

"Come into my humble abode. Careful not to step on any needles."

Hanna pushed Cole from behind, not wanting to be the first one to enter. Inside the apartment was a table with three chairs, a broken down sofa with a mismatched stained recliner that set with its back to a hallway. Shoved in a corner were a gold metal TV stand and a small flat screen television. The TV looked strangely out of place in the disarray and filth of the apartment.

Sitting in the middle of the room was a woman of indeterminate age. Her hair was fiery copper on the bottom four or five inches and a dingy, six months of grey growth coming from her scalp. Across her lap was a knitted throw and a skinny black and white cat.

The woman didn't change her expression or greet Lindsey and her guests. The woman's eyes were a milky blue and void of life. At first, Cole thought she was blind, but then she looked up at him.

"What's all this?" the old woman said.

"These are my new friends, Grandma. This is Cole Sage, the famous newspaperman. "And this," Lindsey said, putting her hand on Hanna's shoulder, "is his assistant."

"What have they got to do with you? Why'd you bring them here?" The Grandmother's expression changed to one of suspicion and anger.

"Nice to meet you. Lindsey has told us a lot about you." Cole smiled and gave the woman in the wheelchair a nod.

"They are going to help me become a real writer."

"Bullshit. Nobody does nothin' for nobody in this world. What's your angle?" The woman glared up at Cole. "What's she got to do with anything?" she asked, jerking her head toward Hanna.

"She thought it would be good if she came along since I'm a girl."

"You afraid he'll touch my Lindsey?"

"Hardly," Hanna said firmly. "These days appearances are everything and it is better for young girls not be taken places alone with men."

"Grandma, the reason they're here is to get you to sign some papers for the school and the newspaper saying it's OK for me to go after school for work experience."

"You get paid?"

"No, it's for school credits. I have to go to school as part of the deal."

"Then that damned attendance woman will stop calling?"

"Yes."

"Well, that would be something."

"Here's what we've got," Cole said, slipping two sheets of paper from an envelope he took from his jacket pocket. "On this form, you give your permission for Lindsey to come to my office after school. This form is from our personnel office, registering her as an intern." Cole handed the papers to the grandmother along with a pen.

"Why wasn't I invited to the party?"

A bone-thin woman stepped in from the hallway. She wore a grimy pair of red Forty-Niners sweatpants and a man's sleeveless undershirt. Her sagging breasts were evidence of her lack of undergarments. Her arms and neck were covered with purple and greenish bruises. Her neck bore signs of being choked, and the right side of her face was in the final recovery days of a black eye.

She moved across the room and extended her hand to Cole. "I'm Natalie." She turned and glared at Lindsey. "House rules, girly, you turn tricks, I get half."

She stood uncomfortably close to Cole and he could smell the acrid stench of methedrine. Her face was worn beyond her years and her dancing eyes and dilated pupils showed she was heavily under the influence. She looked up at him and smiled revealing a mouth missing two teeth and a serious lack of oral hygiene. "You're kind of cute. You and I could have a real grown-up party. None of that kid's stuff. I know things we can do that she's never dreamed of. Fifty bucks and I'll turn you inside out. Whaddaya say?"

"I say you are embarrassing your daughter to death. I'm here to get her guardian's signature for her school and my newspaper, for a work experience program." Cole stepped back.

"I guess if you're hittin' at that, you don't need to pay after all." Natalie turned and grinned at Hanna. Hanna stood by stoically.

"Have you signed the papers?" Cole turned back to the grandmother.

"There you go, my best Marie Schoenberg."

Cole reached down and took the forms and slipped them back into the envelope. He turned and smiled at Lindsey. "All done."

As he turned to go, Natalie reached out and grabbed Cole's arm. "I got an idea. A hundred bucks and all four of us can go back to the bedroom and get really acquainted. We can get naked and I'll have you clawing the wallpaper off the walls."

"You are about the most disgusting piece of...." Hanna was silenced by a man coming from the hall.

"What's going on here? Who the hell are you?" The man's tone was hostile and threatening. His greasy hair hung far below his shoulders. He wore a beard that only in patches covered his raw meth-induced acne.

"If I were the least bit interested, I would ask you the same." Cole glanced at Hanna, signaling it was time to go.

Before anyone had a chance to move, the man crossed the room and shoved Natalie out of the way.

"Stevie!" Natalie squealed.

"You hittin' on my old lady? Who do you think you are?"

Cole chuckled at the stupidity of the question. "If she was the last woman on earth, I'd consider a gay lifestyle. On the other hand, I might just kill myself." Cole laughed, shook his head and gave the man a sneer.

"You gonna let him insult me like that, baby?" Natalie's voice went up an octave with the possibility of her honor being defended.

"I think you need your ass kicked to teach you some manners." Stevie's fists were clenched and he was tensed, ready to strike.

"Let's go," Cole said to Hanna.

"What about Lindsey?" Hanna asked.

"Up to her." Cole looked at the girl and saw fear in her eyes. "Maybe she better come too."

"Says who? Stevie stepped closer to Cole.

"Look, Tiger, we don't want any trouble. We came here trying to do the kid some good."

"I don't think so."

"You tell him, baby!" Natalie chimed in.

"You really don't want to get involved. Just pay Natalie here the twenty bucks for her services and leave well enough alone."

From his back pocket, Stevie pulled a knife. In a heartbeat the blade was open and he waved it in front of Cole.

"Stevie, you stop it now!" the grandmother shouted. "Natalie, make him stop!"

"I'm thinking I'm going to show you what happens when you wander into places you're not welcome."

"It strikes me that thinking may not be your strong suit, so I'm going to give you a moment to reflect on what is obviously going to be a bad decision."

"You think you're better than me, comin' in here insulting my woman, showing off for your lady friend and...." There was a long pause while Stevie tried desperately to remember Lindsey's name. Finally, he said, "The kid there. I'm going to beat you blind."

"You really don't want to go there. You won't beat me like you do her," Cole said fiercely.

Stevie jabbed the blade at Cole. Cole stepped back. The knife slashed through the air, to the left, and then the right. With each jab and thrust of the knife, Cole stepped back. He felt his leg bump something behind him. He spun and grabbed a cushion off the back of the sofa.

"I'm gonna gut you like a fish," Stevie growled.

"Are you serious? That's the best you got?" Cole taunted, circling Stevie. "How about something like, 'I'm going to slice you like cheap salami' or 'You ever heard steel hit bone?' No, no I got it...'Prepare to be served tartar!'" Cole shot the cushion out toward the waving blade.

"Slice him, baby! Make him show some respect," Natalie screamed.

"Cole!" Hanna took Lindsey by the shoulders and moved toward the door.

At that moment Stevie lunged full force at Cole. The cushion swallowed the knife blade to the hilt.

Cole lifted and twisted the cushion. Without warning, Cole released his left hand and punched Stevie hard on the chin. He grabbed the cushion again with both hands and wrenched the knife from his hand. Cole threw the cushion towards the door.

Stevie swung at Cole, but Cole pulled back and Stevie's fist lightly grazed his cheek. Cole hit Stevie hard with a right jab and then a left. Stevie staggered and Cole hit him with a devastating right uppercut to the jaw, sending Stevie staggering backward into the recliner. The worn-out old chair collapsed, leaving Stevie with his legs pointing at the ceiling.

Cole walked over to the ridiculous site of Stevie struggling to right the chair. Cole put his foot on Stevie's throat.

"Different when you try to hit a man, huh? If I ever see a bruise on Lindsey, I'll be back, and I'll throw you out that window."

Stevie growled and grunted out some tough guy bravado, but Cole pressed harder.

"I don't think you're listening."

Natalie rushed up behind Cole and hit him in the back of the neck. Without turning, he threw back his elbow and caught her square in the nose. She screamed and threw herself across the sofa.

"You just better pray I never come back. Got it?" Cole took his foot from Stevie's throat.

"OK, OK," Stevie gasped.

As Cole turned and walked toward the door he looked at Lindsey's grandmother. She smiled at Cole and from hands inconspicuously resting on the arm of her wheelchair, gave him two thumbs up.

Cole bent down and pulled the knife from the cushion and opened the door. He placed the knife blade just above the center hinge and slammed the door hard as he jerked the handle backward snapping off the blade. He turned and threw the bladeless handle back at Stevie.

When Cole got to the door at the bottom of the stairs Hanna and Lindsey were already at the car.

"Well ladies, that was certainly an adventure." Cole grinned and rubbed the knuckles of his right hand.

"Are you OK?" Hanna asked.

"Yeah, fine. Nothing a little ice won't fix."

There's blood on your hand," Lindsey said.

Cole chuckled. "Just a flesh wound."

"I had no idea you could…" Hanna began, but Cole cut her off.

"There's still some fire left in this old man. Just glad it didn't take long." Cole winced as he opened and closed his right hand.

"What are we gonna do with you?" Hanna said to Lindsey, as she opened the car door.

"I'll be fine. This kind of stuff happens all the time, really. Don't worry. They'll cool down in a while. I'll just disappear for a bit." Lindsey tried to be convincing but it didn't work.

"Under the circumstances, I think it might be a good idea if you come home with me," Hanna said.

"Can I have a word with you?" Cole said to Hanna.

The pair walked just out of hearing distance from Lindsey.

"Are you nuts?"

"What is that supposed to mean?" Hanna snapped.

"You can't just take a strange kid home with you," Cole replied.

"She needs help."

"So do a million other kids. Take a step back. She starts off with the mother of all attempted con-jobs. She lives in a cesspool with a couple of violent Tweakers. You've got a great heart, but we do not know this kid. Enough to help her, sure, but not enough to house her."

"You don't think she's a good kid?" Hanna questioned.

"I'm not saying that. I'll bet there are a half-dozen laws, violations, and restrictions you're breaking by taking a minor into your home, without, I might add, the knowledge or consent of her guardian." Cole cleared his throat. "Look, just don't make any promises until we make a few calls, alright?"

"I know you're right, but the poor kid is a nuisance to them." Hanna's voice showed her emotion.

"Kelly has a friend at Child Protection Services. I'll call her and get the guy's name and number. Is that fair?"

"You're the boss." Hanna walked back to Lindsey.

The two exchanged a few words, then, Lindsey turned and wandered up the street.

* * *

"How soon does the next movie start?"

The young man behind the thick glass was so focused on his cell phone texting he didn't bother to look up.

"Excuse me, when is the next movie starting?"

"Six minutes, screen four, Midweek Morning Classics, five-fifty." The texter-cum-ticket seller glanced at the computer screen for the time and then back down to his phone.

A five-dollar bill was slipped under the glass. Moments later, a ticket lay in the metal tray. The young man didn't notice he was shorted fifty cents, and never looked at the patron standing in front of him.

The 1:50 showing on a Wednesday afternoon apparently wasn't high on anyone's list of must-do activities. Add to it, it was a screening of Alfred Hitchcock's *Rebecca,* a dark 1940, gothic romance, and it didn't have much of a chance for big-ticket sales.

Near the middle of the small screening room generously called a theater, in the center seat of the row, sat a man in a business suit, slouched down, and trying to appear incognito.

"Looks like we're the only ones who care about a classic," the voice behind him offered.

The businessman didn't turn around to see who was speaking to him.

"It's a good place to hide." The voice was thickly slurred and the smell of bourbon hung in the air.

"From work or family?" asked the newly arrived patron.

"Both." The businessman rasped out a loud phlegmy cough. "The wife wants to go to Bermuda, the kids only make contact when they run out of money, and the tuition, my God, what am I, Donald Trump?"

"What do you do?"

"Sales, what else? You want to buy a copy machine?" The man in the business suit replied sarcastically as the lights went down.

The heavy, faded, red and gold, art deco curtain parted and a World War II-era Pathé newsreel lit up a perfect square in the center of the screen. Seven minutes later, an explosion of Technicolor animation splashed across the screen. The room was illuminated enough for the salesman's whiskey bottle to show clearly as he took a sip and screwed the cap back on.

By the time the bells of the black-and-white Selznick Studios logo chimed out, the salesman's head bobbed three times. He would either be asleep or passed out in a matter of moments. The opening scene of the film was so dark, any image was hard to make out. Female narration helped to identify the approaching gate on the screen. The salesman took another pull on his emptying bottle. This time he didn't replace the cap.

Up on the screen, a foggy path wound its way to a clearing and the sight of a large English manor house. The ice pick slipped easily out of the patron's jacket sleeve in the darkness.

Standing silently behind the salesman was death, but he neither saw nor felt the arm come down in the old theater. The tight fist grasping the ice pick felt the hair of the salesman as the thin spike pierced through the top of his skull all the way to the handle.

"Now you have no more complaints," the voice from behind the salesman whispered softly.

A quick hard twist and the deed was done. The last thing the salesman saw was a chrysanthemum of light exploding in his brain and the voice of the film's narrator saying "The moon hovered an instant like a dark hand before a face."

Everything in the salesman's world ceased to matter. The whiskey bottle made a hollow clank on the floor that no one heard except the killer who glided out of the aisle and down to the musty curtain below the pale red exit sign to the right of the screen. Seconds later, the muted light of the alleyway next to the theater greeted the killer.

At ten-thirty that evening, the killer was already tucked into bed and enjoying a good night's sleep.

The salesman's body would not be found until after midnight when the theater closed for the night. A young man in a blue vest tried to wake the motionless body. When he couldn't be roused, the young man called an ambulance. The police arrived a little after twelve-thirty and agreed with the paramedic that the man, now identified as Kenneth Allan Dwyer of San Mateo, was definitely dead. It wasn't long after that Mr. Dwyer's wife was notified of his death.

The next morning, the medical examiner would discover a hole in the top of Dwyer's head, and his brain was scrambled.

* * *

Kelly Mitchell sat on the wooden bench, twirled the combination on her lock, and opened the locker door. The chatter of women in the locker room drowned out her gasp as she stared at a long-stemmed, red rose. Kelly sat motionless for a moment taking in the site of the rose sticking out from the back pocket of her jeans. She took the towel from around her head and squeezed her wet hair.

"Oooh, secret admirer." Claire Muir spoke from behind Kelly.

Claire was in her late thirties and single. She and Kelly had hit it off instantly the first day of the "Pilates for Lunch" class. They laughed and joked their way through the class and even went to coffee a few times. Hanging out with Claire made Kelly feel a bit younger and she liked it.

"I'm not so sure I like the idea of my locker opening so easily," Kelly said.

"Those old things are probably all set to the same combination," Claire laughed. "Is anything missing?"

"It doesn't look like it."

"Good. It's your turn to buy coffee. Have you got time?"

Kelly took the rose out of the locker and examined it. "It is lovely. But it is kind of creepy don't you think? I mean, there's no one here but women."

"Didn't you experiment in college? A drunk night with the girls that got out of hand?" Claire inquired.

"Heaven's, no!" Kelly exclaimed. "First off, I have never been drunk. I occasionally have wine with dinner, but never to the point of intoxication. Secondly, I have no interest or desire for women in that way."

"Then it must be from the janitor!" Claire laughed heartily at her own joke.

The wind outside the gym was cool and refreshing. The two women walked the few yards to Cup O' Heaven coffee shop in silence. The smell of freshly roasted coffee made Kelly breathe deeply and double her need for a large steaming mug. With their order placed, and Kelly paying the bill, they made their way to a seat by the window.

"So, how is that fiancé of yours? What was his name, Carl?"

"Cole, and he is wonderful," Kelly said, holding up her engagement ring. "I just picked it up from being sized. What do you think?"

"Gorgeous! It must be love," Claire offered.

"It truly is. I feel really blessed."

"You must have got the last good one out there." Claire looked out the window.

"Oh, I don't think so. There are a lot of nice guys. You just have to look in the right place."

"I've turned over every rock from here to Berkeley looking for a guy. Every one of them has nothing but bugs and creepy crawlers under it." Claire chuckled.

"As I said, you've got to know where to look. There are a lot of great guys at my church, waiting to meet a nice girl," Kelly offered.

"Oh, no. No church for me. I don't believe in fairy stories."

"Here you go." The barista set two steaming mugs on the table.

Claire blew across the top of her mug and took a sip. "Yuck! What is this supposed to be?" Claire stood and charged the counter. Over the next minute, she berated, abused, and insulted the young woman behind the counter.

Kelly stood and walked to the counter. "Claire, Claire!"

Claire whirled around, "What!"

"It is just a cup of coffee," Kelly said softly.

"Nobody can do anything right! Not even a stupid cup of coffee." Claire's anger burned red hot.

"Go sit down. I'll sort this out. Take a deep breath."

"Demand a refund. I am never coming back here."

"Yes, you will, you love this place. Just have a seat. Everything will be fine."

Claire stomped back to the table, mumbling and sputtering all the way.

"I am so sorry about my friend. I'm so embarrassed. Please forgive her, she's not normally like that." Kelly tried her best to soothe the feelings of the barista.

"Yes, she is." The young woman shot back.

Kelly frowned and said softly, "Is what?"

"Like that. I'm going to ask the manager if we can refuse to serve her. She is such a bitch, and we all hate her. She disturbs our customers and just makes us crazy. That order was right. I did it myself knowing how she is."

"I am dreadfully sorry. I had no idea," Kelly said humbly.

"It's not your fault."

"No, but it reflects badly on me because I am with her. I feel bad."

"Thank you for trying to help, but she's not worth it." The young woman was kind but firm.

Kelly went back and sat down at the table. Claire sat with her arms folded, her face still flushed with anger.

"It wasn't really the coffee was it?" Kelly began.

"What do you mean?" Claire said sharply.

"It was a cup of coffee. The order was wrong, or it didn't taste right. The girl who made it wasn't trying to poison you, didn't insult you, she just brought you coffee."

"It was wrong," Claire said defensively.

"So is human trafficking, ISIS beheading Christians, mass murders, and the way the Giants have been playing." Kelly smiled. "A cup of hot water and roasted bean grounds shouldn't cause that kind of rage. So, it wasn't really the coffee was it?"

"I am just sick of nobody doing anything right."

"You are a strong, intelligent, attractive woman, with a good job. Why does that bother you so much?"

"Why doesn't stuff bother you? How do you always stay so cheerful? You never complain about anything, the damp towels in the gym, the fat lady that farts during yoga, anything!"

"A lot of things bother me. The difference is I don't let them overtake me. There are so many things in the world I have no control over. If I get angry or upset, who does it affect? Nobody but me, and the people around me. The thing that upsets me doesn't change. There are too many good things to dwell on, so I push the things I can't control out." Kelly shrugged and took a sip of her coffee.

"Yeah, but you don't have to work."

"That's right, because my husband, who I loved dearly, died. I would gladly trade all he left just to see him for a little while. But I can't.

"You have a fiancé now. You're not lonely."

"I wasn't before. I had family, friends, and wonderful neighbors. Cole was a part of God's plan for my life I never saw coming."

"Oh, come on, Kelly, really. You really think some invisible Santa in the sky, out of all the people on the earth, sees you? Do you know how silly that is?"

"No sillier than screaming at that poor girl behind the counter over a cup of coffee. I see it this way: everybody bets their lives that either God exists or he doesn't. Even if there is a small chance that God exists, wouldn't a rational person live as though He did? I mean, if God doesn't exist, a person will have only given up a few fleeting, worldly pleasures. But, if He does, look at the upside, an eternity in Heaven and avoiding an eternity in Hell. To me, the choice was, and is, easy."

"I don't buy it," Claire said.

"OK, then let just say I'm too blessed to stress."

The barista that Claire berated approached the table with a fresh cup of coffee and set it in front of Clair.

"Thank you." Kelly smiled.

Claire didn't say a word.

"My pleasure," the barista said with a big smile as she walked away.

Claire sipped at the coffee silently, having no idea that the barista spit in it.

Chapter Four

Cole turned down Lombard Street and watched the stream of tourists wind their way down the "Crookedest Street in the World" in front of him. Being a landmark navigator, he didn't bother to write down the number of the house where Kelly was staying. Luckily for him, there was a blue glass ball on a pedestal next to the front door. He signaled and slowed nearly to a stop before turning to assure the carload of touristas from Ohio didn't rear-end him.

Cole rang the bell and heard the first few notes of Beethoven's Fifth faintly through the front door.

"Hello, stranger!" Kelly said, as she wrapped her arms around Cole's neck and kissed him warmly.

"It has been a week of unparalleled turmoil. How 'bout I tell you in the car? Ready to go?"

"Spoken like a true journalist. Just let me grab my purse."

It was several minutes before either spoke. The traffic was fierce, and talking could be a dangerous distraction. Kelly let Cole bob and weave through the early evening traffic. The stereo played low and seemed a strange soundtrack for their drive to Erin and Ben's.

"Leonard Cohen? Are you feeling suicidal?" Kelly teased.

Cole laughed and reached over and turned the volume off. "Sometimes you just need to know somebody else is worse off than you are." Cole chuckled. "Leonard always does the trick for me."

"So, what's going on?" The traffic was thinning and time for talk.

"You first," Cole yielded, "you said on the phone you needed to tell me something."

"It may be nothing," Kelly said, then sighed. "But, I've had a couple of weird things happen at the gym and it is kind of creeping me out."

"Like what?"

"Well, first, there was a single red rose in my locker. And yes, I have a lock on it. It was stuck in the back pocket of my jeans. Then there was this." Kelly held up a small sheet of rose-bordered stationery. "It's a love poem. I found it under my windshield wiper today." Kelly began to read:

> *The seasons of life, though filled with strife,*
> *Bring us love in places we might never have looked.*
> *I have found you and the vision of the perfect wife,*
> *Your beauty and laughter leave me captivated and totally hooked.*

"It's certainly not Shakespearean, but it does make me feel neglectful." Cole joked to ease Kelly's concern.

"You have been, but that's beside the point," Kelly teased, but Cole could tell her heart wasn't in it.

"Do you have any idea who it could be?"

"The thing that makes me really uncomfortable is I think my admirer is a woman."

"What?" Cole didn't see that coming. "Because…?"

"It's a women's yoga studio and health center. There are no men in the building. Very feminist, a women's empowerment kind of place."

"Well that fits you perfectly," Cole said sarcastically. "Why did you pick that place?"

"It is rated very highly, it's close to the house, and it's the cheapest monthly fee I could find.

"OK, now that really makes sense."

"I'm being serious and you make jokes. Don't you find it weird?"

"Not particularly. You are a beautiful, charming, witty, woman. This *is* San Francisco, after all."

"Meaning?" Kelly pressed.

"Oh, come on Kell'. This is a Mecca for Gays and Lesbians from around the world." Cole was shocked at her naiveté. "Look, if you are approached by this person just politely decline her advances. It's not uncommon for straight women to get hit on, just tell her you're in a relationship with a handsome, manly man."

"Funny. It still makes me terribly uncomfortable. Even Claire, my new friend from the gym, thought the gifts were kind of odd. But, then she acted like I was weird because I had never 'experimented'."

"Things are a lot different than when we were young…younger," Cole quickly amended.

"I know, I know. Sometimes I wish things *were* like when we were 'younger.' Your turn, what's going on? I haven't seen you in nearly a week."

"I think it's time for me to leave the paper," Cole blurted out.

"Whoa! Where did *that* come from?"

"We have a new editor. Chuck got canned, and there was a monsoon of pink slips this morning. I got called in to meet with Chuck's replacement, and quite frankly, I'd love to shove him out the window just to see what kind of pattern that kind of snake makes when it hits the pavement."

"Cole!"

"OK, not really, well maybe…no, not really, but what a pompous jerk he is. He has no background in the newspaper business. As a matter of fact, he doesn't even read one. He gets his news from the phone that's grown to his palm." Cole felt his anger rising and tried his hardest to appear calm, but it wasn't working. "I was informed that from now on my stories will come from his pointy little head, and will be things he thinks are in keeping with the pulse of our readers. Get this," Cole stuttered, "I'm supposed to write a piece on how wonderful it is that San Francisco is a sanctuary city! Anyone who reads my column knows I'm opposed to that idea. I'll look like a sellout, or a liar, or a lame combination of both."

Kelly sat quietly. It was a couple of blocks before she said, "Are you through or just taking a breath?"

"Taking a breath," Cole grunted.

This was new territory for Kelly. Cole was angrier than she had ever seen him. She slipped her hand over and patted him on the thigh. He sighed and stared straight ahead.

Cole began with renewed vigor. "Oh, and get this! I had a guy try and stab me today. You see, that's what happens now when you try to do a good deed."

"OK, Sport, let's park on that one for a minute. What is that supposed to mean?"

Cole suddenly laughed. He ran his hand through his hair and said, "I must sound nuts."

"A bit goofy, but nuts is a little strong." Kelly smiled, grateful the rant was over.

"Sorry, the whole situation just makes my blood boil. I have an idea that might lead to a new beginning. I tried to…"

Kelly cut him off in mid-sentence, "Stabbing? Knife, sword, plastic fork? You can't throw that out and then change the subject."

"This little girl, teenager actually, came into the office pretending to be my niece. She wants to be a writer. She bluffs her way as far as Hanna. Cute kid. Raised by druggies, but really bright, and quite talented."

"She tried to stab you?" Kelly interrupted.

"No, no," Cole laughed. "Her mother's boyfriend."

"She tried to stab her mother's boyfriend?"

"OK, stop, I'll start over."

"Thank you!" Kelly smiled.

"Her name is Lindsey. She showed up with a backpack full of notebooks. Her writing is nothing short of brilliant. She's written this whole collection of stories called *Life in the City*, or something like that. Sketches of people, places, observations—just wonderful."

"High praise," Kelly interjected.

"And well deserved, I might add. That's the good news. The bad news is her home life is horrendous. Her grandma's in a wheelchair, her social security pays the bills, and she's treated like a houseplant. Her mother is a part-time hooker. The mother's boyfriend is an off-the-rails tweaker who thought I was hitting on to mom!"

"Were you?" Kelly giggled.

"Funny." Cole chuckled. "I suggested that the girl, Lindsey, do an internship after school at the paper. I got the paperwork from HR and Hanna went with me to take her home and get the permission papers signed. Easy, huh? *Au contraire*. The mom's such a screwball she can't sign stuff, so we put a pen in grandma's hand and had her do it. That's when Stevie, the boyfriend, enters the scene and pulls a knife on me." Cole sighed.

"For a writer, sometimes you are a really lousy storyteller."

"See, that's where you're wrong. I'm saving the wild finish for last, with a pause for dramatic effect," Cole teased.

"Since you're still here I can surmise he didn't kill you. So how did our hero escape? And what about his female companions?"

"Well, Super-News-Guy, that's me, grabbed a cushion off the couch and the villain stabbed it, giving our hero the chance to knock his block off!"

"Cole, this really isn't funny. I'm joking to keep from crying, or throwing up, or both. He could have really hurt you. Killed you even! Did you call the police?"

"Hanna took the girl to the car when the trouble started. Do you still have that friend at Child Protective Services?"

"Terry? Yeah, he's still there. What about the police?"

"I need his number?"

"And the police?"

"They wouldn't have done anything. Besides, I taught Stevie not to play with knives. Besides, he might lodge a complaint about the way I handled him." Cole reached over and patted Kelly's leg.

"I love you, but these daring deeds of yours are going to get you hurt one of these days."

"What are you trying to say?"

"Well, grandpa…."

Grandpa! Cole thought. The word stung but not in a hateful way, not in a way that he resented, but the accolade carried with it the realization there was a lot less of life in front of him than there was behind.

Cole used the volume control on the steering wheel to turn up the stereo as Leonard Cohen's Titanic-deep baritone sang the first line of *Dance Me to the End of Love*. It seemed to him that Cohen was just the thing for that moment. The pair rode for seven minutes and forty-three seconds in silence, as the lilting waltz took them to places neither spoke of. Kelly's words sent a message to Cole that was long overdue: he was indeed getting old.

As the song faded, Kelly said softly, "Will you dance with me soon?"

"I can think of nothing that would give me more pleasure and you more embarrassment. Can we do it in private?"

"So long as you hold me tight."

The remainder of the trip was spent with Kelly's head leaning against Cole's shoulder. He changed the music to a jazz station he knew she liked and the two rode along in silence.

As a bluesy tune played, Cole's thoughts drifted back to a small blues club on Maxwell Street in Chicago. He saw a flyer for an appearance of Howlin' Wolf, the legendary bluesman. *One Night Only!* The words seem to shout off the paper and Cole thought, *I'm in!*

The place was almost narrow enough for a tall man to reach from wall to wall. It was as if it were built in the gap between two buildings, not far from Halsted and Maxwell Street, almost to the freeway. Cole smiled at the thought of the way it looked then, before the University of Illinois bought up every building in sight and turned it all into a red brick mall.

Out in front of the place—Cole wished he could remember the name—sat an old black man with a small barbecue grill and an ice chest. For a dollar one could buy a length of Polish sausage topped with grilled onions and yellow mustard tucked in a chunk of Italian bread. The length of the bread depended on the length of your cut of sausage. Cole got the eight inch, dollar size, and went inside.

There was a man in a gray, shark-skin suit who claimed to be Howlin' Wolf's manager just inside the door collecting three dollars from everyone who came in. There couldn't have been more than a dozen people in the tiny place and most were at the bar. Cole chose a table down in front, just a few feet in front of the double-stacked pallet and plywood stage. At the right end of the bar was a tall glass-front cooler. Cole left his sandwich and went to get a bottle of RC Cola.

"You be by yo' self, up there, son," the bartender said as Cole put fifty cents on the bar.

"Yes, sir. Best seat in the house." Cole smiled at the bartender as he popped the cap off the soda.

"How in the world did a white boy like you find out about this place?"

"I work at the *Sentinel*, somebody had a flyer pinned to the wall of their cubicle. I wasn't about to miss a chance to see the Wolf in person."

"Well, you stick around, son, 'cause Willie Dixon be showin' up, later on, to sit in on a few numbers.

"I think I've died and gone to heaven!" Cole said, giving the bar a slap.

The bartender reached out his hand, "Name's Edgar, this is my place."

"Cole Sage. Nice to meet ya."

Several of the older men at the bar looked Cole's way. The bartender gave them a grin and said, "There's at least one white boy in Chicago who knows what's good!"

The men at the bar nodded with approval.

At straight up 9:00 a large, greying man with ebony skin came out from the back room with an acoustic guitar in his hand. He stopped at the edge of the stage and then looked down at Cole.

"Can I borrow this?" the man asked, in a voice like gravel crunching under tires.

"Absolutely," Cole said, indicating the chair in question.

"Thanks, 'preciate it."

Cole watched as Howlin' Wolf, the man he first heard years before with the Rolling Stones and Eric Clapton on a scratchy LP called *The London Sessions* in a friend's dorm room, took the stage.

"I want to thank my cousin Edgar for having me here tonight."

"You owe me, Chester! You owe me!" Edgar teased, using his cousin's real name.

Behind Cole came whoops and hollers from the men at the bar. The irony of Wolf's opening was not lost on them. He reached in his pocket and pulled out a harmonica. He started with a low, mournful wail. The notes seemed to bend, contort, and moan with grief as he played a blues number that Cole didn't recognize. When he finished, Cole applauded enthusiastically.

"Thanks, son, but it's just you and me. No need for that."

Cole turned and looked back at the men at the bar.

"Don't give them any mind, they're just old friends. You're the audience tonight." The big man on the old chrome chair didn't seem disappointed. *This is what he does*, Cole thought, as he smiled and nodded accommodating Wolf's request.

"Now, what would you like to hear?"

"*Spoonful?*" Cole asked.

"How 'bout we wait until Willie gets here. His song, you know."

"*Killing Floor?*"

"There ya go! That one's mine."

Cole sat for nearly a half hour mesmerized by the swirling vocal shouts, stomps, and blues harp. Howlin' Wolf's guitar was more for rhythm than melody, and Cole smiled as a string broke and was simply wound around the head of the guitar. Wolf kept playing on the five that were left.

The big man shifted on his chair and stretched his leg out. He winced in pain. "It's a bitch to get old, boy."

A group of voices rose above the respectful chatter and soft laughter at the bar. Cole turned to see five young, black men enter the tiny club. They were loud and swaggered with cocky intent. Cole turned back around and tensed as he heard chairs scoot across the floor. A large, boney knuckled, hand slapped Cole across the shoulder.

"You in my seat white bread."

Cole looked up into the angry face of a tall, thin man with a huge Afro and eyes that looked like they were about to bleed. The man wore a broad-brimmed hat and a wide-collared, polyester shirt. Cole didn't move for a long moment trying to decide what to do, so as not to completely humiliate himself, and still get home alive.

"You wrong, boy. This young man's been in that seat from the start. I suggest you find yo'self somewhere's else to listen." Wolf's words were firm but friendly.

"You think so?"

"That's what I said." Wolf nodded and winked at Cole. He started to hum low, and blow the familiar introduction of *Moanin' at Midnight*.

"Hey, bartender! What is this shit? We came here thinkin' we'd hear some real music, not this field nigger shit." The voice behind Cole did not belong to the one who slapped his shoulder.

"Bring us some beer here," shouted another voice.

As he nervously looked to the door that Howlin' Wolf entered from, Cole wondered if there was a back door out. The tone of the young men and their loud, mouthy attitudes made it clear to Cole that it wouldn't be long before he was going to be in an unhealthy situation.

"Who payin'?" Edgar growled, bottles clanging as he set a tray with five bottles on an unoccupied table.

"Start a tab."

"We don't do tabs."

"Taylor, you pay the man," one of the young men shouted.

"Why me?"

" 'Cause you been drinkin' free all night."

The group laughed and Taylor, the one with the reedy voice asked, "How much?"

"Ten," Edgar said.

"Ten!"

"Dollar for the beer and a dollar cover charge."

"The guy at the door already got three! A piece."

"That's for the talent," Edgar replied.

The young man lifted two fingers holding a twenty dollar bill. "Shee-it! This place ain't worth ten bucks, chairs and all."

Edgar took the bill. "If you want change, you best follow me."

"You can't bring it back?"

Edgar just glared at the young man.

All the way to the bar Edgar listened to the swearing and complaining of the young patron.

"If you don't like it, then you best leave." Edgar's voice deepened and his hand casually reached below the bar. "Here's your ten," Edgar began.

"You listen to me, boy, that man on the stage is a legend. I suggest you show him some respect. Otherwise, you'll be sportin' some serious scarring on the pretty face of yours. You get my meaning?"

"We ain't lookin' for no trouble."

"I hope not," Edgar nodded. Howlin' Wolf played on.

The strong, angry eyes of Howlin' Wolf looked straight at Cole as he slapped his harmonica on his thigh. The unspoken communication was a combination of reassurance and response to insult.

"Next up, an old thing called *Little Red Rooster*." Wolf looked at the man returning from the bar and began the song.

"Play some Marvin Gaye!" one of the young thugs barked.

"Wilson Pickett!" shouted another.

The voices behind Cole taunted. Wolf jerked his head to the right sharply, and then to the left and Cole could have sworn he heard his neck crack.

"I can't see! White bread gityo' ass out my chair." It was the voice of the Slapper.

Cole ignored the request and didn't move.

"This ol' man's caterwaulin' makin' you deef?"

The group laughed and chimed in with catcalls and profane remarks.

"Thought ya said you boys didn't want no trouble. Time for y'all to leave." Edgar was back and his voice showed negotiation was out of the question.

"Says who?" said the slapper.

It was time for Cole to move. He stood and backed toward the side of the stage.

"Me," Edgar growled like an old lion claiming his territory. "I own this place and I choose who stays and who goes."

"You kickin' us out and you lettin' white bread stay? What kind of Uncle Tom bullshit is that?"

"Boy, I just 'bout had enough of you and yo' mouth."

"Zat so?" The Slapper stepped toward Edgar and gave him a shove. "I think we'll stay."

The older men at the bar slowly stood. From their pockets, a variety of knives, straight razors, and brass knuckles appeared. They quietly made their way toward the tables unnoticed, as the group of five young men taunted and insulted Edgar.

"OK, that's enough!" Wolf shouted from the stage. He stood at the edge of the tiny platform, and Cole could see what a big, big man he was. "I said, that's enough!" His voice seemed to fill the small club like thunder from above. He handed Cole his guitar.

"Whatchu gonna do 'bout it, gran'pa?" The slapper scoffed and laughed, pointing at the big grey-haired man on the stage. "I don't think so."

A blanket of uneasy silence seemed to cover the small club. The Slapper's four friends directed their attention to Wolf. All wore smirks of "you're gonna get it now" across their faces. The Slapper took two steps toward Wolf.

Cole looked at Edgar who had just been handed a sawed-off, double-barrel shotgun one of the old men brought from under the bar.

"You want us to teach 'em how to behave?" a big-bellied man asked from behind the five unwelcome patrons.

"Nope, I got this," Wolf said calmly.

Without another word, Wolf reached back and pulled a .32 automatic from his waistband. It was a finely etched, nickel-plated "Tuxedo Colt" with mother-of-pearl hand grips. Wolf pointed it, full arm's reach, straight at the slapper's forehead.

"Hey, now! Hey, now!" Slapper said with hands raised high. "We don't want no trouble!"

"Y'all have a funny way of showing it. First, you put hands on my friend here," Wolf gave a quick flick of the gun towards Cole, "and try and take his seat, then you insult my cousin, and then…and then, worst of all, you call me Gran'pa! It's time for you and yo' jive-ass friends to get on back to your cradle, yo' mama's waitin' supper on you."

"Hey man, no need ta point no gun at us!" Slapper protested.

"Tell you what, skinny, you git out an' never come back b'foe I have you kiss my wrinkly ol' black grandpa ass." Wolf jabbed the gun towards the slapper. "Now git!"

Slapper turned and gave his friends a jerk of his head and started for the door. The old black men from the bar formed a gauntlet and slapped their palms with the razors, brass knuckles and knife blades they held, ready for use.

As slapper reached the front door, Wolf fired hitting the header just above the open door. Everyone behind the slapper began to shove and break ranks running out the door.

The club filled with the uproarious laughter and comments of the men from the bar. Wolf looked down and smiled at Cole.

"Shall we continue?"

Cole handed the big man his guitar. Before he could be seated a large group of men started through the door. In front was a man in a grey fedora that looked as big around as he was tall. Behind him, a younger man carried a standup bass in a brown canvas cover.

"Willie!" Wolf shouted.

Through the doorway flowed men carrying guitar cases, amps, drums and for each one there seemed to be two women dressed up for a night on the town.

* * *

"Where have you been?" Kelly asked interrupting Cole's memory.

"Chicago." Cole smiled and signaled to turn on Ben and Erin's street.

Dinner at Erin and Ben's was always a pleasure. Cole loved having a family. After spending years alone, his daughter Erin entering his life was a surprise gift that erased all the loneliness. The addition of Ben's mother Kelly to the mix was a blessing he would never have dared to dream of. They were indeed a blended family.

Then there was Jenny. Cole's granddaughter was a constant source of wonder and delight. She was seven, going on sixteen. She could talk circles around both her mother and grandmother, which is no small feat. She always kept Cole on his toes and his pockets empty of change.

Cole rang the doorbell.

"I bet they're going to tell us they are naming the baby Cole," Kelly teased.

"I'll take that bet!" Cole laughed and turned to Kelly. "My money is on Grace Kelly Mitchell."

The door opened and squeals of "Grandpa! Grandma! You're here!" filled the air.

"Hey, sport, how you doin'?" Cole responded.

"You guys want to see my new books? I got three. One is about a boy who can fly in his lawn chair with balloons tied to it."

"How about after dinner? Then you can read it to us," Kelly said, going in the house.

"Works for me!" Jenny spun around and disappeared before Cole made it through the door.

"Hi. Long time no see," Ben said, giving his mother a peck on the cheek.

"In here," Erin called from the kitchen.

"Sounds like a cry for help," Cole said, making his way to the kitchen.

"Father, dear, can you come to taste this?" Erin called out with an unfamiliar pleading in her voice."

The counter and stove looked like a food truck exploded in the housewares department of Macy's. Cole tried to assess the damage and figure out what Erin was attempting to prepare. Her cookbook was speckled with a Jason Pollack abstract of spattered grease and a palette of crimson sauces.

"This isn't working."

Cole smiled. "Depends on your objective."

"That's not funny!" Erin burst into tears.

"Sorry." Cole crossed the kitchen and took Erin in his arms. Her ever-growing baby bump took Cole by surprise.

"Stupid hormones! I can't think straight. Stupid tsp and Tbsp!" Erin tossed the measuring spoons on the counter behind her.

"I know a great little Mexican place. I'll pay. Kelly and I will clean up this..." Cole paused, as Erin began to laugh.

"Pretty bad, huh?

"I've made bigger messes, but they usually involved motor oil. What are you fixing?" Cole asked, fearing another flood of tears.

"Goulash with handmade Spätzlenoodles."

"So, what's the problem?"

"I saw paprika and grabbed cayenne out of the cupboard. They are kind of the same color, right? Anybody could make that mistake, right?"

"Anybody with company coming, a high-maintenance, seven-year-old running around, and who's six months pregnant, sure."

"There is even more to it than that," Erin said softly. "Can you have Kelly come in here, please?"

"Hey, Kell'! Can you give us some input here?" Cole called toward the family room.

Cole realized the dinner disaster was not the root of his daughter's stress.

"They're watching the game. Thanks for saving me!" Kelly entered the kitchen.

Erin turned and pushed her hair behind her ears, and smiled sheepishly at Kelly.

"Did I miss something?" Kelly asked.

"We're suffering from a hormonal spike," Cole offered.

"It's not just that," Erin started sobbing again.

"Oh, sweetie." Kelly moved to where Cole and Erin stood in front of the stove. "Group hug?"

Erin planted her face into Cole's shoulder and sobbed quietly. Kelly looked at Cole with a raised eyebrow, what-is-this-about, look. A few moments later Erin pulled back and wiped her eyes.

"Sorry."

"No, no, it's OK. Let it out if you need to."

"It just all too much. The baby, the house, keeping up with Jenny, and then Ben drops the atomic bomb on me last week, and I'm just overwhelmed. And just look at this kitchen!"

"We can deal with the kitchen. What atomic bomb?" Kelly asked, fearing the absolute worst.

"He was waiting until tonight to tell you."

"Tell us what?" Cole questioned, sensing Kelly's apprehension.

"We're moving to Texas!" With that, Erin began sobbing again.

Kelly leaned back against the counter. "What?"

"Ben was offered a job at Texas Children's Hospital, in Houston, as head of pediatric cardiology. We leave in a month. I don't want my baby born in Texas. I don't want to live in Texas. I don't want Jenny to grow up in Texas. This is my home, and this is where you guys are."

Cole felt like he swallowed a grapefruit. He looked over at Kelly who was leaning against the counter, milliseconds from crying.

"Come, sit." Kelly reached out and took Erin's hand and directed her to a chair at the kitchen table. "Let me tell you a story."

Erin drew squares, then circles, with her finger on the top of the table.

"A nice young man from Connecticut came to Colorado to do his residency at St. Francis Hospital in my hometown of Colorado Springs. He was tall, handsome, and my Prince Charming. I think you know the rest of the story. The point is, he was offered a teaching fellowship in San Francisco. I cried, pouted, sulked, and begged that we not leave. In the end, I realized my selfishness was standing in the way of a tremendous opportunity. I prayed and prayed and asked God to give me peace and a willingness to give up the life I always loved for a new life, full of new opportunities. If I hadn't, we wouldn't be sitting here, any of us. We don't know God's plan, we only know what we are comfortable with."

"How did you leave your family?" Erin sniffed and looked deep into Kelly's eyes.

"It was then I realized that Peter and Ben were my family. I know the hurt, and feeling of separation. It was during those five years I became the woman I am today. I was forced to grow in ways I never knew even existed. We're here, and we'll be there, as often as you want us."

Cole took a seat next to Erin and put his arm around her shoulder.

"Oh, Daddy." Erin buried her face in Cole's shoulder.

Cole closed his eyes fighting back tears. Since Ellie, Erin's mother, introduced him to his daughter, shortly before she passed away, Cole lost his one great love and Erin lost her mother. In the years since, as they grew together as father and daughter, Erin only once before called him Daddy.

"I love you, sweetheart," Cole whispered. His heart sank, and a dark blanket of sorrow enfolded him, as the dread of their separation swept over him.

Chapter Five

Cole awoke sideways in his bed with the top sheet wound tightly around his left arm. His night had been a succession of fitful dreams, nightmares really. Erin and her family, in Texas, was the constant. Fits and starts of dream images, buried memories, and gooey fragments of things real and imagined. His dreams felt like the sabotaged niceties of his waking hours, postcards from his subconscious, subway posters of dread and guilt. The triggers were many and the manifestations painful. In the last seven hours, Cole Sage tossed, turned, sweated, and trembled his way through hellish tableaus, Technicolor Imax memories, and had returned exhausted.

His life didn't pass in front of him, but rather he relived moments of terror, bravery, and shameful cowardice. Cole didn't dream often, seldom would be more accurate; during the night he made up for the long period of peaceful sleep.

As he lay drifting in that cloudy, nearly awake place between getting up and nap, snippets of dream images shot across the ceiling above. The room still was awash with the gray shadows of early morning. The digital clock's red number reported 5:40 and Cole rolled onto his side hoping to capture a few more minutes of sleep before the alarm would force him to face the day.

Sleep is the great deceiver and hider of time. Moments could pass for hours, undisturbed—one never knew. The chirp of the alarm seemed to erase the tormented sleep from Cole's mind. He sat and rubbed his hands briskly up and down on his face.

"Up, up and way!" Cole mumbled, standing, and making his way to the shower.

One and a half bagels, and a hot, steamy mocha later, he was on his way to see what the new day would bring. He kicked the paper on the porch aside. Untypically, he turned on CNN and forgot to get the paper earlier. He missed the front page story about the strange rash of fatal stabbings in the city. With the turmoil at the paper and the introduction of Lindsey to the media mix, news of the city was the last thing on his mind.

Arriving early at his office, Cole was ready to do his part. As he waited for someone to pick up at Child Protective Services, he shuffled a stack of notes for his Sanctuary City story.

A pleasant feminine voice greeted him: "Good morning, Child Protective Services. How may I direct your call?"

Cole scrambled through the pile of notes for the scrap of paper where he wrote the name of Kelly's friend.

"Yes, good morning. David Elmore, please."

After a brief wait, a different woman's voice said, "Mr. Elmore's office, Faith speaking."

"Good morning, Faith, Cole Sage calling, is Mr. Elmore in?"

"Cole, Kelly's friend, right?" Elmore said picking up the phone. The voice was strong, confident, and a rich baritone. "She e-mailed me and said you might be calling."

"Yep, that's me." Cole knew he was going to like this guy.

"What can I do for you?"

Cole gave Elmore the *Reader's Digest* version of Lindsey's story and asked how to get Hanna appointed Lindsey's guardian."

"Damn." Elmore sounded suddenly deflated.

"Can't do it?"

"No, it's not that. I was hoping you were calling to do a story on us."

"We can do that, too."

"Sounds good."

"What's the angle?" Cole inquired.

"Understaffed, budget cuts, and an explosive increase in kids who need help."

"My kind of story."

"We have two supervisors that are more interested in getting their names in the paper supporting various causes, than allocating funds for the real programs that help real kids in real danger." David Elmore was getting excited and switched to full fighting mode. "But, first things first: tell me about your friend."

"Hanna Day, my secretary, slash, assistant: stable, street smart, no-nonsense fighter for truth, justice, and the American way," Cole chuckled. "She has a two-bedroom apartment, a good income, no criminal record. What else ya need?"

"Address, phone, and e-mail."

Cole gave Elmore the contact information and his too, for good measure.

"OK, she's good to go."

"That's it?" Cole said, a bit shocked at the lack of red tape.

"Lindsey's in a bad place? Hanna is willing to take care of her and make sure she's in school? Feed her? Give her a real bed to sleep in? Isn't in it for the money?"

"Well, ya, of course. I mean, no, money doesn't enter into it."

"Then Hanna is a better guardian than 90% of the people I deal with."

"When should she come in to sign papers or whatever?"

"No point. I'll put something in the file. It will take six months to get to the top of the pile. Nobody'll know the difference." Elmore sighed. "That's what I mean, between the foster care system and the county referral program, money gets the wheels to stop squealing. 'Where's my check, I've had this kid two months!'—I hear it every twenty minutes. Tell Hanna she'll have an emergency check by the weekend. I'll fax you over the docs so she can get on the list at Lindsey's school."

"Wow, I don't know what to say." Cole was truly shocked at Elmore's handling, or not handling, of Lindsey's case.

"Say you do your magic and fry the hides of those two publicity hogs on the Board and get us some attention. My door is wide open and I'll get you complete access to anything in the building."

"Deal!" If Cole could tie the two supervisors to the Sanctuary City mess, it would kill two birds with one stone. "How about I come in this afternoon?"

"Come at noon and I'll buy lunch!"

"You're on."

* * *

As planned, Lindsey met Hanna promptly at 7:15 in front of the *Chronicle*.

"Do I really have to go to school?" Lindsey protested. "I could just work at the paper with you. I could file things, and go get stuff. I could be your gofer!"

"A deal's a deal. You go to school, and *then* you can come back to the paper. Grades up, perfect attendance, and you're set. Screw up, and back to mom you go. Got it?" Hanna was bluffing about the back-to-mom part but on the rest…she meant business. "Let's get rolling. I can't be late for work."

"OK, Mom!" Lindsey teased, but deep down she was thrilled with the image she saw. She was living in a scene from a TV show with a normal mom and her teenage daughter.

The halls of Lindsey's school were old and dark. Butcher paper signs for an upcoming football game and class elections were the bright spots as

Hanna and Lindsey made their way to the attendance office. The hallway was packed and the roar of a thousand kids on their way to class was deafening.

"This looks just like my high school. Time doesn't change some things," Hanna said over the noise of the crowded hallway. They approached the window marked A-G.

"Good morning," a dark-haired woman with bright eyes and a big smile said in welcome.

"Good morning. We need to clear up some absences, and get me added to Lindsey's emergency contacts list."

"Are you mom?"

"No, I'm a temporary guardian."

"Oh, for the safety of the student, may I have your paperwork, please.

"That's being processed." Hanna felt problems looming.

"Sorry, I can't help you because you're not on the emergency list. As soon as you have your paperwork though, we'll get you all squared away."

"I'm sorry," Hanna began, "What did you say your name was?"

"I'm Pamela."

"Hi, I'm Hanna Day. Is there some way we can have me as a contact until we get the papers to you. I should have them today."

"Great, then just bring them in. Until then, I'm sorry, I can't add you to the list."

"Look," Hanna lowered her voice to almost a whisper. This child is in a scary place. We really need to make sure she's safe. In case of an emergency—meaning her mother—I need to be notified."

"I understand. Until I have a CPS, Welfare, or a court document, my hands are tied."

"Is there someone else I can speak with?"

"Sure," Pamela smiled brightly, never showing the least bit of irritation. "Sydney, can you help this nice lady?"

"Be right there."

"OK, Lindsey," Pamela said, "what's your ID number?"

"Uh, 648332, I think."

"There you are. Lindsey Frost. Oh my, you have missed a lot of school. What's the problem, sweetie?"

"I'm not a big fan of organized education," Lindsey answered with confidence.

"Well, in the last three weeks, you've only been here three days."

"Menstrual cramping."

"No…I said you've only *been* here three days."

"Yeah, I heard you. It's hard to be out on the street those days, you know. Good clean bathrooms in the gym here and you guys always give me free pads."

"I see." Pamela's cheeks colored a bit. "Lindsey, I hate to, but I'm going to have to give you three days of Saturday school. You should get twelve, but…."

Lindsey, cut her off. "You do realize I won't go. It is a kind gesture though."

"Then you'll get in-school suspension."

"Have you ever thought how silly that is? A kid like me doesn't come to school, and then you stick them in the 'jail room' when they show up? You should be celebrating the little victories, not making it even less inviting to come."

While Lindsey and Pamela were speaking, a petite, athletic, woman, stepped up to the counter.

"Good morning, I'm Sydney Stephens, can I help?"

"Good morning, I hope so." Hanna could see this was where the buck stopped. "I'm Hanna Day, here is my ID and press credentials. I am Lindsey's temporary guardian. Due to the violent nature and unstable situation at home, I need to be contacted if the mother or her boyfriend try to remove Lindsey from school. How can we get this arranged?"

"We will need a request from her legal guardian or documents confirming your status as guardian. Until then, I'm afraid we can't help you. It's State law." Sydney's voice and demeanor made it evident they weren't going to budge.

"I see. I will fax them to you as soon as I get them."

"I will need to have you bring them in, I'm afraid. Papers to sign. You understand how it is."

"Indeed I do." Hanna hated bureaucracy and it showed. Hanna turned to Lindsey.

"Is there anything else, Pam?" Sydney inquired.

"I think everything is working out on this end," Pamela answered brightly.

"Thank you, Pam, for your help. I hope we won't have to be dealing with our wandering girl anymore."

"That's what I like to hear." Pam was pleased with the support.

"Here you are, Lindsey," Pamela handed her a pink slip of paper. "You just used up all your last chances," she whispered. "If you need someone to talk to or have any problems, I'll be right here."

"Thank you, Pam." Hanna sensed an ally, despite the confines of red tape.

"No, *thank you*. We need more adults involved in getting our kids to school."

"I'll pick you up after school. 2:10 right?" Hanna turned her attention back to Lindsey.

"I'll be out front where we came in. And I get to stay at your place tonight?"

"That's the plan."

"Awesome!" Lindsey gave Hanna a high five.

Hanna turned and walked toward the exit. Behind her, she heard Pam telling Lindsey to hurry or she would be late for first period. *Ahh, high school*, Hanna thought.

***

The killer was thankful for remembering to bring a cap. The outdoor seating at the Café Puerta Dorado followed the sidewalk and into a shallow alcove. The sun was warm and glared hard against the whitewashed faux adobe wall. The food was good and they made a fresh *pico de gallo* that was plentiful, and the chips were free—a rarity in San Francisco. The peace and quiet of the little side street taqueria was its greatest asset. There were never more than one or two patrons outdoors this time of day, so the privacy added to the draw.

The wait staff changed frequently. There was no rush, no recognition, and no reason to think it would change. The young man who drew the outside serving stations was efficient, not friendly, and hadn't been back since the second refill of chips. The check—for a Coke and two of the lunch-special tacos—came to just under five dollars. It fluttered occasionally in the light breeze under a red and white striped peppermint. Everything was perfect until a man was seated just on the other side of the alcove.

His voice was deep and loud. Before the server arrived at his table, he bellowed out an order for coffee, and a Chili Colorado Burrito. The man's order blasted into the alcove as if the wall didn't exist.

Then, everything went back to the warm, voiceless peace. After about five minutes, the serenity was again shattered by the man's bellowing voice.

"Excuse me! Where is my coffee?" There was a five-second delay and then, "Hey, can I get my coffee?" The tone and inflection made it very clear the man was not pleased.

"Here you are," a waiter said.

"What? You forget I was here?" The man barked.

"No, sir. Sorry for the wait." The words from the waiter were correct, but his tone reflected his disdain for the way he was being spoken to.

Indecipherable mumbling continued for several seconds after the waiter walked away.

The quiet time of a good, cheap lunch and reflection was gone. The killer twisted the bright yellow print napkin.

"Hey!" the man suddenly blurted out. "Hey, look at this table cloth! When was the last time it was changed?"

The waiter walked back to the table. "Just before you arrived. I changed it myself. What's the problem?"

"What the hell is that then?"

"I would say a little berry from the trellis there blew onto the table. I think you may have smashed it with your arm."

"Looks like bird crap to me."

"Would you like to move, sir?" the waiter offered.

"No, just pick it up. That's a nasty thing to have in a restaurant," the man grumbled.

"We *are* outdoors, sir." The waiter cleared his throat. "I'll check on your order."

He didn't say it loud, but the killer heard the man grumble, "Idiot."

It wasn't very long before the waiter returned. "Here you go, sir."

The patron didn't respond.

The killer tapped the table softly with the edge of a spoon. The mood of the day was destroyed. The sun was warm, the gentle breeze barely ruffled the edges of the table cloth, but the serenity during the late morning snack was ruined.

"He has given me indigestion," The killer softly said, tapping the table a little harder with the edge of the spoon. "Why must people complain? It's a beautiful day. How will I be productive when my guts are churning? I could have complained about the lack of meat in my taco, but I didn't. Life is just that way. Next time I'll get extra. Things always even out." *I'm mumbling,* the killer thought.

The handle of the ice pick felt sensuous in the killer's hand. Taking it out was always a rush. Under cover of the table cloth, square wooden handle gently turned over and over. With fingers nearly trembling with anticipation the killer stroked the cold steel shaft of the ice pick. The excitement of what was to come brought a wide smile that was hard to contain. This would be a present for the waiter. The outdoor space was empty of other customers. The man who disturbed the peace sat with his back to the alcove. The waiter was nowhere to be seen. No customers were visible through the windows.

The loud, nasty man was much smaller than his voice would suggest. A couple quick, silent steps were all it took to be behind him. Tightly grasping the man's soft, clammy forehead with one hand, the killer drove the ice pick into the top of the man's head with the other. Three rapid rotations of the handle and the man went limp. With a quick practiced purpose, she took the man's head in both hands and gave him a forceful pull upwards, straightening his position in the chair. Then, as if setting down a valuable vase, she gently leaned the victim's head forward to a napping position.

She wiped the bloody shaft of the ice pick on the man's shoulder and backed around the corner to the alcove. Quickly, but naturally, she walked up the street.

"I love that place. I'll have to go back tomorrow."

* * *

"Hi!" Hanna called from her VW Bug window.

Lindsey came running up to the passenger side of the car with a big smile on her face. "Right on time!"

"Hop in."

Lindsey tossed her backpack on the back seat and buckled her seat belt. "I usually get stood up."

"It's a new day," Hanna said as they pulled away from the curb.

At 3:30 Cole stood from his desk and stretched.

"I'm off to give this to our illustrious new leader, Cole said waving several sheets of paper. "Be back in a few."

"You could e-mail it," Hanna said as he passed.

"I want to force him to read it on paper."

"Would you like to check on our intern in the break room?"

"On the way back," Cole called back.

Cole approached the scowling woman guarding Faraday's door.

"Special delivery!"

"I'll take it."

"No, it has to be delivered in person by hand to Mr. Faraday."

"Who are you again?" The secretary sneered.

"You first." Cole smiled broadly.

"You really do think you're cute, don't you?"

"I know I am. My girlfriend tells me so all the time. Anybody tell you lately you're cute?" Cole grinned.

"No," she snapped.

"Thought not. Please let Mr. Faraday know I'm waiting," Cole said firmly.

The secretary picked up the phone and punched three numbers. "There is a man here with something he needs to deliver to you personally…I tried…no, he wouldn't give it to me."

"I bet you wish you hadn't come along with your boss now." Before Cole could continue the door of Faraday's office flew open.

"You!" Faraday said in disgust.

"Me," Cole replied brightly.

"What is it?"

"Since you are now handing out the assignments, I figured I would hand them in to you as well."

"Don't you have a computer?"

"Of course. How do you think I printed this?" Cole gave Faraday his best, "Are you an idiot? Look."

Faraday turned and went back into his office, "Come on."

Cole smiled at the secretary. "I think you're cute."

As the door closed behind Cole, Faraday asked, "What's that all about?"

"Poor thing is having appearance-related issues. Nobody has told her she's cute lately. Frankly, I just think she's homesick."

"She's ugly as hell. Got a face like a dried apricot. Don't be filling her with nonsense. She has a lot of work to do." Faraday took a chair behind his desk. "So what have you got?"

"My column for the Sunday." Cole handed Faraday the folder he carried.

"Good, I don't have to look at it now. I'll get back to you."

"Fine. Just didn't want it falling into the wrong hands." Cole went to the door.

"What is with you anyway?"

"How do you mean?" Cole said turning back to face Faraday.

"It seems you just go out of your way to antagonize everybody."

"Not everybody," Cole said as he turned and went out the door.

Faraday cursed at Cole's back but the closing door blocked the editor's voice. The folder Cole had delivered was tossed on a stack of files and papers waiting on Faraday's desk.

As Hanna dumped the envelopes and junk mail on the desk her cell phone rang. On those less than frequent occasions when it did ring, it usually was either a solicitor, a wrong number, or a political robocall. The number was unfamiliar and Hanna answered grudgingly.

"Hanna?" the voice was loud but broken up with buzz and crackle.

"Lindsey? Is everything OK?"

"Better than that!" Lindsey sounded happy and excited. "Hold on." Fifteen or twenty seconds passed. "Is that better? I went outside. You were breaking up."

"Yeah, lots. What's going on?"

"I wanted to warn you that the guidance counselor is going to be calling you. I gave her your work number. I hope that's OK. She has some good news. Great news!" The sound of the passing bell drowned out Lindsey's next few words. "Gotta go, bye!"

"Bye," Hanna said into a silent phone. She smiled and slipped the phone back into her pocket. "This is what it's like to have a kid, I guess." Her smile broadened.

For the next hour, Hanna froze every time the phone rang and sighed deeply when it wasn't the counselor. Finally, at a couple of minutes after two, the call came in.

"Hi, is this Lindsey's mom?" The voice was cheerful and a low register for a woman. "This is Penny Crawford, Lindsey's counselor."

"I'm her guardian." Hanna was a bit taken back, wondering if Lindsey told the counselor she was her mom.

"I have some wonderful news. In our most recent round of STRA and TVI testing, Lindsey had nearly perfect scores!" Penny made it sound like

Lindsey won the lottery. "We have an Articulation Agreement with several outstanding schools for gifted and talented students. The schools can be the gateway to opportunities not usually available to our students."

"Wow." Hanna was impressed, but still working on STRA and TVI.

"Yes, indeed. I wanted to let you know that Wellsburg Academy in Virginia has shown a great deal of interest in Lindsey. They've offered her the chance to sit for their entrance exam."

"Great. When is that?"

"This Saturday. She will need to report to the testing center at the University of San Francisco. Would that be a problem?"

"Not at all." Hanna was getting excited. "What does she need to do to prepare?"

"Other than get a good night's sleep and a healthy breakfast, a smoothie, juice, fruit—something like that, nothing heavy. She has everything it takes already in her head!" Penny laughed at her own attempt at humor.

"Sounds easy enough. So, if she does well...?" Hanna inquired.

"She could be offered a spot at Wellsburg!"

"In Virginia," Hanna said with a total lack of enthusiasm.

"Isn't it fabulous?" Penny's cheerleader exuberance was wearing thin on Hanna.

"Is it expensive?"

"Can one put a price on a child's future?"

"So, it's *really* expensive." Hanna was realizing this was nowhere in the realm of a possibility.

"It *is* an exclusive private institution." Penny's tone showed her displeasure with Hanna daring to bring up cost. "Then there is the fee for sitting for the exam." Penny sounded like a used car salesman who figured he was losing a sale and might as well let the fine print out, too.

"And that is…?"

"Two hundred dollars."

Hanna felt like she was drowning. She won the dream house only to find out she couldn't pay all the taxes. Her emotions, already swirling in a confused spiral since the visit to Lindsey's apartment, were once again rearing her fight or flight response mechanism. Her initial commitment was to save a young girl from a hellish situation, to bring Lindsey into her home, feed her, clothe her, and provide a safe haven. Hanna was prepared to pack lunches, run her to school, guide her, direct her, and keep her out of trouble.

Hanna knew the effects of an unstable, dysfunctional family. She lived it, she bore the scars. Fear of commitment to relationships, fear of not being able to break the cycle of alcohol, abuse, and cruelty. Hanna was now committed to saving Lindsey from the pain, fear, and effects of the life into which she was born.

The pain of expectations and disappointment flowed just below the surface of Hanna's cool, self-confident façade. On occasions like the conversation with Penny, a scene or an incident in her past would come to mind, as clear, vivid, and painful as the moment it happened.

A vision of high school rose to the front of Hanna's memory. During her junior year, she was asked to the junior-senior prom by a handsome young man named Michael Brimm. He was quiet, kind, and not one of the in-crowd. Hanna took all the babysitting money she hid in a mayonnaise jar in her closet that was wrapped in a too-small PE sweatshirt and went to town.

She could see the bright spring day as if it was that morning. The smell of jasmine and sweet peas planted along Main Street sweetened the air. She remembered going through the door of Dee Ann's Formals feeling like she stepped through the looking glass. She usually wore clothes from discount stores and thrift shops. She couldn't remember ever having a new dress, let alone a formal.

A beautiful woman with silver hair greeted her about ten feet inside the door.

"Prom time!" the woman said cheerfully.

"Yes. I need a dress," Hanna replied.

She could feel the clerk's eyes look her over from head to toe. Hanna suddenly wished she hadn't come into the shop. She was ashamed of her clothes and panicked at the thought of seeing the pink price tags that hung from all the gowns.

"With a cute figure like yours, we can find something that will knock your date's eyes out! Ready to have some fun?"

"Oh, yes ma'am!" Hanna's fears melted away and she was swept up in the clerk's enthusiasm.

Dress after dress, Hanna tried on gowns and formals. Sleeveless, long lacy sleeved, floor length, and almost indecent minis—it was like the best game of dress up ever.

Finally, she found "the one": a strapless, lavender dress that clung like a spider web. It showed off her pretty legs, but not too much. It displayed just a hint of cleavage and made her feel very grown up.

On the way to the counter, Hanna noticed the dress had no price tag. Some of the other dresses she loved were way out of her price range. Why didn't she look? What if it cost more than she had? She still needed shoes. Hanna felt her face redden and her neck go splotchy like it always did when she was embarrassed.

"What's your shoe size, hon, about a seven?" the pretty clerk asked.

"Yes, exactly," Hanna replied softly.

The clerk reached under the counter and pulled out a shoebox. She removed the lid as if she was opening a treasure chest, and indeed she was. Inside the box was a pair of elegant lavender high heels. They sparkled with a glittery sheen that matched the trim on her dress. Perfect.

"Oh, my," Hanna said, gazing down at the shoes. "I don't know..."

The clerk cut her off, "Oh, you must!"

"But I don't have a lot of money," Hanna replied sheepishly.

The clerked laughed with a beautiful musical quality. "I completely forgot to ask your budget! Please forgive me. What do you have to work with?"

"One hundred and twelve dollars." The thrill of shopping in this fairytale store was gone. Hanna nearly ran from the store. She realized her pittance of savings probably would only pay for the shoes. "I'm sorry, I think I have wasted your time." Hanna gently laid the dress across the counter. She let her hand softly stroke the satiny material one last time. "Thank you. I'm sorry." She turned and started for the door.

"Where are you going? We haven't rung up your dress." The smile on the clerk was dazzling.

"But...."

"No buts. Let's see where we are before you panic."

Hanna stood nervously watching as the clerk flipped through a three-ring loose-leaf binder. Page after page she turned. The sheets were filled with handwritten lines of numbers and descriptions.

"Here we are. Lavender Bridesmaid Gown, number 12238." The woman turned the pages to the back section of the binder where the shoes were listed. "Lavender size seven, three-quarter heel! That's us."

The woman took out a sales ticket and began to write.

What is she doing! Hanna thought.

"OK, here's what we've got. The dress and shoes were ordered for a wedding that was canceled. The bridesmaids all came in and picked up their dresses early. But one girl was coming from out of state. When the wedding was canceled, she canceled her trip. We were stuck with the dress. We agreed to sell the dress on consignment. So you are the winner!"

"How do you mean?"

"I really like you, sweetie, what's your name?"

"Hanna."

"Well, Hanna, I'm Dee Ann and since this dress has been here passed the six-month agreement, and she hasn't bothered to make contact or extend the consignment, I've decided it should go on sale!" The clerk smiled. "I was thinking seventy-five percent off."

"Really?" Hanna nearly screamed with excitement.

"So, let's see." The clerk entered several numbers into the calculator on the counter. "How does $106.38 sound?"

"Oh, yes! Oh, yes! That's awesome!"

Just the memory all these years later made Hanna flush with embarrassment.

Bringing her thoughts back to the present, Hanna realized she was smiling at the memory. It was one of the happiest moments of her life but, like Lindsey's chance at a Virginia Prep school, it would soon be shattered.

Now, one phone call shattered the peace she felt by giving Lindsey stability, safety, and love.

"Would you be able to provide that much money?" Penny was questioning and condescending all in the same sentence.

"I am able," Hanna snapped, a little harsher than she intended. "I'm not sure if it's something I am willing to do, at this point."

"I see," the counselor said flatly.

"I don't think you do. Lindsey has just come out of a life of abuse, neglect, and a total lack of parental involvement. I've taken on the task of providing stability and care. I'm not sure if it would be wise to dangle the carrot of one more dream that can't come true."

"That is a very shortsighted way of looking at an opportunity like this."

"Is it? I will pay for the test, I can get her there, and I can certainly encourage her to do her best. The rest of the picture is very uncertain."

"All I can say is that this kind of offer won't come again. For a student that lacks credits, has horrendous attendance, and frankly is in danger of not graduating, to be offered this kind of opportunity is unheard of. Think about what you would be throwing away. Have a nice day." Penny was gone.

Hanna was overcome by guilt, shame, and a feeling of utter defeat, just like she felt on prom night so many years ago.

Another memory now came to Hanna. This time it was pain when she took the dress and shoes home. Along the way, she treated herself to a double scoop of Butter Brickle ice cream at the Thrifty Drug Store.

When she got home, her mother was passed out on the couch with an empty vodka bottle lying on the floor next to her. Hanna took the dress and put it in her closet. In two days she would surprise her Prince Charming with her beautiful dress.

The afternoon of the prom, Hanna took her dress from the closet and laid it out across the bed and set her shoes on the floor below.

Her mother had slept in and when she awoke she was as mean as a badger. She screamed and berated Hanna all morning. Hanna did her best to avoid her, but it was a small house. Normally, her father would have been there to buffer some of the abuse, but he was on a sales trip and would be gone for a week.

She only needed to avoid her mother for another two hours and then Michael would come to pick her up.

"Hanna! Where have you snuck off to?" Her mother's voice sounded shrill and angry.

"I'm going to shower. It's time for me to get ready," Hanna called back.

"Ready? Ready for what?" came the angry reply.

"The prom, Mother! You know that," Hanna said cheerfully.

"No, I didn't know that!" Her mother was drunk or would be soon.

Hanna scurried down the hall to the bathroom and locked the door. From the other side of the door, she could hear her mother yelling. Hanna couldn't make out what she was saying, but "Prom" and "Who do you think you are?" came through clear enough. She was glad the sound of the shower drowned out the rest.

Several times, as she showered, Hanna heard the sound of fierce pounding on the door. As she turned off the blow dryer, she could hear screaming and banging down the hall.

Hanna stood for almost a minute before she summoned the courage to open the door.

She quickly moved down the hall. The house was now quiet. As she stepped into her room, she let out a tormented cry from deep in her soul. Her dresser drawers were lying in various places in the room and their contents scattered. Her pictures and posters were torn from the walls and shredded. The mirror on her wall was shattered from the blow of her mother's fist.

On her bed, her beautiful lavender dress lay in tatters. Her mother had slashed and cut the gown with a razor or sharp knife. The beautiful lavender gown was pieced back together with a one-inch space meticulously left between the ribbons of satin. The dress was destroyed. Hanna fell across the bed gathering the pieces of her gown and holding them to her breast. She howled with despair, hate, and devastation.

Down the hall she heard her drunken mother scream, "I never got to go to no Prom! I was pregnant with your ugly ass. If I didn't get to go, you sure as hell ain't goin' Miss Priss!"

Hanna didn't move until she heard the doorbell ring.

"It's your fancy-pants boyfriend! Get the door!"

Hanna rose from the bed still clinging to the remnants of her gown. As she turned to leave the room, she saw her wonderful shoes sparkle from where her mother shoved their heels through the sheetrock. She walked to the door in a daze, still wearing her robe, clutching her dress like a bouquet.

She opened the door to the shocked look of her date.

"I'm sorry, Michael. I won't be going to Prom," Hanna said blankly.

"My God, what's happened, Hanna?"

"My mother...." With that Hanna closed the door.

Hanna wiped the tears from her cheeks and cursed her mother one more time.

Chapter Six

Hanna arrived at her desk shortly after 8:30. Cole was working the phone gathering background for his Sanctuary City story. He found himself hoping for facts supporting his view with each successive call.

"Cole, there's a News Talk radio guy on line one. Do you want to take it?" Hanna gave up completely with the intercom. She hated hearing Cole's voice in both her ears.

"Sure," Cole said, pleased with the distraction. "Cole Sage."

"Ralph McCormick, KSFO, we've bumped into each other from time to time, not sure you'd recall."

"I do. You guys are the number one button on my car radio. What can I do for you?"

"As the city's leading voice in the press, I want to get your take on the buzz in town about the bloodletting at your paper. We're doing a series on the state of the media, and newspapers in particular. OK if I record this?"

"You know, Ralph, I'm not sure how much, if anything, I can tell you."

"Off the record, how bad is it, just between us old timers?"

"Bad." Cole Sage offered.

"Percent?"

"A third."

"Tape rolling. The current lack of trust, combined with the Internet has dealt quite a blow to radio and print news alike. The closure of newspapers nationwide and the decline in AM listeners is reshaping the way people are finding their news. As someone who has won numerous awards, and is considered a dean of American journalism, where is all this headed?"

"We're in a digital age of micro-second news and misinformation," Cole said. "Never before in the history of news has the old adage, 'don't believe everything you read' been truer. Anybody with a cell phone and a blog can report any rumor as fact, or make up a story of their own. Like they used to say on KSAN news in the sixties, 'If you don't like the news, go out and make some of your own!' I don't think they had this kind of reporting in mind." Cole laughed.

Ralph was silent for a long moment. "But the marketplace is changing."

"Sure. Craig's List, Facebook, and eBay have all but killed classified advertising. *Drudge Report, Politico, Huffington Post*, and a lot of serious bloggers report and comment on the news. Every major television network news department has a webpage." Cole cleared his throat. "Papers can't compete with instant. Local news, features and human interest stories are what sustain the newspaper. Radio news has it easier, they can report up to the minute traffic, weather, but so can the phone in nearly everyone's hand."

"Tape off. That gives me some great sound bites and background. Thank you."

"I'd like to say my pleasure, but it was a pretty grim pronouncement."

"What do you make of all these random murders? One of my people got it from a coroner's deputy that the killer is using an ice pick or something similar."

Cole panicked. He didn't have a clue what Ralph was talking about. *Murders? Ice picks? Where have I been?*

"The world's gone nuts." Cole figured that blanket statement would cover about anything.

"You got that right. Are you going to be working the story?" Ralph expected a positive response.

"I fear that will be up to the new editor," Cole replied.

"You sound none too happy, my friend."

"The times they are a changin'."

"Then you better start swimmin' or you'll sink like a stone!"

"Quoting Dylan lyrics first thing in the morning! And we're both over thirty, how can we trust each other?" Cole said.

"Old habits die hard." Ralph laughed.

"We are getting old."

"And pot is legal!"

"Who would ever have believed it? Peace, brother!"

***

"How about a smoothie at the juice bar?" Claire panted. "I'm buyin'."

"Yes, yes, yes!" Kelly wiped the sweat from her neck with a white towel.

Fifteen minutes later, showered and refreshed, Kelly and Claire took a seat at the gym's Juice Bar counter.

"Tell me about your boyfriend's writing," Claire said.

"He is a newspaper columnist for the *Chronicle*. He's won lots of awards, worked at *Time*, *Wall Street Journal*, and *Chicago Sentinel*. Let's see, he writes mostly about people who need help in some way. Gee, I don't know…he's pretty wonderful."

"I detect a strong dose of prejudice there," Claire teased.

"To tell you the truth, before he came to San Francisco, I really didn't know that much about him. I remember reading some of his stuff. He's my daughter-in-law's father. I told you that, right?"

"Yeah. That is so weird…how you two got together, I mean."

"Why do you ask?" Kelly took a sip of her smoothie."

"You promise not to laugh?"

"Sure." Kelly was intrigued.

"I want to be a writer. Not for newspapers or magazines. I want to write books, mysteries. Murder mysteries."

"Really? That's cool. Have you written anything? I mean, that's ready to publish?"

"I'm working on something. I think it is going to be really good. At least I hope so."

"I'd love to read it. What's it about?" Kelly smiled.

"You know the ice pick murders in the news? I'm writing the story as a mystery novel."

"Really? I'm curious. How did you decide on that?"

"Well, it's a cool way to kill somebody. It's like old time Chicago mobster stuff, you know?"

"Pretty heavy subject matter. Wow, Claire, I had no idea you had a literary side to you."

"There's a lot about me you don't know." Claire looked down at her smoothie. "I'd love for us to get to know each other better."

Kelly felt a little uncomfortable with Claire's response. "So, who is the killer going to be?"

"She's got to be really smart. She doesn't get caught, and she's killed how many people…five or six now?"

"Why do you say 'she'?"

Claire laughed, "Because in my book I would make the killer a woman. I thought I could get in the killer's mind and tell the story from her side, kind of a first-person point of view."

"That's creepy."

"Why, what's wrong with creepy?" Claire snapped.

Once again, Kelly got a glimpse at the rage simmering just below the surface of Claire's happy go lucky demeanor. The whole conversation was taking an uneasy turn. Kelly wanted to leave, but she had more than half of her smoothie left.

"Nothing. I just can't imagine wanting to identify with someone so evil," Kelly replied.

"We don't know she's evil. There could be circumstances that drive her to kill. People are way too quick to assign good and evil to everything."

"I think killing people is evil. That's an easy one." Kelly tried to sound as cheerful as she could.

"Is the army evil? Cops? They kill people all the time."

"That's different."

"You said, 'I think killing people is evil.' Killing is killing. I'm saying this person might be under a lot of stress, have some kind of medical condition, I mean, who are you to judge?" Claire was on the edge of a full-on rant.

"Sorry. I didn't mean to start an argument. Let's just finish our smoothies."

"I'm done." Claire stood and walked to the exit without another word.

"There is something wrong with her," the Juice Bar server said. "A few days ago she was screaming at some ladies who were chatting in the lobby. I had to call the manager. I'm sorry. I was kind of eavesdropping once she raised her voice. I'm with you…there is a difference between murder, and the army or the police."

"She is so angry," Kelly said.

The server wiped down the surface of the counter. "I apologize if she's your friend, but she's about to get her membership revoked. She's been warned twice."

"I just know her from yoga. We've had coffee after class a couple of times. It's really sad when someone is so full of bitterness, or anger, or whatever brings that on."

"Kind of scary."

"Hey, really good smoothie by the way," Kelly intentionally changed the subject.

"Thanks." The server moved to the other end of the counter to help a customer.

Kelly sat at the counter until she finished her smoothie. She really didn't want it anymore. Claire's rant gave her a knot in her stomach. She was really just waiting until she was sure Claire was in her car and gone.

***

It isn't every day that someone can talk Cole Sage into stepping outside his comfort zone. Cole isn't a joiner. Clubs, societies, causes, crusades, fraternal groups, or gatherings of people that pay dues, have secret handshakes, elect sergeants-at-arms, fines for people getting a promotion or, a new car, or clubs whose members wear funny hats and march in parades—as far as Cole was concerned, these groups were to be avoided at all costs.

Cole took great delight when invited to join such an organization, in quoting his hero, Groucho Marx: "I would never belong to a club that would have me as a member." That usually got him off the hook.

There were, however, always those occasions when a zealous recruiter wouldn't take "no" for an answer and pressed Cole with "Why not?"

"Because," Cole would retort, "their standards aren't high enough."

Somehow Hanna convinced Cole that he would enjoy Facebook. She stressed the importance of networking in today's society.

"It could be a great place to gather ideas for stories, reconnect with old friends, keep up with the people he left behind in Chicago, or interact with people who like your work."

"What if I don't like it?" Cole asked, hoping that question was an easy out.

"You quit."

"But don't they gather all kinds of personal information about you? What about identity theft?"

"They can only gather what you give out. I don't think Facebook is on the frontline of identity theft." Hanna thoroughly enjoyed giving Cole the sales pitch.

"I'll think about it," Cole conceded.

Hanna knew that "I'll think about it" meant the patented Cole Sage way of politely saying no.

"I'll even help you set up your page," she said. "I think you'll love the site if you'll just give it a chance."

Cole knew he was beat. "OK, but can we keep it simple?"

"You're the boss!" Hanna replied victoriously.

"You'd never know it," Cole grumbled, still unconvinced.

It only took a few minutes to have Cole up and running on Facebook. Hanna "friended" him and then he sent a "friend" request to Erin and Kelly. Hanna took a picture of Cole sitting at his desk and used it for his profile. She typed and he answered the profile questions. Per his request, she kept the information to a minimum and blocked anyone from posting anything to his page. The search feature intrigued Cole and Hanna showed him how to locate old friends. Together they sent several "friend" requests, and to Cole's amazement, almost instantly got back three accepted requests.

"Anyone else?" Hanna asked.

"There are a bunch people I've lost track of over the years that might be nice to hook up with." Cole was starting to get the bug.

Within ten minutes, he found an old colleague from the *Wall Street Journal*, a high school classmate, and three or four other people he always wondered about. To his delight, he found Olajean Baker and sent her a "friend" request. *Maybe I will enjoy this,* Cole admitted to himself.

"Welcome to the twenty-first century, Mr. Sage!" Hanna proclaimed, as she triumphantly returned to her desk.

A message popped up on Cole's screen:

Roland Thompson used your phone number to reach you.
Soldier at U.S. Army

Lives in Aleppo, Syria
11:01 AM

"That was fast," Cole said softly at the monitor.

RT: Hello

Cole stared at the pop-up window of the "private message." *Now what do I do?* he thought. Frantically looking over the pop-up menu, he saw the pale gray text *"Type a message…"* in the box at the bottom of the message window.

CS: Greetings.
Cole leaned toward the monitor.
RT: Hi how are you

"I guess we don't use punctuation," Cole mumbled.

CS: Well, thanks.
RT: And I'm Roland, and you?
RT: And tell me more about yourself
CS: I'm a journalist. Live in the USA. And you?
RT: I'm a US military man and I'm in Jordan on a peacekeeping mission

That's cool, Cole thought, *my first new friend.* Before he could respond another message popped up.

RT: And are you male or female?
CS: Who's that working out?

"Oh, crap," Cole muttered. "Typo."

CS: How's
CS: Sorry

"Note to self, don't hit the return key." Cole was now speaking out loud.
"Did you need something?" Hanna called from her desk.
"No, just stumbling through a message," Cole replied.
"You'll get the hang of it," Hanna said.

RT: Why sorry
CS: Misspelled How's

There was something not quite right about this conversation. For an American, this guy's grammar was really weird. Cole was starting to see red and yellow flags going off in his head.

CS: How is it that you are writing to me if you don't know who or what I am?
RT: I'm looking for a good friend who I can trust
RT: And be a good friend to
RT: And tell me are you single?
RT: And how old are you?
CS: I make a poor friend...sorry.
RT: Why did you say that?
RT: I will make you rich okay

RT: Tell me more about yourself and your family

CS: No thanks. Goodbye

RT: Why good-bye?

Cole put the cursor on the X in the top corner of the monitor and clicked the mouse. Facebook was gone. *How did that guy choose me?* Cole wondered.

The idea of a fun place of reunions and catching up with old friends was replaced with uneasiness, of being spied on. Someone somewhere picked Cole to run a scam on. It wasn't the Nigerian Prince of the spam e-mail. This was a living, breathing person, sitting at a computer who knows where just pretending to befriend him. Hey, little boy would you like some ice cream? Just get in my car, Cole thought. There was something so perverse about the experience that made Cole shudder.

"That was weird," Cole muttered.

"Line one. Kelly," Hanna called.

"Finally, a ray of sunshine!" Cole said brightly into the phone.

"Maybe not." Kelly's mood was obviously low and her voice near trembling.

"What's going on?"

"That's what I would like to know. I am so freaked out. I just want an end to this. I don't understand why they are doing this to me." Kelly's voice was a mix of anger and panic.

"Who? What? Slow down, sweetie. Now slowly, what's the trouble?"

"I was just sent a picture. It's me! It's me naked in the shower at the gym. What am I going to do? Who did this?"

Cole could hear Kelly sobbing.

"Who sent it?"

"The return says anonymous."

Cole's mind flashed back to Chicago and the day Tom Harris brought an intercepted envelope of kiddie porn to his office that was found shoved into his mailbox. The revulsion of the material combined with the detective's suggestion that Cole could be on some pervert's mailing list terrified him. Terry Kosciuszko, the twisted sadist, who held Cole captive for over a month in his cellar, planted the horrific pictures to discredit, humiliate, and terrorize Cole.

The propensity of evil being to shatter the lives of innocents never left Cole. A photo, in the days of Facebook, Twitter, and Snapchat could destroy the reputation and privacy of the unsuspecting, right along with the foolish. Cole's first thought was to get Randy Callen to identify the sender, then call Leonard Chin.

"We need to identify the sender," Cole said. "My research guy, Randy, could hack the President. He can find who did this. I'll see if he can delete it. Then we'll call Leonard Chin."

"I'm not showing this picture to anyone!" Kelly said.

"Kelly, it is a crime. You need to report it."

"No."

"You want another one? You want this on the Internet? I understand your embarrassment. The only one who will see it is Randy. I won't, Chin won't.

Randy will give the, whaddya call it, IP address to Chin. He'll know what to do. This must be done for your own safety and peace of mind. Please don't argue. There's no room for discussion." Cole was afraid he was coming on too strong. "I love you, Kell, please, let the authorities do their job."

"Alright, but please don't look at the picture. I would be mortified."

"I bet it's lovely," Cole said gently.

"Please don't say that."

"We'll talk later." After giving Kelly the personal email address of Randy Callen, they hung up.

Cole quickly dialed Randy's extension.

"Research."

"It's Cole. Don't talk, listen. There is an e-mail coming to you, a picture. I need you to promise to not forward it, post it, or whatever you guys do. Do I have your word?"

"Of course. What is the picture?" Randy asked.

"A friend of mine. It was taken while she was showering at her gym. I need you to find who sent it, track it, destroy any postings if they exist, then send me the address of the sender. Can you do that?" Cole pressed.

"Of course I can *do* it. It is illegal as hell. Are you good with that?" Randy was surprised at the force of Cole's request, and anger in his voice. The sense of urgency was something new, even the touchiest of inquiries were normally tip-toed around by Cole.

"I don't care. I want whoever did this burned at the stake. Infect their computer, erase their hard drive, make their life a living hell."

"Who is the picture of?"

"Don't ask...now or ever. You got me? When you're done, destroy the picture. Do I have your word?"

"Have I ever let you down?" Randy pushed back.

"Do I have your word?"

"Of course. You wouldn't ask if this wasn't something beyond important. I swear."

Randy's phone vibrated on the desk. It's here. Cole, have you seen the photo?"

"No. How bad is it?"

"If it were me, I wouldn't give it a thought. It is the back side of a tall, thin woman. No face, just a nice figure, and wet hair. You still want the nuclear treatment?"

"Yes. People can't do this kind of thing and get away with it."

"What will you do with the address? When I'm done there will be nothing left."

"Nothing? This is just between us."

"Tell Kelly not to worry. I got this," Randy said reassuringly.

"How did you...?"

"You two are hopeless at being sneaky. The sender's name and address are on her e-mail."

Cole took a deep breath. "I guess we are. Later."

"I'll let you know what I find out."

The phone rang almost immediately. After the third ring, Cole looked out at Hanna's desk. Empty.

He picked up the phone. "Cole Sage."

"Mr. Sage, my name is Jim Tamarance, I am the chair of the Journalism Department at Stanford. Do you have a minute to chat?"

"Sure. What can I do for you?" Cole said fumbling for a pen and notepad.

"Media is changing, Mr. Sage."

"Don't I know it? Please, call me Cole."

"Thank you. You and I have seen a monumental shift in the way that Journalism is approached and, quite frankly, the shift disturbs me. Our program here focuses on multimedia, data-intensive, entrepreneurial, influenced by design thinking." Tamarance paused for effect. It got just the one he wanted.

"In English, please," Cole said, not hiding his aversion to academic speak.

"No need, since it is to my point. You are one of America's greatest journalists, in the old-school tradition of beat the bushes, find the story, ruffle a few feathers along the way, and print the truth. More than that, you are a great writer. We are losing the journalism battle to Internet research—slanted, phone it in, or rather, e-mail it in, unsophisticated writing. Not to mention that our students, some of them, really have a spark for words, phrases, and the beauty of language."

"You sound like an English professor," Cole responded. "I appreciate the kind words but…." Cole's words drifted off.

"Let me get to the point," Tamarance jumped in. "First congratulations on your Ph.D."

"What?" It was Cole's turn to butt in.

"No need to be coy, Cole. Academia is a small place, really. I have a friend who has a friend that you know. My old roommate is at the University of Chicago, and he told me about you getting the honorary degree. I think it's brilliant. Anyway, before it really gets into the wind, we wanted to make you an offer. I know it's early, but there are rumblings already."

"I'm not sure I...," Cole stammered.

"I understand you'll want to explore your options, but, hear me out. You are a West Coast guy, born and bred, working in the east doesn't make you Ivy League any more than sleeping in the garage makes you a car. You know what I mean?

We want you on our team. According to what we pulled together, your son-in-law is at UCSF Medical, and you have a lovely daughter and granddaughter that are in the Bay Area. Being a grandfather myself, I know I wouldn't dream of leaving them. Oh, and I understand that congratulations are in order, with number two on the way? So you see, we're the home team." Tamarance chuckled at his remark.

"Look, mister, uh, Jim, I am a bit surprised at all this."

"I appreciate that and I knew it was a gamble but I wanted to be ahead of the curve. We need a strong writing element here that we are currently lacking, Peter Chase is retiring in a few weeks, and we think his spot is perfect for you. As far as money goes, I know our offer more than doubles what you are currently earning, not that money is everything. I realize that there is "the love of the game." We offer a place for you to share your vast knowledge with the next generation of journalists, and instill a love of writing, truth, and the high ethical standard we need to instill."

"Can I be frank, Jim?" Cole gave a nervous chuckle, at the sound of the request.

Tamarance got the pun and replied, "You can be anyone you like."

The laughter the men shared momentarily relieved the tension both felt. Cole was literally dizzy at the news this unexpected call brought. Stanford? Ph.D.? U of Chicago? Thoughts were jumping synapses and making their own blurring connections.

"I am flattered and very honored, that my work over the years has garnered this kind of attention. To be truthful, I'm really kind of thrown off balance by your offer."

"Please don't feel any pressure. I, we, want you to be comfortable with your decision. I kind of came on a little strong. It's just the idea really is an exciting one for us."

Cole looked down at the name he scribbled on the notepad in front of him, "I tell you what, Mr. Tamarance, you have my word I will not make any decision lightly and not without conferring with you and your colleagues. Is that fair?"

"It is all I could wish for. We would like to meet with you as soon as we can for an informal gathering to introduce you to our staff and let you see if we are a good fit. May I call your secretary later to make the arrangements?"

"That would be fine. Let me ask you something." Cole cleared his throat and took a long moment to gather his thoughts. "If I decided to join you, would there be, that is, could I bring my secretary, and key researcher with me?"

"Secretary without a doubt. Researcher is the magic word around here. I can almost guarantee it. But, let's save that for next time."

"Well, this has been most enlightening. I look forward to our getting together," Cole offered.

"As do I. Until then...." With that Tamarance was gone.

Cole put his hands on top of his head and leaned back. He was having a hard time breathing. Did that guy just offer me a job at Stanford? Cole played out a hoax scenario in his head. He didn't know the voice. Who would do such a thing? It's just too random to be a joke.

"I'm back! Had to run to the Ladies Room."

Cole was too deep in thought to respond for a moment and then: "Did I miss any calls?"

Hanna approached Cole's door. "Are you OK?"

Cole sat up and looked at her. "Why?"

"I don't know, you look kind of funny."

"Clown funny?" Cole tried to shake off his shock.

"You're fine." Hanna rolled her eyes. "You just look pale."

"I've had a bit of a surprise and I'm still trying to process it."

"I'll leave you to it then." Hanna smiled. "You're sure you're OK?"

"Never better. Truly, never better." Cole reassuringly returned her smile.

For more than an hour after the call, Cole daydreamed, doodled, and thought about what it would be like to teach the thing he loved most. Oddly, the thought never entered his mind before. Over the years when he got really fed up, with a boss or the assignments he was given, and especially during the dark years before Ellie came back into his life, he sometimes plotted running away and becoming a beach bum or hermit. Even then, writing was always the heart of the plan.

He rehearsed in his head how to break the news to Kelly. He thought about taking her to the reception at Stanford and making it a surprise. *Bad idea* was his almost immediate second thought. Call her and tell her? Not after her day today. He wanted and needed to tell someone. It couldn't be Hanna, although she would be the most convenient, then he'd have to explain why she got to know first. Ugh, women.

He dropped the whole line of thought and shifted to Chicago. When were they going to tell him? How did Tamarance's friend know? Was he on the selection committee? It was several months to graduation. He would worry about it then, he thought.

"Hey, Hanna! Come here for a minute."

"What's up?"

"I've never been to your place. Do you like it?"

"It's OK. What is going on? You are being just plain weird."

"I wasn't fishing for an invitation. I just wondered if you liked living where you live."

"Are you considering buying an apartment building?" Hanna quizzed.

"What, with my good looks?"

"You're right, it would have to be really little. Seriously, why do you ask?"

"I got some really incredible news earlier. I can't tell you because, if I told you before Kelly or Erin, I'd get killed. But it might involve you if you're interested."

"Are we moving to Hawaii?"

"No."

"Well, then it depends."

"Full circle: Do you like where you live?" Cole asked again.

"Not especially. It is nice for what I can afford."

"Thank you. So, if the right set of circumstances occurred you would not be opposed to relocating?"

"No. You want to stop playing games and tell me what's on your mind?"

"I can't. But, if there is an opportunity coming up...."

"I'm in." Hanna interrupted.

"Awesome, I think you'll like Bakersfield." Cole laughed at his joke. "Relax, when the time comes I'll tell you. There is no sense getting excited about something that might not happen. I just wanted to know how settled you were."

"What about Lindsey?"

"She's the big X in the equation."

* * *

"Where is that bus?" A thin black woman wiggled on the bench and resettled her purse and shopping bag. She turned and looked up at the bus schedule with a scowl. "Ten minutes late. I ain't got all day ta be sittin' on this damn bench."

"It kind of feels good just to relax a bit, don't you think?"

"Relax? Who got time to relax? I need ta git home and fix dinner. My old man be mad as hell, his supper ain't on when he walks through the door." The woman was getting angrier by the second.

"Maybe waiting would be a good lesson."

"You crackers think you know everythin' 'bout everythin'.

"Just because I'm white doesn't mean I don't see things like they are."

"So, what you sayin'? You feel my pain? Ha! That's rich."

"I'm just saying it matters the way people are treated. It sounds like your husband doesn't appreciate you. That's all I was trying to say."

"So now you know all about my old man. What you need to know is that white folks never understand what it is to be Black in America. To me, Black lives matter more than all that cracker we-all-created-equal bullshit I had to swallow knowin' ain't nobody believes it."

"Forget it. I was just trying to be nice."

"Why, so you can go home to yours, and tell how you talked to a real Black woman today? Will that make your Obama-lovin' family feel like they helpin'?

Let me tell you somethin': Obama ain't black, and he ain't helped us a damn."

"Fine, I'll shut up."

The woman didn't respond. She just stared straight ahead with her chin held up in an unnaturally stretched position. She mumbled something under her breath and moved the shopping bag from her lap.

The cold steel shaft of the ice pick made the killer smile. Three fingers tapped the handle like a trumpeter's big solo. With movements smooth and fluid, the ice pick was slipped out and held tight.

Glancing to the left, then to the right, there were no bus, no cars, and no pedestrians. The stoplight up the block was red, and the traffic was still. With the speed of a cobra's strike, the ice pick slammed into the woman's heart. The shaft sank so deep, her fist hit the woman's chest with a thud. It felt good. It felt solid. She loved the sound, the feel, the rush of burying the shaft deep into the heart of the woman. So much in fact, in less than a moment, she removed the ice pick and thrust it even harder into the woman.

"Wrong. Your Black life doesn't matter, at least not to me. Let's see how your old man likes going without dinner, permanently." The killer mocked and chuckled. The thin black woman's head fell back against the Plexiglas wall of the bus stop cover. Her muscles relaxed and she looked calm. Her stress and anger were all gone.

"Well, well, here comes the bus," the killer said, standing. Feeling elated, and with a sense of accomplishment, she turned and walked up the street toward the oncoming bus.

Chapter Seven

A pair of well-dressed Chinese women in their late forties sat on a sunny bench on the edge of Buena Vista Park. They chatted, laughed, and ate their lunch from bright white Styrofoam containers. They slipped in and out and back and forth from Chinese to English.

The killer ate a banana and watched the women with a combination of envy and disdain. "Nothing is that funny," she said.

The two benches set slightly off at parallel angles. The killer was to the right and slightly behind the pair of women. As she watched she quietly grasped a brand new ice pick and slowly withdrew it from her jacket pocket. It was a constant source of amusement that she could go through her day and no one noticed the nine-inch tool in her pocket.

"I think I can do them both," the killer spoke aloud, knowing the women couldn't hear her. "The little one is nearest. Top of the head would be the only way. Bam, bam, one after the other. A second hit if they move. Shouldn't though, no one else has."

She watched the women closely. They were so involved in their conversation that they were unaware of her existence. The park was fairly busy during lunch hour. But as it was nearly one o'clock, the office workers and couples meeting for lunch were beginning to thin out. The women didn't pay any attention to people passing by. They just laughed, giggled, and continued talking.

I need to get moving, the killer thought. I have things to do. I'll wait for a few more stragglers. She sat scanning the park and watching people pick up their trash, lunch bags, and water bottles.

"Mind if I join you?" A man's voice broke into the killer's thoughts.

Hell yes, I mind, the killer thought, but she didn't speak. She quickly put the ice pick back in her pocket.

"Beautiful day isn't it." The man took a seat on the bench. "I was watching you eyeball those two over there. I thought I'd come over and see what was so interesting. I was kind of lonesome over there by myself anyways."

"They're so noisy. I couldn't help it."

"I'm kind of the un-appointed mayor of the park."

The man was relatively clean. At least he didn't stink. The killer judged him to be at least sixty, but it was hard to tell with street people. He wore a pair of green plaid dress slacks, a gold polyester shirt, and a brown knit tie. If it were 1975 he would be right in style. As it is, he looked like the mannequin in a thrift shop. His hair was mousey gray and greasy. He wore a pair of high-top lace-up climbing boots. At one time he might have been good looking, but the ravages of alcohol and life on the street were written on his face in deep creases and scars.

The killer didn't respond to the man. She was about to stand when he suddenly grabbed the back of her neck. His grip was like a clamp suddenly ratcheting down on her muscles.

"Let go of me!" the killer groaned.

"My other hand's got a knife in it, so don't move. Why looky there, your friends are leaving."

The killer tried to scream, but his grip was so painful she was finding it hard to breathe.

"If you settle down, I'll let up. If you try to run, I'll gut you like a fish. M'I clear?" He eased his grip slightly.

"OK, OK."

"I just want to have a little chat. Other people 'round here have always got somebody to have a little talk with. Not me, I try to be friendly but people act like I got leprosy. I don't. I got needs. Everybody's got needs. Am I so gross or hideous to look at? I bathe, my clothes are clean. I just need someone to talk to, maybe fall in love with. Is that so terrible? Shouldn't I have that chance?" The man's voice was a harsh whisper and his breath smelled of alcohol. "So I decided since you were alone, and I was alone, that we needed each other. Now, you gonna sit still and let us get to know each other?"

"Sure, no problem. Just let go," the killer said, trying to sound calm.

"Alright then…" the man slowly let go of her neck but left his hand resting on her shoulder. "Let's start over. Hello, what's a pretty little lady like you doing here?"

"I like to come here at lunch," she replied softly.

"I love this park. The trees are like old friends to me. I always love it when the city guys come and mow the lawn. The smell of cut grass reminds me of home. Do you like the smell of cut grass?"

"Yes. And the flowers are nice this time of year, too."

"If we get to be friends I could bring you flowers. I think flowers are romantic. You don't have a boyfriend or anything do you?"

"No, not right now."

"That's good, that's good. Now, you say something to me. Say something like people do." The man's voice rose with anticipation of a conversation.

"Have you been to the flower show at Moscone Center? I was there last year and I'm really looking forward to it." The killer's voice quaked in fear, but her words were just what the man craved.

"Perhaps we can go together. We could go and then take a stroll afterwards."

"We just might do that. I do have some obligations coming up so I'll have to check the dates." The killer tried to sound like the woman of his fantasy.

"You see, we are getting along real well. I had a girl back home. Sheila was her name. We were going to get married…had to, if you know what I mean. I didn't mind. I loved her like the stars above."

"She must be lovely."

"You think I'm making it up," the man said angrily. "I'm not! She got killed in a wreck comin' home from work. She died, her and my child inside her. You need to think before you speak."

"I didn't know, I'm sorry."

"Let's start over. That's a pretty jacket you have on."

"Thank you. I like your tie. I think knit ties are very handsome."

The man let his hand slip from her shoulder. He sat quietly just looking ahead. "People should consider what a person's been through before they judge them. I used to have a job at the Safeway stocking shelves. The young guys always made fun of me. They weren't considerate like you."

"You're right. People are too quick to judge others."

"Can I kiss you?"

"Not yet. We just met. Maybe later, when we get to know each other better," she said softly.

The killer crossed her legs and scooted slightly away from the man as she changed positions. He looked straight ahead. Suddenly he seemed miles away. She moved as slowly as she could. She was afraid to speak for fear of him noticing the distance that was growing between them.

"I'm leaving this city soon. I'm going back home. You'll like it there. I've decided we should go together."

"How long has it been since you were there?" She took the opportunity to slide a slight bit further away.

"Thirty-seven years, I think. I am not so good with dates anymore. July sixteen, I remember and April twelve. Those are good dates."

"I like February tenth," the killer replied.

She slipped her hand gently into her pocket. Her friend, the ice pick, was cool and confident.

"I've been thinking about that kiss," she said. "You're a bit older than the guys I usually go for, but why let that get in the way of love, right? Like they say, age is just a number."

The man smiled. "I'm ready any time. It is up to you. This is me being considerate. Do you like it?"

"I think I'm ready. But you have to close your eyes. I'm kind of shy."

The man closed his eyes and puckered his lips. The killer almost laughed, as she drove the ice pick into his chest.

"Wha, what are you...."

She withdrew the shaft from his chest and stood. Without hesitation, she drove the spike through the top of his head and rotated it three times.

"Say hello to Sheila, asshole."

The killer took the man's tie and wiped the shaft of the ice pick clean of his blood. She got to the sidewalk as the Muni bus approached the Buena Vista stop. The doors opened and she got in unnoticed. Through the grimy window, she looked back and saw the man in the green plaid pants dozing on the bench, dreaming of his Sheila.

* * *

Lindsey Frost was the only person in the breakroom when Cole arrived. She was staring off into space and didn't notice him until he was nearly to the table.

"Getting anything done?"

"Not much," Lindsey replied.

Cole pulled out a chair and seated himself across from Lindsey. On the table was a biology book, a history text, and a spiral notebook. The books were closed the notebook was open.

"Finished the biology?" Cole inquired.

"Huh-uh," Lindsey said without looking at Cole.

"History?"

"Huh-uh."

"Well, this is supposed to be a time to get your homework done, and then get some tutoring in writing."

"I know."

"How 'bout I help you with your homework. Kind of get you started?"

"Whatever."

"I have a better one. *Whatever* seems to be the problem?"

"School sucks. I hate it. They don't do anything important. I hate the stuck-up kids, the know-it-all teachers, and all those bitches in the office that are always just...*trying to help*. I don't need it. I know how to write, and I know what I want to do. They are in the way." Lindsey's eyes blazed with rage.

This was a side of the girl Cole hadn't seen. He didn't like it.

"So our deal's off?" Cole pushed back his chair and stood up.

"I didn't say that." Lindsey was taken back by Cole preparing to leave.

"Let's see, and I quote, I don't need it...they're in the way, end quote. Sounds like you've made up your mind. That's your right. Come back and see me when you get published." Cole turned and started for the door.

"Wait! Where are you going?" Lindsey cried out.

"Back to work. That's what they pay me for. Not babysitting."

"I didn't say I was quitting. I said it sucked and I hated it. There is a difference."

Cole turned and walked back to his chair. He grasped the back with both hands. This feral kid was showing her true colors and they weren't going to be easy to take. He looked at her for a long moment. Cole hated to be conned. Lindsey Frost was a con-artist from the ground up. She smiled a smile as beguiling as any demon. Two can play this game, he thought.

"There are two things in this world I hate," Cole began. "A thief, and a liar. If you expect to continue in my good graces, and as a work-experience intern, you better not turn out to be either one, a thief or a liar. You got me?"

"Yeah," Lindsey said with a shrug.

"You have a great opportunity here if you are really serious about being a writer. You got a chance to have a safe home life with Hanna. This test coming up on Saturday, if you do well you can write your own ticket. Thing is, kiddo, it's entirely up to you. This time last week I didn't know your name, next week it could be the same way."

Cole scooted this chair closer and rested his elbows on the table. He interlaced his fingers and paused long enough to gather his thoughts. "You looked like you needed a helping hand. I reached out and so did Hanna, but if you are unwilling to make some changes in your attitude, attendance at school, and grades, you're showing us you don't want help. *Take*, is not something to strive for, but *give*, is. As I see it, you got it backward. We're willing to help, but you have to be worthy of our efforts. That make sense?"

"Yeah, but you don't get it. I know what I want. The teachers don't know or care. There are three thousand kids at that school. Teachers just do their thing, period after period, day after day. They hate that place as much as I do. The difference is I have the freedom to do something else. For them, it's a life sentence. If being a writer means being trapped in a cage, I'll find another way.

"I appreciate what you and Hanna are trying to do for me, "Lindsey continued. "Really I do. But, I know what I can do, how to live, eat, sleep and survive. I've been doing it since I was ten. You talk about *take*? Ain't nobody ever given me anything, I take what, and when, I need to. You talk about liars and thieves? I can read. The people running for president are all liars and they must be thieves because their only job is politics and that doesn't pay millions. Even *I* know that." Lindsey stared up at Cole. "So let's get this clear: What is it you want from me?"

"Respect, and a lot of hard work."

"What's in it for me?" Lindsey didn't flinch. "I want to be a writer. You said you'd teach me. School is bullshit. I've never had a father, and the mother I have sucks, professionally. Hanna is a nice lady, but I don't want another mom."

"So what are you saying? You done? You quit? What?" Cole pressed.

"I'm saying I will do my best to comply with your rules," Lindsey answered without a smile or the least hint of sincerity.

"And the test? Are you going to blow that off? It is worth thousands, and a prep school like that on your transcript will get into some amazing colleges. Probably scholarships too. *I've* never had a chance like that. Ever."

"I'll see what I can do."

Lindsey's noncommittal, who cares attitude frustrated Cole almost beyond its limits. Cole never dealt with a teenager on a long-term basis before. He didn't like what little exposure he was privy to. He saw talent in Lindsey's writing. Her ability to write clouded his view of who she was. He should have realized when they went to the hell hole she called home that nothing good could come out of it. Hanna played the maternal nurturing card. Cole was a sucker for a good rags-to-riches, pulled-up-by-their-own-bootstraps, against-all-odds story. He built a career on telling those stories. But he wasn't part of them.

If Cole Sage was anything, it was certainly not a hand holder, babysitter, enabler, or co-dependent. His work ethic and moral compass were unfaltering and unwavering. More often than not he was let down and disappointed by people who had received his trust. It seemed very few people could or would do what they say, when they say, and get the job done to the best of their ability.

Cole was aware of his faults. He spoke too soon, often wishing for an immediate retraction. When he felt he was right, he would fight to the death for his position, alienating co-workers and management alike.

His attributes, by far, outweighed his faults. Cole Sage was generous, compassionate, loyal to a fault, and a man of his word. Truthfulness seems to have fallen out of favor in modern day America, but since rededicating his life to the faith of his youth, keeping the Ten Commandments seemed a sacred bond between him and the Almighty. He probably wouldn't have felt he needed church, or religion, in his life as much as he did, until he met Kelly.

Her faith, that of her son, and most of all his daughter Erin made Cole feel there was a hole in his soul, God-shaped and needing to be filled. He wasn't preachy in any way, shape or form, few knew he attended regular services. His faith was his own and seemed to grow as time went by.

His desire to help Lindsey Frost perhaps came from the knowledge of how a life can be lifted from the darkness. He wanted to set a good example for her. He could be a mentor to her. He would do everything he could for her, but only if she was willing to comply with their agreement.

Cole looked at Lindsey and thought of Anthony Perez. A harder case you would be hard pressed to find, but he reached out to Cole. He wanted what Cole had, an education and a career in journalism. Their friendship was a treasure. Cole looked at him as the son he would have wanted. What was the difference? Was Anthony older, wiser, wanting to change? Lindsey, during their short relation, had never given Cole a reason to want to help her…other than her talent.

Cole felt a sense of disappointment as the girl grudgingly opened her biology book.

"I gotta do these questions."

"Do you need me to help?" Cole asked softly.

"Nah. They're easy."

"How about History?"

"It is just reading the chapter. You can go back to work." Lindsey's inflection betrayed her resentment at being subjected to Cole's tough love.

"Alright. Come up to my office at about five to five. I'm sure Hanna will be ready to go." Cole chuckled and gave her a grin. "I'll be long gone. See you tomorrow. Let's get your work done early so we can talk writing."

"Yeah, that would be good." Lindsey didn't look up.

As Cole left the breakroom he breathed a prayer, "God, help me. I'm not sure this was a good idea."

Cole needed to think. He took the stairs instead of the elevator. He didn't want to deal with people. He sat down on the landing between floors. The step was cold and the updraft of cool air felt good on his flushed cheeks. With elbows resting on his knees, and his face planted in his palms, Cole sighed deeply. This whole mess is my fault, he thought.

If he hadn't been so blown away by Lindsey's writing, he may have taken a few extra minutes to assess her personality. The chit-chat over lunch and that crazy encounter with her mother and Stevie didn't exactly make for getting acquainted.

He closed his eyes and tried to relax a bit before going back to face Hanna. A few minutes later, above him, he heard the metallic click of a door opening. Moments later it clicked shut and the sound of approaching footsteps ruined his solitude. Before he could stand, a man plopped down on the step next to Cole.

"What are you doin' here?"

"Trying to get a little privacy," Cole said coldly.

"Sage, right?" The man fished a package of cigarettes out of his shirt pocket. "O'Malley, Circulation."

"Nice to meet you." Cole offered his hand.

O'Malley shook hands with a firm enthusiastic grip. "No, it's not. I interrupted your peace and quiet. Mind if I smoke?"

"Kill yourself," Cole quipped.

"Ha! That's good." The man lit the cigarette and blew smoke upward. "Natural ventilation in the staircase."

"I noticed," Cole replied. "You know…this is a no-smoking building."

"I sneak in here a couple, three times a day. Used to be, we could smoke at our desks. That seems like ancient history," O'Malley mused, ignoring Cole's admonition.

"Been here a long time?" Cole liked the man's energy and realized talking to a stranger was a pleasant distraction.

"Started as a paperboy when I was twelve. Market and Battery was my domain." O'Malley chuckled. "I fought off bigger kids and news guys for three years. I got noticed by the distribution manager and got a job indoors. Stacker-bundler—I did that all the way through high school, every morning before school. After I got home from 'Nam, I got a spot in classified. Stayed there until last month. 'Circulation or retire' they said. Can't do that quite yet, so I'm back where I started. Ironic, huh?"

"Certainly is."

"We are the last of a dying breed. Real newspaper people. I expect a pink slip any day. Everything's online. No customer service anymore." O'Malley took a long drag on his smoke. His energy seemed to drain away as he thought of the future.

"You know, O'Malley…"

"Please…call me Tim."

"I was sitting here wondering what I am still doing here. You're right. We are two of a kind. I don't really know anything else," Cole agreed, more to himself than his new friend.

"You met Waddell's replacement?"

"Yep. Now, there is a guy who wouldn't know a scoop if it ran up and bit him on the butt."

Both men laughed then sat in silence, enjoying the peace of the staircase as O'Malley finished his cigarette."

Finally, O'Malley said, "I better get back before they figure out nobody pees for ten minutes. Little snitches will squeal, sure as hell."

"Here." Cole handed him a stick of gum. "Don't give them any ammo!"

"Nice to meet you, Sage. Want to bet on which of us leaves first?" O'Malley said with a wry grin.

"Sucker bet," Cole smiled.

O'Malley stood and ran up the stairs. Cole stood and made his way to his office.

"Where have you been? Randy has called three or four times," Hanna asked as Cole approached her desk.

"Went to check on your little darling."

"And?"

"You're going to have your hands full with that one." Cole took a deep breath. "I feel like I owe you an apology for dragging you into this. If I hadn't…"

"I'm a big girl, Cole. It was my decision. If you recall, it was you who told me not to jump into anything." Hanna smiled but it was weak and not at all convincing.

"Just the same, I feel partially responsible."

"OK, I'll let you be a little miserable." Hanna smiled, this time it was real. "I appreciate you trying to take the blame. I need to work through this one myself. Maybe it is just the new environment, all the changes for her, you know, structure. Can you imagine going from the mess she was into where two real grown-ups are willing to look after you? I was thinking this morning: she now has breakfast, lunch, and dinner, a bed, a shower, and thank God, shampoo, and deodorant!" Hanna laughed. "Now, I just need to get someone to do something with that hair of hers and she might look a little more domesticated."

"Good idea. It looks like it was cut with a lawnmower."

"How do they always know when you're back? Except for Randy, the phone hasn't rung once." Hanna answered the phone. "It's Randy."

Cole sat at his desk and counted to three and answered the phone. "Hey."

"OK, here's what I got. Nothing. The picture came from a burner phone, pay as you go, disposable kind of thing. I've been able to obtain a list of numbers from the phone. We are in deep, black water here, Cole. I can do a back-trace and find out who the person called, but here is the thing: We are crossing the line between the abusive sender, to the privacy of the people whose numbers are on the phone. Doesn't sound like much, but to the Feds, it is a big deal legally."

"So what are you saying?" Cole asked.

"I'm saying the only way to find your photographer is to find the friends and acquaintances whose numbers I have. FYI, Kelly's number is on here, but only the one call was made."

"Then what you're saying is, we can find out who else the person called, then we can try and identify…"

"We have to call them…" Randy said.

"…and ask if they know this number."

"That's about it. How to do that is way out of my wheelhouse."

"How many are there?" This was a natural for Cole's bag of tricks.

"Six."

"E-mail the numbers to me."

"No dice. I write them down and bring them to you. No trail, Cole, this can't come back to us. I'll be right up." Then there was just dial tone.

"Can you come here a second?" Cole called to Hanna.

A moment later Hanna appeared in the doorway, notepad in hand.

"How would you like to do some of that undercover work you love so much?"

"Yes! Please!" Hanna replied. "I'm all caught up and have absolutely nothing to do."

"Alright, here is the deal. I need you to make six calls. Use any guise you want. I suggest a legal secretary from Oui, Cheatam, and Howe."

Hanna laughed. "Not sure about that one, maybe Howard, Fine, and Howard?"

"Love it. Anyway, we need to find out if these people recognize a phone number that I'll give you. If so, who is it? On and off as quickly as possible, no gabbing, all business."

"Sounds easy enough. Why do we need to find this person?"

"Can't tell you," Cole said dryly.

"Can't or won't?" Hanna pushed.

"Your choice."

Randy Callen appeared at the door and his presence stopped Hanna from responding.

"It's OK. Cole looked at Hanna and waited for an answer. She's part of the plan. Doesn't know why or what, but she's in. Right?"

"I guess so."

"Here is the list. And this is a little present." Randy handed Cole an old flip phone. "I don't know where it came from. I've never seen it before, and I never want to see it again. When you're finished doing whatever it is you're going to do, break it in two, throw the battery in one place, fold the sim card and burn it, and throw the phone parts in two different places."

"A little paranoid, are we?" Hanna said sarcastically.

"I like to think of myself as cautious," Randy responded.

"You're serious then," Cole said, sitting a little straighter.

"Serious as a pink slip on your time card."

"Then that's what we'll do."

"Do I ever get to know what this is about?" Hanna's voice was showing serious concern.

"Maybe, but it isn't up to me," Cole answered.

"Don't look at me." Randy's eyes met Hanna's inquisitive stare. "If there isn't nothin' else…"

"No, thank you. I'll let you know what we find out."

Randy left the office. Hanna didn't move. Cole looked down at the list.

* * *

"There's something we need to talk about," Cole said. "It's kind of a five-hundred-pound cannoli in the room."

"A cannoli?" Kelly sounded confused.

"I didn't want to say elephant or gorilla. I'm kind of hungry, and that's what popped into my head." Cole shrugged. "Silly, huh?"

"Just a bit." Kelly cocked her head slightly and gave Cole a long, thoughtful look. "So what's going on?"

"When we get married, I mean, well, we've never talked about money, budgets, you know, a couple's finance stuff." Cole cleared his throat. "I have spent very little in my life. I mean, I eat well. I have a nice place to live, but I don't spend a lot of money. I've traveled the world, but it was always paid for. My folks left me some money, and I bought a new TV, but other than that I've never touched it. I have a bit of a pension from the *Sentinel*, not much, Social Security, and a 401K. When I retire I think we can live comfortably—not extravagantly, but we won't starve or have to move in with the kids."

Kelly gave Cole a wide smile. "What is this all about?"

"I want to leave the paper."

"OK."

"I've been offered a teaching job at Stanford."

"That's wonderful, Cole!"

"I haven't told anybody. Just you."

"Go on, go on!" Kelly scooted to the edge of the sofa.

"I'm worried. It is an amazing compliment that they think I could teach journalism. But, getting married is a huge step for us. I know we love each other, but I don't know if I'll be able to take care of you. I mean, if it doesn't work out. I want to be a good husband, a good provider. If I fail we could be in trouble. The thing too is, I want to give you all of my attention, you know. What if the job requires too much time? I wouldn't do anything that might come between us." Cole looked deep into Kelly's eyes, he wanted her to know how sincere he was.

"I am so proud that your brilliant mind and wonderful writing is being recognized. You will be an amazing instructor, professor…whatever it is. Cole, I have a lot of money. Some might say I'm rich, I don't, but I'm certainly well off. We have nothing to worry about."

"I know it's old fashioned, but I've always believed it's the man's job to support his wife."

"Really? Did you park a buggy outside? I think we're way beyond traditional spousal roles, don't you?" Kelly frowned. "Is that what you're worried about?"

"I want to feel like I'm making a decision that's sound, one that doesn't put undue strain on our relationship, or makes me look like a kept man if I flop."

"Cole Sage, have you no respect for me? I am an independent woman of means. I have nowhere to live, therefore, I have nothing. I will let you carry me across the threshold of your beautiful home when the time comes. *That* tradition I love. I'll admit I will want to buy a few things. Your taste does tend to run a bit on the leather and wood side. Things could use a bit of brightening up. But, I am about loving you.

"The reason we have never had this talk before is that it doesn't matter," Cole continued. "I can live here in the city or move to that awful Central Valley. I don't care as long as I can call you mine. I am so proud of you for loving me enough to worry about supporting us, but if you retired tomorrow, we wouldn't feel it."

"Stanford University won't know what hit them! You will be amazing. I am completely dumbfounded that you doubt yourself!"

"I just want to make sure," Cole said. "I have only ever had to look out for myself. I've always been a newspaperman. I never imagined doing anything else. I never dreamed I wouldn't be the breadwinner."

"You aren't supposed to eat a lot of carbs anyway!" Kelly stood and moved toward Cole. "I think this news needs a celebration kiss."

Cole stood and embraced Kelly. He held her tight, her head lying against his shoulder. They swayed gently. After a long moment, she raised her head and looked him in the eyes.

"I love you broke, unemployed, or as an old grey professor." Kelly closed her eyes and Cole kissed her.

Chapter Eight

The lobby of a large city newspaper isn't anyone's idea of a beehive of activity. But as they say, to every rule there is an exception.

Thirty high school journalism students can make quite a racket even when they whisper. When left alone, while their teacher is chatting with their tour guide, things can get cheerfully exuberant.

Laughing, talking, and excitedly waiting for the tour of the biggest newspaper in the city, none of the students noticed a wiry, thin man, with the greasy ponytail, enter the lobby.

Security guard, Craig Simmons, watched the kids from the vantage point of the security entrance of the first-floor office area. As they teased, poked, and good-naturedly flirted, Craig thought of his own kids at that age. He smiled as one smaller than the rest, a redheaded boy, approached a pretty Asian girl and attempted to strike up a conversation. Oh, to be that age again, the guard thought.

"What have we got here?" Hanna asked as she approached the security guard.

"High school field trip. Great bunch of kids. Where are you off to?"

"I have to drop off some papers at Lindsey's school."

"What a weird turn of events that is! I pick up the stray, and you take her home!" Craig laughed merrily.

The redheaded boy seemed to have said something right because the pretty focus of his attention pushed her long raven hair behind her ear and smiled. The bellowing of a big kid in a letterman jacket drew Craig's attention. No one saw Stevie Quint and his greasy ponytail, ragged jeans, and flip-flops move to the center of the lobby.

Stevie repeatedly licked his lips and tightened the thin elastic band on his ponytail. The receptionist shoved her finger in her ear, in an ineffective attempt to block out some of the noise in the lobby.

As he approached the reception counter for the first time, he spotted the security guard by the door. Stevie tapped the counter with the fingertips of his right hand.

The manic action caught the attention of the receptionist. "How can I help you?"

"I want to see that Sage guy. The writer. Or, or, or…his woman, the one who works for him. I don't know her name." Stevie was agitated and showed signs of being under the influence of methamphetamines.

The receptionist looked toward the security guard. Craig was enjoying chatting with Hanna and watching the kids, and didn't see her panicked look.

"Call 'em. What are you waiting for?" Stevie demanded.

"I'm not sure if Mr. Sage is in today."

"Call the woman then!" Stevie was trying to hold it together but his voice began rising.

"How can I call someone when you don't know their name?"

"Does he have a secretary? All big shots have a secretary. He's a big shot around here, right? Mr. Im-por-tant Wri-ter, right? That's him, right? Call his secretary then."

"Please sir, lower your voice or I'm going to have to ask you to leave." The receptionist sat a little taller in her chair. Her new found bravado was lost on Stevie.

"I'm not going anywhere until I talk to one of them. They stole my kid and I want her back!" Stevie was now screaming at the woman behind the counter.

For the slightest moment, the lobby grew quiet. The eyes and ears of more than the thirty students were all directed at the screaming tweaker standing at the counter. Craig Simmons' attention was taken from Hanna and went on high alert as his eyes met those of the receptionist.

"Craig, that's the boyfriend of Lindsey's mom," Hanna whispered.

Never one to rush into a situation, Simmons took in the sight of the man at the counter. Though standing still, Stevie seemed to be running in place. His muscles twitched and pulsed from head to foot. As Simmons approached the counter, Stevie turned to face him. It was then Stevie spotted Hanna.

"What do you want? I'm not doing anything that concerns you. Go mind your own business."

"The lobby does concern me. You see, it's my little peaceful part of the world. I noticed you are a bit upset. Your volume seems to be giving my friend Keri a bit of concern. Now, why don't you and I step over here and see if we can work out whatever it is that's upsetting you?" The security guard spoke softly, firmly, yet with a friendly tone.

"She just needs to call Sage or better yet, bring her over here." Stevie pointed at Hanna. "This isn't any of your business. She and I will do fine without you buttin' in."

Hanna took several steps towards the reception desk. The security guard turned and gave her a sharp shake of his head.

"Does Mr. Sage know you?" Simmons asked.

"See this? This is his work!" Stevie raised his index and middle finger to the large purplish green bruise on his cheek. "He did this. Sucker punched me."

"I hate it when that happens." Simmons gently put his hand on Stevie's shoulder and tried to direct him away from Reception.

"Get your hands off me!"

Simmons put his hands up, palms facing Stevie, in a motion of compliance. "OK, let's just calm down a bit. Now tell me what the problem is. Why is it you need to see Mr. Sage? Maybe I can help."

"He and that woman over there came to my old lady's house and beat me up and took her kid. They're trying to get our welfare cut off, that's what. I want the kid back now!"

"You know, I've known Cole Sage a long time and I never knew him to be a kidnapper. Do you suppose this is just some kind of misunderstanding? Who is this kid, anyway?"

"She's my old lady's kid. She lives with us at her grandma's place. We all live together."

"What's her name?"

"Um, she goes by, uh, her name's...."

"Let's start with her mom. What's her name?"

"Natalie," Stevie answered.

"Pretty name. What's yours?"

"Stevie."

"Well, Stevie, how 'bout I call Mr. Sage and see if he can straighten this out for us."

"That's all I want. That's all I'm askin'. I don't need all this other crap."

"None of us do. You stay right here and I'll go call."

As he approached the reception counter Simmons said, "Keri, can you ring Mr. Sage for me?" Then, in an effort to keep Stevie from hearing he whispered, "Keep an eye on me. If I give you the nod, call the police."

Keri smiled and nodded. "Mr. Sage? We have a bit of a problem. Craig needs to speak to you." Keri glanced up and the security guard, then said, "Here he is."

Keri handed the phone to Craig.

"Hi, Cole. I have a fella down here in the lobby named Stevie. He's pretty upset. He says you and Hanna took his daughter or something."

"My old lady's daughter!" Stevie shouted.

Craig turned to check on the kids from the field trip and saw a couple dozen phones filming and snapping pictures as fast as they could. Terrific, he thought. Hanna stood wide-eyed and gave Craig Simmons a what-do-I-do shrug.

"I kinda figured as much. What do you want me to do? I can do that. Yes, sir, that's what I'm here for." Craig handed the phone back to Keri. "Remember what I said."

"Well, Stevie, it seems Mr. Sage is pretty busy. He asked me to tell you he has nothing to say to you. The girl is in a safe place and is being taken care of. So I'll need you to leave."

From his baggy jeans pocket, Stevie pulled a knife and with a flick of the wrist the blade was out and his hand waved it in front of Craig Simmons.

"You call him back, you hear? You call him back and tell him I'm not going anywhere 'til he mans-up and comes down here and faces me man to man. I want the girl, I want the money, and I want to give Sage a dose of this!"

The guard looked at the receptionist and gave her a nod.

"I'm afraid that just isn't going to happen. Now, put the knife away and leave peacefully while you still can. You really don't want to get locked up over this, do you?"

"Don't talk to me like you know me! What the hell do you know? That girl is our meal ticket. I can't work, and her mother is a twenty-dollar street whore. I want that girl back! Grandma's her guardian! She'll tell ya what's what!" Stevie was burning with rage and his movements were erratic.

"OK, we're done here. Out you go!" Craig's voice now boomed with authority and reflected his physical dominance over Stevie.

Stevie started to move on Simmons's, then without warning darted to where Hanna watched the scene and grabbed the front of her jacket.

The knife swung through the air wildly, "You want me to cut her? Is that what you want?" Stevie swung around behind Hanna and pressed the knife to her throat.

With precision and well-practiced fluid motion, Craig Simmons un-holstered his revolver: "Let. Her. Go." There was no question as to Simmons's meaning or intent.

"Get Sage!" Stevie screamed hoarsely.

"Let her go." Simmons turned to the group. "Get out of here, kids."

Like a huge jellyfish, the thirty students seemed to move as one freeform body running toward the door. Simmons circled, his back to the kids, assuring them that Stevie couldn't get to them.

"I'm going to ask you once more," Simmons said firmly.

"What are you gonna do, shoot me, Rent-a-Cop?"

"Hanna, stay calm," Craig said, hoping to calm her and keep her from doing anything to provoke Stevie.

"Cool as a cucumber," Hanna said in a trembling voice.

"This guy's a bully. He's a coward or he wouldn't have grabbed you. Don't worry, he's not going to do anything to you." Simmons continued to circle. "Have you read any of Sue Grafton's books?"

"Yeah," Hanna replied.

"Shut up and get Sage!" Stevie yelled. "This ain't a Book Club!"

"What do you suppose Kinsey Millhone would do in a situation like this?" Simmons smiled reassuringly.

"I said, shut up!" Stevie turned slightly and directed his attention to the receptionist. "Call Sage! Now! I'll slit her throat! Call him!"

In that slight moment of distraction, Hanna stomped her heel hard on the top of Stevie's bare foot. A second later, she went limp, dropping to the floor, and rolling away from her capturer. Nothing registered with Stevie. In his drug muddled mind, his plan was unraveling, and he was unable to process the situation. In his fury, he focused on the source of his plan's disintegration and rushed Simmons. The knife slashed through the air and he screamed with the rage of a wounded animal. Unflinching, the security guard fired, dropping Stevie on his third step.

The bullet hit just above Stevie's knee shattering his patella at the joint. The sound of the shot echoed in the lobby like a clap of thunder. The room suddenly roared with Stevie's guttural screams. Simmons approached Stevie with confidence and determination. He kicked Stevie's hand, sending the knife sliding across the floor.

Simmons holstered his weapon, took several steps back, and stood with his arms at his sides watching Stevie writhe on the floor.

"You shot me! What the hell, man?"

The security guard did not respond. Soon Stevie's screams turned to moaning and Simmons realized he was crying.

Hanna was on her hands and knees looking up at Craig. Her face was the color of Wonder Bread.

"Can I go out to the kids?" the voice from behind Simmons stopped him from going to Hanna's aid. "They must be freaking out."

The teacher who watched the scene from behind the locked security door approached Simmons with the tour guide from the PR office.

"Yeah, go ahead."

Before the teacher reached the door, it burst open with the full force of four SFPD officers. From Keri's initial call it took the police approximately six minutes to arrive. A tall, raw-boned officer in street clothes and a badge dangling from his neck rushed to Hanna.

"Are you hurt, ma'am?" His voice was deep but full of concern.

"Just my pride," Hanna said raising to her knees.

He reached out and took Hanna by the hands. His large rough hands totally engulfed hers.

"What's your name?" He smiled for the first time. A salt and pepper stubble covered his face. His hair was cropped short and showed white at the temple.

"Hanna."

"Well, Hanna I think you were brilliant. Where did you learn that move?"

"Too many detective movies." Hanna smiled and shrugged. "You saw that?"

"Those big glass doors make a good vantage point. I arrived just as you did your stomp, drop and roll. I'm Detective Winston Salem, by the way, I guess this gave that away." He held up his gold shield.

"Detective?"

"Yep. Let's go sit over here. I need to ask you a few questions."

Hanna and the detective went to a group of chairs and a black and chrome couch that surrounded a short, newspaper-covered table. They both seemed to want to sit on the couch but Salem yielded, taking a chair to Hanna's left.

"So, let's start with the basics," Salem said taking out a small well-worn leather notebook from his hip pocket. "Hanna?"

"Day. Hanna Day."

"Address?"

As Hanna answered she couldn't help but notice the detective's eyes. They were a deep blue, almost black. A thin scar ran through the lid of the right eye and on to his cheek.

"How about a phone number, where you can be reached?"

"I'm here Monday through Friday. She wanted to give him her cell number but didn't want her voice to show how smitten she was becoming in the policeman. "Do you want my cell?" She said a little more excitedly that she intended.

"That would be nice."

Nice? Hanna thought. Did he mean nice, *nice*, or just nice? She gave him the number without looking up.

"That's the easy stuff. The guy that grabbed you..."

"Stevie," Hanna interrupted.

"Stevie. He seemed to know you."

"Well..." Hanna tried to gather her thoughts. "It's kind of a long story."

"I'm salaried. Take all the time you need." Detective Salem smiled for the first time.

Hanna told the story of Lindsey coming to the paper, her trip to her house with Cole, the fight, and Lindsey coming to stay with her.

"What does your husband think of all this?" Salem asked.

"I'm not married. Haven't been for...I'm not," Hanna stammered.

"So, this Stevie character thinks you want the girl for the welfare payment?"

"Honestly, I was just doing what I thought was right. Money never entered into my thinking. The poor kid was in a terrible home situation, and before I knew it, and against Cole's advice, she is staying with me.

"...and Cole is?"

"My boss. Sorry."

"No, no, it's fine. Does anyone know you have taken in…what's her name?" Winston flipped back a page in his notes. "Lindsey?"

"Oh, yes sir," Hanna handed the detective the envelope she was taking to the school.

Salem took out the papers. "Signed sealed and delivered. Well done again. Let me ask you something. Do you intend to adopt this girl? I'm kind of fuzzy on the arrangement here."

"No, I mean…I…no! No adoption. I haven't really thought it out that far in advance. I just took her in temporarily. So she had a safe place to stay and would get her back in school. She was wandering the city, going anywhere she pleased, and school was the furthest thing from her mind."

"Gotcha. You have no kids of your own?"

"No," Hanna said softly. Funny question from a cop, she thought. What's that got to do with Stevie?

There was an uncomfortable silence. Salem stared down at his notes and Hanna looked down at his left hand. No ring.

"Winston."

"Sorry?" Hanna didn't follow.

"My name…or what people call me." The detective was suddenly blushing.

"Oh, I see. Sorry, I thought it was police jargon for end of the interview or something, like Roger or Wilco or…I'll shut up now." Now Hanna's face flushed.

Winston Salem laughed. His wonderful speaking voice transformed into an infectiously delightful laugh.

"Dumb, huh?" Hanna said, embarrassed at her blunder.

"No, not at all. I thought it was absolutely delightful." The detective looked into her eyes and Hanna shuddered.

"Are you from North Carolina?"

"It's kind of a funny story if you're into dark humor, but I'm not telling unless I get to buy you coffee."

Hanna tried really hard not to let her delight show, but it was no use. Her face beamed with possibilities that coffee with the handsome cop presented.

"I take it from your smile the idea is not totally out of the question."

"I would be happy to suffer through coffee to be able to crack the secret of your name," Hanna teased.

"How about I help you deliver those papers and we grab a coffee on the way back? You feel up for that?" Winston paused for a long moment. "Or maybe we should do it another day. You've been through a bit of an ordeal this morning."

"Oh, I'm fine now. I think coffee would be nice." Hanna wasn't about to let the chance to get to know this man with the star get away.

"Great. You sit tight, and I'll see what I need to do to wrap up my part of the show and we'll be on our way.

Keri followed emergency protocol to the letter and, within moments of the police's arrival, Craig Simmons, Hanna, and the high school teacher were joined by a trio of middle management personnel.

The aftermath of the disturbance lasted far longer than the incident itself. Stevie was taken away by ambulance, Simmons was interviewed, and Cole Sage came down to answer a few questions from the police. After an hour, the police left, management returned to their respective offices, and the janitor arrived to mop up Stevie's blood. Keri went to the third-floor cafeteria for her break, to bask in the glory of her "cool head" and her "courage under fire." Still excited and recounting the story, everyone went back to work except for Craig Simmons and Keri, the receptionist, who were sent home for the rest of the day.

The teacher and the PR department guide decided it might be a good idea if the tour was rescheduled. There was no argument from any of the kids, and they eagerly boarded the bus for the trip back to the school, bouncing off the walls from the excitement.

"All set. Ready to go?" Winston's smile was no longer just good cop.

"Ready." Hanna stood next to the detective for the first time. Nice fit, she thought.

Out on the street Detective Salem directed citizen Hanna to a dark green sedan with blacked out windows.

"Company issue. Hop in." He opened her door.

The car was outfitted with every kind of radio and scanner that could possibly fit on, and under, the dashboard. A clipboard sat in the passenger seat. Hanna picked it up and slid in.

"Just toss that in the back. Try not to hit the guy sleeping back there."

Hanna's head snapped around to find the back seat empty, except for a jacket.

"Gotcha," Winston teased.

"You're pretty funny for a detective," Hanna replied.

"And you're kind of funny pretty for a secretary," Winston shot back.

"I'm not quite sure how to take that."

"You are very pretty, in a different kind of way. I mean, there are a lot of kinds of pretty, but you are different. Your face makes me smile. I didn't mean you are funny looking." The detective frantically tried to talk his way out of the clumsy compliment.

"And you are humorously handsome." Pause. "Shall we change the subject?" Hanna beamed like a school girl who just got her first, *I like you. Do you like me?* Valentine from the cute boy in class.

As the car pulled away from the curb, Winston asked, "Where are we going? I mean, what school? Not coffee, there's only one place in the city to get coffee, right?"

"Wallenberg High School. Do you know where it is?" Hanna really wanted to ask about the coffee but sat silently.

"Sure do. So, where are you from, I mean originally?"

"The mid-west. My dad was in sales so we moved around. I've mostly lived in Utah, and California as an adult."

"Mormon? Huh…not that there's anything wrong with that. It's just that, I mean…."

Hanna guided Winston out of another minefield. "Nope, father was Jewish, my mother was a devout alcoholic."

"Giants or A's?"

"Cubs, I have a soft spot for lost causes. I don't have to keep track, whatever it is, it's going to be bad."

Winston turned and smiled at Hanna. "She died. Two years ago. A crazy undetected liver cancer, then it spread everywhere. She was a fighter. They told us six to nine months, she lasted a year. Sally-Ann Marie Tyler, Texas girl. Prettiest thing I ever saw." Winston cleared his throat. "There you are. Got that out of the way. You are the first woman I have even spoken to since, socially I mean. No flirting, nobody's been in my car, no dates, no nothin'."

Hanna for once was at a loss for words. Detective Salem looked straight ahead.

"Michael Robert Garner. Broke my heart, left me with sixty-thousand in debt, and a house I couldn't pay for. He skipped town with a cute little salesgirl from the radio station. The last guy I dated turned out to be married with three kids. That was five years ago. Now we're up to speed on me."

"Any big rush to hand those papers in?" Winston asked.

"What do you mean?"

"Let's get coffee first. Best coffee in the city is on the way to the school. Sort of."

"Alright."

Dynamo Donut and Coffee is truly a hole in the wall, or rather a roll-up door. It sets between a palm reader's place and a Mexican church on 24th Street near Potrero. To both their surprise, there was a parking space just up the block.

Hanna was unusually quiet. She felt at ease with the handsome policeman and felt comfortable enough to not fill the silence with meaningless chatter. Winston was going through his own processing of this impromptu coffee date. He was at turns excited and guilty, elated and terrified.

They walked past the crowd at the walk-up counter and went inside.

"Hi, Tessa!" Winston called out cheerfully.

"Hi yourself. What'll you have?" The woman behind the counter turned and gave Winston a big smile and Hanna the once-over.

"Gibraltar with an extra shot and a chocolate rose."

"And for the lady?" Tessa asked.

"The same," Hanna replied.

"Better keep it to one shot the first time. You'll be cleaning house at two a.m."

"That's one way to get it done."

"We'll be out back." Winston led the way to a door at the back of the building. The sunlight shone brightly through the open door, and Winston motioned for Hanna to go through. To her delight, her new friend brought her to a quiet little charming courtyard full of tables and umbrellas, right in the middle of the city.

"Surprise!" Winston sang out.

"You are full of surprises. This is wonderful. How did you ever find it?" Hanna inquired.

"I'm a detective. Where would you like to sit?"

Hanna looked around the patio and spotted a corner table under a bright green umbrella with giant yellow daisies. "That looks springy." Hanna headed toward the corner.

So are you going to tell me about your name or did you get me here under false pretenses?" She took her seat.

"It isn't nearly as interesting as you might think. My father chain-smoked Winston cigarettes. My mom hated it. So she named me Winston. She thought it might make him quit."

"Did he?"

"Not until he died of emphysema," Winston chuckled. "The Salem part is just a wicked twist of fate."

"Do you go by Winston? I mean, is there a shortened version?" Hanna wasn't fond of the formal sound of Winston.

"Like Winnie?"

"No, but what did your mother call you?"

"She called me 'Honeybunch.' Would you like that better?" Winston shocked himself with the boldness of his joke.

Hanna felt her face flush and hoped it wasn't as red as it felt. "No, seriously."

"I am serious. That's what she called me…unless I was in trouble, but that name's not proper in front of a lady."

"OK, I give up."

"Tell me about the girl, Lindsey." Winston changed the subject.

"Cop questions? I thought we were having coffee." Hanna flared.

"No, it is a get-to-know-you-better question. I was wondering what about this kid appealed to you enough for you to take her in the way you have."

"I have been wondering the same thing."

"How do you mean?" Winston showed concern and his voice showed it.

"She's been through a lot for a kid. She tends to bristle easy. Hates school, she'd rather wander the city writing in her notebook. I don't know why exactly. My do-gooder side, fear for her safety, you met her mom's boyfriend. Maybe I was lonely. Whatever it was, I'm not sure." Hanna paused as if searching for the right words. "Maybe I haven't thought it through good enough. Now I feel trapped. Not trapped exactly…that's an awful thing to say. It's just that she's…I mean…I…I don't know what I mean."

"You're conflicted. I get it. I had the same experience with a dog. A big Golden Retriever, beautiful animal. Chewed up my favorite shoes, crapped all over the apartment while I was at work, and everything I owned was covered with hair."

"What'd you do?"

"Shot her," Winston said.

"What!"

"Just kidding. I took her back to the animal shelter."

Hanna leaned her head a bit to the right and looked at Winston for a long moment. "Well, it may come to that."

"Shooting her?" Winston teased.

"Here you are," Tessa interrupted. Two chocolate roses and two Gibraltar's with an extra shot. Can I get you anything else?"

"This looks great," Hanna replied.

"I think we're fine. Thanks, Tessa."

Hanna looked down at the short clear glass tumbler.

"Two shots of espresso and milk," Winston sensed Hanna's confusion.

"In a glass?"

"I don't like drinking out of a mug. I make it this way at home. Not the espresso part, but coffee."

"Works for me." Hanna reached out and took the glass. "Whoa, that's hot."

"That's the only drawback." Winston smiled.

"How long have you been a cop? Is it OK to say cop?" Hanna winced.

"Just don't say 'pig'." Winston smiled. "Seems like forever." Winston was more relaxed now, and very comfortable with Hanna. "I was an MP in the Army for twelve years. When I met Sally-Ann at Fort Hood, I knew I was done with the Army. I left the service when we got married. A buddy of mine was on the force here and, voila! And you? How long have you worked for the famous Mr. Sage?"

"Almost three years. Best job I've ever had. I'm just afraid it isn't going to last. The newspaper has laid-off so many people. Cole was asking me the other day if I liked where I lived. He's been acting kind of weird. I really hope he's not thinking of leaving. He hates the new editor. The old one was a good friend of his, and this new guy is a corporate hatchet man. Not a good combo."

"Jake."

"What?" Hanna said, taken off guard.

"That's what my friends call me. My middle name is Jacob, after my grandfather. Please call me Jake."

"I like that," Hanna said softly.

They chatted for almost a half hour when Jake got a call. Cutting their time together short, they drove to Lindsey's school. Hanna ran in with the documents and then went back to the paper.

"This was very nice," Jake said as they pulled up in front of the *Chronicle*.

"Very." Hanna smiled.

"How about dinner next time?"

"I would love that."

The radio squawked and the dispatcher gave the details of a one-eight-seven and an address.

"187…a homicide." Jake offered. "I'll call you."

Hanna opened the door and said, "Thank you. Talk soon."

"Soon," Jake said as the door closed.

When Hanna returned from coffee, the incident with Stevie was far in the past, that is until Cole began to grill her. Without actually saying so, his voice and attitude displayed a forceful I-told-you-so. He was genuinely concerned for her safety.

"Look," Cole summarized. "This kid has more baggage than a Greyhound bus. You are a single woman. A formidable advocate, and a little more than able to get out of a scrape. But, when is this going to end? Are you prepared to put up with the kind of crap this girl brings with her? Sure, she a terrific kid, and shows incredible talent for someone so young, but geez Hanna, it is a lot to take on."

"I've really gotten myself into something, haven't I? What's the matter? You think I can't deal with it?"

"What? Second thoughts?" Cole was surprised by Hanna's response. "It seems a bit late for buyer's remorse. Do you want to send Lindsey into foster care? Send her back home? What are you saying?"

"Well, no. I mean…not that. It's just…are these crazies going to terrorize us forever?"

"Well, little Stevie will be going away for a while. Grandma isn't getting out of her chair any time soon, so no, I think this is the end of it…for now."

"What about her screwball mother?"

Cole smiled, unwilling to say what he was thinking. Lindsey's mother was still in the mix. Without Stevie egging her on, perhaps she would realize she would lose on every front if, and when, the question of Lindsey's guardianship ever went to court. For now, the storm had passed.

Hanna went back to opening and sorting the mail. She didn't mention having coffee with the handsome detective. Cole returned to his office and continued to work the phone. He was committed to writing a strong piece on the state of the Child Protective Services, even if it proved to be his last.

Chapter Nine

Hanna poured the coffee into the cup of Cole's morning mocha mixture.

"I can't wait until Friday," she said to the redheaded man with the lame excuse of a beard standing next to her, pouring the third packet of sugar into his coffee.

"Almost there. It'll be TGIF before you know it. So you'll just have to be happy with sure happy it's Thursday."

Hanna didn't respond. Just stirred the mocha.

"Get it? Sure Happy It's Thursday. Get it?"

Hanna turned and looked at the grinning redhead and said, "No." Not wanting to give him any encouragement for his dirty little joke. "How are you enjoying junior high?" She asked as she turned and walked away.

"What do you mean? I don't get it."

Cole's smile was worth the daily walk to the coffee room. Hanna loved her job. For the first time in her life, she felt like she belonged to something.

"You're the best! Have a seat," Cole smiled.

"What's up? If it's about those numbers Randy gave me, I, well, I'm afraid I failed. Three of them wouldn't talk, and the others didn't recognize the number."

"Not what I wanted to hear, but, thank you," Cole sighed. "Actually, I wanted to talk to you about all the changes around here, it feels like we've been silently dancing around them for days. I know it must be scary."

"I've been kind of afraid to even think about what would happen if I got a pink slip, for fear it would happen."

"Here is the deal. I have been offered a position at Stanford, teaching journalism."

"University? Really? That's wonderful!"

"I'm as flabbergasted as you are." Cole smiled. "I will be deciding what to do in the next couple of days. All I have ever known is being a newspaperman. One side of me is terrified. The other side can see the writing on the wall around here. I'm not getting any younger.

Faraday is such a pompous ass. It's all I can do to be civil to him. One of these days he's going to push the wrong button and I'm going to let him know what I really think. That would not be good. I'd be out on the street with no place to go, for a while at least." Cole leaned forward and put his elbows on his desk.

"I can't think of anybody more qualified to teach newspaper stuff." Hanna struggled for the correct wording.

"I am really thinking it may be time for me to do a little to 'pay it forward' as they say. I have asked if I can bring you and Randy with me."

"*That's* why you asked about my apartment?"

"Guilty."

"Would they take me, really?"

"If they want me, yeah. That was one of my conditions: you, my administrative assistant, and Randy as my research assistant."

"I don't know what to say. Stanford? Me? Am I good enough to...." Hanna drifted into her thoughts.

"You're plenty good enough to go anywhere. You don't have to answer now. Think it over. You'll have to move closer to Stanford, I would imagine. It would be a nasty commute."

"I *want* to go. For you. Well, what I mean to say is, I owe you a lot." Hanna saw Cole was about to speak. "Don't say anything, let me finish before I start bawling. You took a chance on me when you could have just got anybody, somebody, with more background and skills than I. You, and you alone have given me a chance to do things I never dreamed possible. I have learned so much. I can't imagine staying here without you. So, yeah, I'm all yours. Thank you so much!" Her eyes teared up. As luck would have it, the phone rang at her desk, giving her an excuse to escape. Hanna jumped up and ran out the door.

"That was easy!" Cole called out behind her as she ran back to her desk to grab the phone.

Hanna grabbed the phone and cheerfully said, "Cole Sage's office!"

"Wow, you do love your job!" Jake Salem said.

Hanna could feel her face flush red. "Hello," Hanna replied in a far more professional manner.

"Disappointed?

"No, no, not at all." Hanna tried desperately to not snap back to the overjoyed excitement of the news about Stanford.

"I was wondering if you would like to have lunch together."

Without hesitation, Hanna said, "Yes!"

"Pick you up at noon?" Jake asked.

"Can't wait."

"See you in a couple of hours then. Bye."

"Bye." Hanna laid the phone down, "Yes! Can today get any better?" Hanna was elated and her voice did nothing to hide it.

"So what now? Win the lottery?"

"No," Hanna said as nonchalantly as possible, "*I* have a lunch date."

"Well, congratulations." Cole smiled and went back to his desk.

With renewed energy, Hanna finished her work in record time. She knocked out a pile of old correspondence and made several return phone calls. The excitement of seeing Jake a second time required several trips to the restroom, to check her make-up, collar, and the crease in her slacks.

The day's mail arrived and Hanna went to work sorting, tossing, and making notes for Cole. As she read a request for permission to reprint a column of Cole's she sensed movement. Standing in front of her desk was Jake.

"Too early?" he asked.

Hanna took a quick peek at the clock on her desk, eleven forty-five.

"Tiny bit. No matter. Come meet my boss." Hanna stood and moved toward Cole's office. "Cole, this is Detective Jake Salem."

Cole stood and moved to the door where the pair stood. "Hello. I think we met briefly the other day after the 'altercation'." Cole offered his welcoming hand.

"I think so. Nice to meet you…again. You're Leonard Chin's buddy. I've heard a lot about you." Jake shook Cole's hand.

"Right, I recognize you from the fracas downstairs. I'm not sure how much he told you would be admissible in court. What can I do for you?" Cole asked.

"Not a thing. Hanna and I are going to lunch." Jake gave Cole a big smile.

"Oh, sorry, *you're* the lunch date!" Cole said, slightly embarrassed by his mistake.

"No problem. I imagine you talk to a lot of cops in your work."

"Too many, sadly," Cole replied.

"Shall we?" Hanna injected, breaking the awkward silence.

"Yeah, lets…. I'm starving."

"Try to be back by sundown, would ya?" Cole teased.

"Yes, boss."

"Nice to meet you formally," Jake said.

"Enjoy your lunch."

Cole smiled as he watched Hanna and her new friend walk away. About time, he thought.

"I'm in the mood for Salvadorian. What do you think?"

"Great," Hanna responded, having no idea what she was agreeing to.

A short drive and lots of give and take later, they arrived at the San Salvadorian Pupusaria.

"What's your pleasure?" Jake asked as they approached the counter in the small restaurant.

"You order." Hanna smiled.

OK, grab a table before it fills up."

Hanna looked around and spotted a table for two in the far corner of the tiny dining room. She left the seat that would allow Jake to have his back to the wall and sat in the other. She turned slightly so she could watch her handsome lunch date at the counter. She smiled at the possible scenarios that bounced around her thoughts.

"Good choice."

"I have to admit that I've been wanting to do this for a couple of days. I just couldn't work up the nerve to call."

"Why?" Hanna asked, a bit surprised by his lack of confidence.

"I don't know. I guess I didn't want to seem pushy, or rush things."

"I am happy you got up the guts. I have wanted to see you again, too. Promise me the next time you get the urge to call, you do it then and there. Promise?" Hanna gave Jake a sweet smile as she looked him in the eyes.

"I promise. So…tell me about Lindsey. How is she doing? Are you two getting used to each other?"

"The good news is she was offered a spot for a placement test from a private prep school in Virginia. She could get a full scholarship, room, board, tuition—the whole enchilada."

"Lindsey, the street kid? Are we talking about the same person?"

"Incredible, huh? She's really smart. Like really smart."

"I sense some bad news is coming."

"We just don't get along. She has these moments of sheer meanness, I just don't know how to react to her, and I usually say the wrong thing. One minute she can be sweet as pie, and the next she's slamming doors and telling me where to get off." Hanna looked down for a long moment before she continued. "The thing is, Jake, I'm hoping she wins the scholarship. Not for her sake, for mine. I just can't do it much longer."

"How soon would she leave?"

"If she scores high, can keep out of trouble, *and* keep going to school, *and* pass *all* her classes." Hanna grinned.

"Tall order?"

"Seems like. If she can do it, I think she'll leave in time for summer session."

"So, like three months," Jake replied.

A young Hispanic woman approached the table with a large tray. "Here we are," she said, setting the first plate in front of Hanna.

"Let me give you a hand." Jake took two glasses of soda from the tray.

"This looks wonderful," Hanna said, excitedly.

"Best in the city!" Jake offered.

"Well, thank you. Can I get you anything else?" the waitress asked.

"Let's see, cabbage, salsa, one cheese, one meat and potato, and one loroco flower and cheese! We're all set." Jake gave the waitress a big smile.

"I'll check on you in a bit."

"Thank you," Hanna responded. "Oh, Jake this is awesome."

"Never had pupusas, have you?"

"No."

"Thought not."

"This stuff goes on top if you want it," Jake said indicating the shredded cabbage and salsa. "You can fold it, use your fork, or whatever. Once they're made I can never figure out which is which, but they're all great."

"Smells wonderful," Hanna said as she took her first bite. "Hmm, good."

"Glad you like it."

"What is going on in your life?" Hanna asked.

"This ice pick killer has been taking over everything. Almost all the departments in the city have been focusing on catching this guy. It's the craziest case I've ever worked on. We got nothin' to go on, not a clue, no DNA, none of the victims have a connection to each other, no witnesses of any kind, sane, or not. It is like this guy is invisible. There have been no defense wounds, the bodies are all just sitting, right where they've been stabbed."

"How many victims?"

"Six or seven…I've lost track."

"Where do you even begin to look? I mean what do you go after?"

"I hate to say it but we're just waiting for him to screw up."

They ate in silence for several minutes. The silence wasn't awkward and Hanna loved just looking up and seeing him there.

"What is a loco flower?" Hanna asked after taking a bite of a different pupusa.

"Loroco flower." Jake chuckled. "I saw it on the menu one day and figured I'd try it. I really like it. They told me it is the blossom of a vining flower that grows wild in Central America. Do you like it?"

"Yeah, it's really a different kind of flavor. I mean, for…I don't know what I mean," Hanna giggled. "I like it. Truly."

Hanna took another bite just as her phone rang. "Nobody ever calls me on this thing."

"Take it, I don't mind."

"Sorry." Hanna winced. "Hello?"

"Ms. Day? This is Pamela at Wallenberg High."

"Is something wrong?" Hanna's voice showed concern. She looked up at Jake and gave him a forced smile.

"I was filing Lindsey's note for her absences and I was wondering…."

"Absences?" Hanna interrupted.

"For the three days this week. You know, she has missed so many days, I just, well, was she really that bad off? I have pretty bad cramps myself, I don't know about you, but I always can make it to work." Pamela cleared her throat. "Then, I saw she hasn't been to classes today."

"What? Three days and then today? I don't understand. I have brought her to school every day. She hasn't had cramps or anything else wrong with her!" Hanna was nearly shouting into the phone.

"I'm so sorry. I'll double check with her teachers, but they can't *all* be wrong."

"No need. She's skipped out again. I've about had it with that kid. Thank you, Pam, for letting me know, I'll deal with it. Sorry for the hassle on your end. I'm sorry I got excited."

"That's OK, I understand. It must be very frustrating. Her behavior is not uncommon."

"I'll be in touch, bye."

"Good luck," Pamela said softly.

"Lindsey?" Jake asked.

"Who else? She promised. I am so frustrated. This is what I was talking about. She promised me, she promised Cole. She's ditched every day this week."

Hanna punched numbers into her phone. After a few moments, she said, "This is Hanna, Lindsey call me. You have broken your promise."

"This is just a thought, but do you think she's ever contacted her mother or grandmother?" Jake asked. "I mean family is family, no matter how rotten they are. It wouldn't be the first time a kid's been taken out of a home by CPS, then tried to go back."

"I never…" Hanna scrolled through her contact numbers, "I'll call grandma." A moment later Hanna said, "Hello? Hello?" She quickly hit the speaker button on her phone.

"Who is it?" The shaky voice of Lindsey's grandmother was nearly buried by the screaming in the background.

"This is Hanna, have you seen Lindsey?"

"I can't hear you. What?" the old woman said.

"Are you OK?"

"Hang that up, you old bitch! Who is it? I told you not to answer." The voice was clearly Lindsey's mother, Natalie.

"I can't talk now," the old woman said. The line went dead.

"What do you make of that?" Hanna asked.

"At best? Elder abuse. Maybe we should go have a look." Jake took a sip of his Coke. "Let's finish our lunch, then, we'll go see what we can find out. Now, take a deep breath, give me one of your pretty smiles and let's talk about something nice."

"You are taking this awfully, I don't know, calmly, or…what?" Hanna was at a loss for words. She was surprised by Jake's matter-of-fact, seemingly unconcerned attitude.

"Look, this is admittedly not a good situation. But nothing will change in the few minutes it takes to finish our meal. It may sound cold, but it won't make any difference if we get there fifteen minutes later."

"Is this a cop thing or a Jake thing?" Hanna asked seeing a side of her perfect man she didn't like.

"It is a reality thing. What people don't realize is that crime, meanness, cruelty—it's all around us." Jake pointed out the door. "That building across the street could be full of abused, misused, abandoned, people. Until someone makes a complaint we will never know."

"But we know," Hanna answered.

"And we will check it out. It is a nasty world out there. You need to realize our time together is precious. I could get called away, at any moment, but when I'm with you, you are all that is important. The hell of this city no longer matters, for these few minutes, it is just you and me. Can you understand that?" Jake reached out and took Hanna's hand. "If this is going to go anywhere with us, you have got to be able to meet me half way."

Hanna sat looking into the face of this stranger who was becoming dear to her. These glimpses into his character were a strange new process for Hanna. She had been alone for so long that a new relationship brings up feelings of possibility and apprehension—all in the same breath. This man sitting in front of her was so kind, so familiar, and yet he has a hard professional side that, though borne of experience and self-preservation, seems so out of sync with the sweetness in his eyes when he looks at her.

She did not want him to release her hand. She put her other hand on top of his. "I can learn."

"Just know, I will never bring my job home, or to lunch or anywhere you are. There will be times I am called away. It will not be by choice. But that is the job. It is hard, I know, I've been here before, but if we can do it, I think we could have something very special."

"Let's eat." Hanna squeezed Jake's hand.

As they drove to the grandmother's apartment, Jake called in for a stand-by back up. As they pulled up in front of the building he called in the address.

"We have a possible elder abuse situation. I'll let you know what I find out. Over."

"We have back up on standby."

The hall was darker than Hanna remembered. From several doors away the sound of a woman yelling could be heard from 213, the grandmother's apartment.

"I'll let you do the talking. Be calm, and let's just see what's going on," Jake said reassuringly.

Hanna stood in front of the door looking straight ahead. She took a deep breath and knocked. A minute passed with no answer. Jake reached out and gave the door a brutal pounding.

"They'll know that wasn't me," Hanna teased.

"Oh, I don't know."

The noise from inside the apartment stopped. The sound of a TV replaced the yelling.

"Who is it?" The voice was unmistakably Natalie.

"It's Hanna."

"Go away."

"I'm worried about Lindsey. Have you seen her? Please open the door, we need to talk. I have some great news."

There was no response. Hanna looked at Jake. He put his finger to his lips.

"Natalie?" Hanna said calmly.

The metallic clicking of the security chain and deadbolt preceded the slight opening of the door. Jake moved to where he wasn't in view.

"Can I come in?" Hanna asked.

The door opened and Natalie stood, one hand on the door and one on the frame, blocking entrance to the apartment. Over her shoulder, Hanna could see the grandmother in her wheelchair. Her face was bruised and her eye was swollen shut.

"So, what do you want?" Natalie demanded.

"Lindsey has ditched school all week. I wondered if you heard from her. I'm worried." Hanna looked at Jake, then continued, "What happened to grandma? Did she fall?"

Jake stepped around to face Natalie. "She looks beat up to me."

"Who the hell are you?" Natalie growled.

Jake pulled back his jacket revealing his badge, Detective Salem, SFPD."

"Shit," Natalie sneered.

Jake stepped into the apartment.

"You know the drill."

"Oh, man," Natalie groaned.

Jake handcuffed her and gave her a quick pat down.

Jake pushed Natalie down in a chair and went to where the old woman sat crying. "Who did this to you, ma'am?"

The old woman looked up, and then to Natalie. No words were needed. Jake removed his radio from his belt. "Salem here, I need an ambulance and back up."

Before he could give the address there was a loud hard thumping on the wall of the adjoining room.

"Stay here," Jake ordered Hanna. The radio crackled as he finished his request.

Jake drew his sidearm as he entered the narrow hallway. The door on his right was locked and at the top was a sliding bolt. He released the bolt, stepped back and planted his foot just beside the doorknob. With the powerful kick the door frame splinted and the door burst open.

"Hanna!" Jake called.

Without hesitation, Hanna ran to join the detective as he stood in the doorway of the small room. There, laying on her back and tied to the headboard, was Lindsey. A crusty trail of blood ran from her nose down her chin and neck. Stuffed in her mouth was a piece of washcloth. Her right cheek was scraped. Above her head, the sheetrock bore the damage of her kicking from her waist, and into the wall above.

Hanna ran to Lindsey and pulled the cloth from her mouth. She frantically tried to untie her bruised wrist from the metal rail of the headboard. She gave a Jake a plaintive look for help. The detective approached the bed and opened a black handled buck knife and, in rapid expert movement, cut her bonds.

"Are you alright?" Hanna asked as she helped Lindsey sit up.

"I'm OK, I guess."

"Your mom do this?" Jake asked.

Lindsey nodded and stood. "Can I go to the bathroom?"

"Sure," Jake said.

The young girl didn't give Hanna any notice. It was as if she wasn't in the room.

"She is in a bit of shock, I imagine." Jake offered reaching out and gently patting Hanna's upper arm.

"I doubt it. She hates me."

"Come on, Hanna, that's a bit strong, don't you think? Maybe she's embarrassed."

"We'll see," Hanna replied.

The sound of approaching sirens came up from the street below. Running water and a toilet flushing could be heard through the thin wall. A moment later Lindsey came back in the room and walked directly to Hanna. She threw her arms around her and buried her face in her shoulder.

"Can we go home now?" Lindsey sobbed.

Hanna looked at Jake in amazement. He gave her a big I-told-you-so smile and nodded.

"We sure can, sweetheart," Hanna said softly.

"Ambulance is here," Jake interrupted.

Two young men in blue jumpsuits wheeled a large aluminum gurney into the apartment. They approached grandma who had dozed off in her wheelchair. Natalie kicked at the gurney and swore at one of the young men who dared step in front of her.

"Ma'am." The taller of the two paramedics gently patted the old woman's hand. "Ma'am, I'm Jamal. We're here to get you some help. Can you stand?"

The old woman raised her head and almost undetectably shook her head.

"Does she look like she can stand up, idiot?" Natalie scoffed.

"That's OK. We'll help." Jamal ignored Natalie. "We need to get you on the gurney for transport. We're going to take you to the hospital."

Jamal's partner took the old woman's blood pressure and heart rate. Natalie continued to badger the paramedics until Jake approached.

"It's time for you to zip it and let these fellas do their work."

"I'm the one who needs medical attention. My heart is racing."

"Meth does that," Jake said, not trying to hide his disgust. "Shut up until my back-up gets here."

"I don't have to shut up. Ever hear of freedom of speech?"

"Ever hear of the law of gravity?" Jake put the toe of his boot under the front brace of Natalie's chair. A quick upward jerk sent her flying onto her back.

"Police brutality! You saw that! You saw him, what he did!" Natalie screamed toward the paramedics.

"Saw what? I've been busy," Jamal said, calmly.

His partner spoke without looking her way, "You've got to learn to sit still, lady."

"I'll sue you idiots, too!"

With swift, careful movements the paramedics got the old woman to a partially standing position, then gently lowered her onto the gurney. She groaned in pain.

"We'll give you something for pain in a minute. Take some deep breaths. We're just waiting for Emergency's go ahead."

"What about me?" Natalie screamed. "I think my back is broken."

The young man at the head of the gurney stroked the grandmother's cheek and said, "Let's get you out of here."

"Wait!" Lindsey cried out as she hurried to the living room.

The girl approached the old woman on the gurney. Tears ran down her face as she stood next to her grandmother. "It's going to be alright. They will get you to the hospital. You'll feel better soon, I promise. She won't be able to hurt you anymore."

With a trembling hand, the grandmother reached up and patted Lindsey's face. She tried to speak, but the dryness of her mouth made her tongue stick to her lips. Her voice was so soft, it was inaudible. Lindsey bent down and kissed her on the forehead.

"We'll take good care of her. Don't you worry," Jamal said, rolling the gurney to the door.

As the paramedics entered the hallway, two uniformed police officers entered the apartment.

"Lieutenant?" A tall African–American officer called out.

"Right here, Combs," Jake called from the hall.

Jake approached Combs and his thick chested partner.

"I need her transported. Mirandize her. We have assault, kidnapping, imprisonment, child abuse, neglect, and anything else connected to it. She abused the elderly woman who lived with her for prolonged periods. I found drug paraphernalia, about a gram of weed, three of these." Jake held up small plastic bags of white powder, "Have it tested. There are several prescription bottles in the back bedroom, I'm guessing Oxy. Too much for personal use, so book her for intent to distribute too." Jake winked at the two officers. "If she gives you any crap, Taser her."

"You can't do that!" Natalie yelled, trying to roll over.

"We got this. We'll see what else we can find."

"Let's see if we can't send her away until this one has grandchildren," Jake gestured toward Lindsey.

The heavier officer moved to where Natalie was kicking and trying to sit up.

"You hear what the Lieutenant said about the Taser?"

"You wouldn't dare!"

"Don't bet on it, lady. Now, I'm going to stand you up. You fight me, you'll regret it. Got me?" The policeman picked her up like she was weightless.

"Lindsey," Jake said softly, "do you want to say good-bye to your mom?"

She glared up at Jake. "Yeah." She moved over to where her mother stood.

"You know I wouldn't hurt you on purpose, baby. But, you fought me. I had to…."

"Don't talk," Lindsey said harshly.

"They were trying to get my welfare. I can't have that. That bitch over there has caused us nothing but trouble."

"I said shut up!" Lindsey yelled at her mother.

Natalie stopped talking and stood with a shocked expression.

"I hope this is the last time I ever see you." Lindsey began.

"Oh, baby don't say that," Natalie begged.

"I'm not your baby. I am not your daughter anymore. You are dead to me. I hope you die in prison. I wish I could see to it myself. I'm free of you now." Lindsey's expression was so hateful and cruel that it gave Hanna a chill.

Without warning, Lindsey spat in her mother face and punched her hard in the stomach. Jake grabbed her around the waist, lifted her off the ground, spun around, and pushed her onto the couch.

"Get her out of here!" Jake ordered the uniforms.

"Lindsey, don't let us part like this! Lindsey, I'm sorry, baby! Please!" Combs took Natalie by the arms and led her from the apartment.

"Lindsey! Please, baby!" Natalie pleaded repeatedly as the officers took her down the hall and to their patrol car.

"What the hell was that?" Jake demanded.

"Not enough!" Lindsey screamed back.

"OK, enough!" Hanna stepped up to where Lindsey sat, arms folded, on the couch. "What is wrong with you? I know you're angry and upset, but that is assault. Do you want to go to jail, too?"

"I don't give a shit," the girl growled.

"Hanna, a word. And you! Don't you move!" There was an ominously implied threat to Jakes command.

Without a word, Jake walked out of the apartment door into the hall. Hanna followed, hesitant as to what came next.

"I know what you're thinking," Hanna said, once in the hall.

"No, you don't. Are you nuts? I hope you're not thinking of taking the monster home."

"She's angry and upset. I can't say I blame her for punching Natalie."

"Did you see the look in her eye? She's psychotic."

"Believe me, I've seen it. Look, she needs to cool down and get some peace and quiet. It will be alright. Really."

"I hope you know what you're doin'. I would strongly advise against it. I think I should call CPS and take you out of the equation entirely." Jake's tone was firm but showed genuine concern.

"I hope so, too. Thank you, Jake, you're a sweetie."

"So, you ready to go?" Hanna could swear Jake was blushing.

"If it's OK."

"Privilege of rank. The guys will do another search, then lock up."

"I need to call Cole real quick."

"No problem."

After filling Cole in on the situation, Hanna went back in the apartment. "Ready to go?"

Lindsey was standing, looking out the grimy window. She turned and nodded.

"Anything you need to grab?"

"Just my backpack, if I can find it."

"Need help? I'm pretty good at searches," Jake said, missing the irony.

"No, I got it."

A couple of minutes later Lindsey came up the hall with her backpack in hand. "It was under grandma's bed. Man, does that room stink."

The trio was almost halfway to Hanna's apartment before anyone spoke.

"Lindsey, how is it that you went to your mom's apartment?" Hanna asked over her shoulder.

"I called my grandma. To check on her, you know? I try to call her every day."

"I didn't know," Hanna interjected.

"She said mom beat her up. She was in trouble. She wanted to leave."

"And you went to help her?" Jake said.

"When I got there mom was freakin' out, screaming and hitting my grandma. I tried to stop her and then she hit me, hard. I tried to fight back but…." Lindsey fell silent.

"It's OK, I see. I'm just glad you're alright," Hanna said softly.

"Me too," Jake chimed in.

Hanna reached over and patted Jake's arm. He smiled and they drove the rest of the way in silence.

The car pulled up in front of Hanna's building and Lindsey got out without saying a word.

"Well, that was quite a lunch date," Jake joked.

"It was the most important one I ever had," Hanna replied.

"How's that?"

"I saw the kind of man you are. And I like it." Hanna leaned over and gave Jake a kiss on the cheek. "Let's talk soon." Hanna got out of the car. She waved as she passed in front of the vehicle.

Lindsey was leaning against the wall next to the door of Hanna's apartment when she rounded the corner from the elevator.

"Are you hungry?"

"I'm kind of thirsty," Lindsey answered.

"Of course. I'm sorry, you must be parched."

Once inside, Lindsey went straight to the refrigerator and got a bottle of water.

"I've been thinking. Maybe we should take tomorrow off and just recharge. What do you think?"

"Won't I get in trouble for ditching?" Lindsey said sarcastically.

"I think I can get this one excused." Hanna smiled and tried her best to show she cared, even though she was torn apart trying to decide if she really did.

Tomorrow they would just hang out together, try to get reacquainted, see if there was a relationship worth trying to save.

"Can I watch TV for a while?"

"Sure, care if I join you?" Hanna replied.

Lindsey just shrugged.

Hanna's cell rang. "Hello."

"Hi Hanna, it's Kelly. I heard you guys had kind of a rough day."

Hanna laughed. "You might say that."

"I was thinking, how would you and Lindsey like to be my guest at my gym for a sauna and massage tomorrow?"

"Oh, Kelly, that would be wonderful. Thank you! What time?"

"Around eleven? You can call me back, and we'll work out the details. I am totally open, so whatever works best for you."

"That is really sweet. Thank you, so much. Let me talk to Lindsey and I'll call you back"

Chapter Ten

"I'm not so sure about this," Lindsey said nervously.

"What's the matter?" Hanna hit the lock on her car key, the alarm chirped brightly.

"I've never been to a spa. In gym class, I always stand against the wall."

"You'll love it! The sauna feels so good. It's hot and steamy and feels like it cleans you to your bones."

"Do I have to get naked?"

"Well, kind of, but you're wrapped in a towel." Hanna tried to reassure her.

"Where do you shower?"

"There is a shower room. But I'm sure it will have a curtain. Is that what you're worried about?"

"I don't like to get naked. I've had some bad times without clothes." Lindsey was unusually subdued.

"If you'd rather not…."

"No, it's OK, if there's towels and stuff."

"You will really like the massage. It is so relaxing. I've actually fallen asleep. It's like all the tension and worries in your life just fade away."

Hanna opened the door to the gym and let Lindsey enter first.

"There you are!" Kelly called.

"Is that Cole's lady?"

"Yeah."

"She's beautiful," Lindsey whispered.

"Sure is."

Kelly crossed the room and joined Hanna and Lindsey. "So nice to finally meet you, Lindsey. Cole brags about you all the time. I guess you're quite a writer."

"I try."

"My friend, Claire, is going to join us," Kelly announced. "I bumped into her on the way in. I hope you don't mind. She doesn't have many friends; I thought it might be nice to introduce you."

"That's fine. More the merrier." Hanna smiled and nodded.

Lindsey looked at Hanna but didn't respond.

In the dressing room, Kelly introduced Hanna and Lindsey to Claire. She was already undressed and wrapped in a towel. Her reception was a bit cold. She shook hands with Hanna without smiling and glared at Lindsey.

"I'll go on ahead. I'm on a tight schedule. I have to get back to work. If I don't get busy I'll be working all weekend." Claire said as she walked away.

"You work weekends?" Hanna asked.

"To be successful, yes," Claire replied in a condescending tone, then turned and walked away.

"I can see why she doesn't have many friends," Lindsey whispered.

"Right," Kelly agreed.

"We'll just be nice as we can and enjoy each other's company." Hanna smiled.

Kelly showed Hanna and Lindsey to their lockers and got them two towels each.

"My locker is just around there." Kelly pointed. "When you're ready just come on over."

Lindsey opened the locker and used the door to partially block Hanna's view as she changed. Hanna was surprised how quickly she got undressed. In her towel, Lindsey was bone thin and showed the deep purple bruises of the beating her mother gave her. She stood quietly looking around as Hanna undressed.

"If these towels were much smaller, I'll need to go on a diet," Hanna teased.

"It's your boobs. I don't have hardly any so the towel wraps around nearly twice."

"You're very generous!"

"You're very nicely... I mean, you look good. You don't need to go on a diet."

"Thank you." Hanna smiled and accepted the compliment. "What do you say we go get sweaty?"

As they stepped into the steam room, Lindsey's eye's opened wide and her head jerked. "It's hotter'n hell in here. Why are we doing this again?"

"Makes our skin pretty," Kelly offered. "Get's all the gunk out of our pores, and makes us glow!"

"If you say so." Lindsey didn't seem convinced.

Hanna took a seat on the bench next to Claire, and Lindsey took a seat with Kelly across from them. They were the only ones in the steam room.

Claire looked across at Lindsey's hairy legs and sneered. Lindsey didn't notice...but Kelly did. Claire was in a mood, dark and unpleasant. Kelly already regretted inviting her to join the group.

"So, are you one of those organic, vegan, earth mother, hippie chicks?"

"Who, me?" Lindsey replied.

"If the hair on your legs gets much longer you'll be able to braid it." Claire pressed.

"Men don't like it." Lindsey glared back at Claire. "They don't like this either." Lindsey raised her arms above her head showing unshaven armpits.

"And girls do?" Claire snapped.

"I'm not into girls!" Lindsey snapped. "So you'd know better than I."

Fearing Lindsey's next move, Hanna changed the subject. "What do you do, Claire?"

"I am a project marketing analyst, for Bio-Therapeutics."

"Here in the city?"

"Yeah, we're in the Market Center."

"What's a project marketing analyst do?" Lindsey injected.

Claire gave Lindsey a harsh look. "I am currently working with a new form of Methylphenidate, it's stronger, and seems more effective."

Hanna and Kelly looked at each other confirming neither one knew what Methylphenidate was.

"So you want to pump more Ritalin into kids so they can be junkies later?" Lindsey's tone and demeanor proved her willingness to go head-to-head with the unpleasant adult.

"Seems some kids should be taking it now," Claire replied sarcastically.

"They tried it. Thing is, I could read the warnings." Lindsey wiped her forehead.

"I wondered how you knew what Methyl... whatever it is...was." Kelly's tone was bright and cheerful.

"What do you do, Hanna?" Claire asked.

"I work for Kelly's fiancé, I'm his administrative assistant."

Claire neither commented nor responded but just stared at the floor. The door opened and a heavy woman in a terrycloth robe came in the sauna. She approached the bench and stood facing Lindsey.

"Can you scoot down a smidge, sweetie?"

Kelly moved first, then Lindsey moved toward her.

The terrycloth robe dropped to the floor, revealing roll upon roll of milky white flesh. Lindsey closed her eyes and shuddered as the woman sat down and her cool, clammy flesh pressed against her side.

"I'm about ready for my massage. How 'bout you guys?" Kelly stood and adjusted her towel.

"I'm with you, Kelly. Wait for me." Claire stood, opened her towel and smiled at Kelly before she covered herself and tucked in the corner.

Hanna grinned with embarrassment and moved toward the door.

Lindsey jumped up and was out the door without saying a word.

The massage room was fitted with eight tables. Four were arranged especially for Kelly's group. The heads of the tables faced each other making conversation easier. Four women stood at the ready, next to small tables each with several bottles.

"Senjah is my favorite," Kelly said moving toward a pretty Indian woman of about twenty.

"I have no preference." Claire moved to the table that faced Kelly.

Hanna and Lindsey stood looking at each other. Neither moved.

"Little one, you come I give you nice massage." A small South East Asian woman offered.

Lindsey climbed up on the table next to Kelly.

Without speaking, Hanna lay down on the table next to Claire. The masseuse did not speak.

Several minutes passed before anyone said a word. Finally, Kelly turned to Lindsey. "So what do you think Lindsey?"

"Feels really good. I didn't think I would like somebody rubbing around on me. But, it's not what I thought."

"I told you you'd like it," Hanna said softly, obviously enjoying the experience.

"I like the deep tissue, right Senjah?"

The masseuse laughed. "You're a glutton for punishment, Kelly."

"I don't think I have any deep tissue." Lindsey giggled.

"You're a funny girl," Lindsey's masseuse added.

"I like peace and quiet," Claire mumbled.

"You're a real grouch today, Claire. What's going on?"

"I just like things a certain way."

"Your way?" Lindsey said into the face hole in the table.

"The adults are trying to talk here," Claire snapped.

"Who put the bug up your ass? You've been giving me shit since I got here."

"Lindsey!" Hanna turned and let the girl know her displeasure.

"I can see that this blend isn't the best. Let's just enjoy our message without visiting." Kelly pleaded.

The small dark woman stopped massaging Lindsey, and bent down and whispered in her ear, "You a tiger. You my kind of girl."

Lindsey let out a near soundless giggle.

The only sounds made the rest of the time were the grunts and groans brought on by the increase in pressure from the masseuses.

Relaxed, dressed, and standing outside of the gym, Kelly stopped to have a few words with Lindsey and Hanna.

"Lindsey, I am so sorry about Claire. Please forgive me. I had no idea she would be so nasty."

"Not your fault."

"But I feel responsible. I invited her to join us. I hope it didn't spoil your good time.

"I'm cool. But, she's not going to live long if she talks to everybody like that."

Kelly gave Lindsey a quick hug. "Next time, it's just us. I promise."

"That would be good. I learned a long time ago with my mom: you can't do anything about what other people say or do."

"You're a pretty smart girl." Kelly patted her cheek. "See you soon."

"And Cole's a lucky guy to have someone like you."

As they said their good-byes, Claire brushed passed the women without speaking. She got in a silver BMW several spaces from where the women stood.

"How'd she get that space?" Kelly pointed as Claire pulled away.

"Dumb luck," Hanna laughed.

"You got the dumb part right," Lindsey scoffed.

"Lindsey!" Hanna scolded.

Kelly laughed and shook her head. "I know I shouldn't laugh but, my goodness, she was really something today."

"How did you two become friends?" Hanna asked.

We had a Pilate's class together and she kind of reached out to me. I keep trying to get her to sweeten up, but she seems to just suck on lemons all the time. It's kind of sad to see somebody miserable all the time."

"I think I would get tired of it," Hanna replied.

"I'm getting there." Kelly smiled and raised her eyebrows. "You two have a pleasant evening. So nice to get to know you better Lindsey. I hope to see you again soon."

"You too. Where are you parked?"

"In the garage around the corner. You?"

"Just up the street. See you later. Thanks again."

"My pleasure."

The women parted company and made their way to their respective cars.

Hanna pulled away from the curb and turned up the radio. "I love this song." She hummed and sang along until "River Deep Mountain High" ended.

Lindsey looked out the window. They drove along for several minutes then Hanna broke the silence. "Wasn't that nice?"

"What part?"

"I don't know...everything."

"Yeah, great, except for that bitch Claire, and the way she was hitting on Kelly."

"You think?" Hanna was shocked at Lindsey's response.

"Oh, Hanna." Lindsey shook her head, the mother-daughter roles suddenly reversed.

"What?"

"You are such a cloud dweller."

"What does that mean?"

"I'm not being mean, but geez, you are so naive. Your head's in the clouds, always trying to see the good, and ignoring the shit in front of your face."

"OK, smarty, how do *you* know *she* was hitting on *her*?"

"Oh, I don't know...the way she flashed her boobs in Kelly's face for one thing. You wouldn't believe the number of dykes that have tried to turn me. It was part of my mother's Use-My-Kid-for-the-Day

Program. Fifty bucks and my little cutie is yours till sundown."

"Oh, Lindsey." Hanna was holding back tears.

When I got older it didn't work so well. I learned to kick and gouge at eyes really good. But on the street, it got worse."

"How so?"

"My butch hair, probably? I dunno."

I've always wanted to ask why you wore it so short, but was afraid to ask for fear of hurting your feelings, or offending you."

"Like Claire with her braided leg hair crack? Bitch."

"That was really rude, but you handled yourself well."

"Lots of practice," Lindsey replied. "Once my mom chopped off a big chunk of my hair when I was sleeping on the couch. Right down to the scalp."

"Why?" Hanna exclaimed in horror.

"She must have thought I was getting too pretty, I suppose. She got mad because Stevie was paying too much attention to me or something. She wasn't having any of it. So she tried to ugly me up a bit."

"Wow. Was he?"

"Who knows? He liked to talk dirty to me. Must have turned him on or something. I just thought he was gross."

"Where was your grandma during all this? I mean did she ever speak up?"

"Oh, hell no. They would have knocked her head off."

"How does a kid protect themselves from all that?"

"Well, I did her one better: I chopped all my hair off." Lindsey made scissors cutting with her index and middle fingers. "Then, as it grew back, I realized I liked it. Wash-and-wear hair, you know? No effort and no time needed. Just wash and go...or not." Lindsey gave a so-it-goes shrug.

"You are really something, Lindsey Frost."

"The question is...what?" Lindsey quipped.

They both laughed as they rode along listening to the radio, heading for home.

A wave of guilt swept over Hanna. What had this poor child endured at the hands of a mother who should have loved and protected her? How could she become so angry so quickly with someone with scars so deep? Lindsey's peculiar set of values, her strength, her skill for self-preservation—these "qualities" were a world far removed from Hanna's own experience.

The mother who verbally abused Hanna was cruel and made her life hell from the time she entered school until she fled at sixteen, but in her wildest imaginings, Hanna knew that her mother would never have beat her or sold her body to the highest bidder. The terror and sexual abuse that Lindsey grew up thinking it was "just the way things are" would have been criminal and totally repugnant even to Hanna's abusive alcoholic mother.

As they drove home in the bright afternoon sun, the radio blasting away, Hanna promised herself to not let Lindsey push her buttons. She knew even with compassion and a desire to understand Lindsey, the girl would once again push all of her buttons. It was just a matter of time.

* * *

"Good Morning. How was your long weekend? Has everything settled down on the home front?" Cole asked.

"Thanks to Kelly for inviting us to the spa. It kind of helped in the bonding department."

"She said it got mixed reviews."

"Yeah, it was OK. Her friend Claire is a real piece of work."

"I heard, sorry." Cole gave an exaggerated grimace. "Other than that?"

"I kept Lindsey on a short leash. Tried to make the weekend fun. Jake came for dinner on Saturday night, and we all went for pizza yesterday afternoon."

"He stayed over?" Cole said in mock shock.

"He most certainly did not!"

"Just wondering."

"Then, last night we watched some awful slasher movie, Lindsey's choice, not mine. I think she might be coming around. I'll tell you though, she is as prickly as a prickly pear."

"Maybe it's just going to take time."

"Exactly. How was your weekend?"

Cole laughed happily. "Mine was nice too. It started out a little rough, but we got through it."

"That's a naughty smile." Hanna teased.

"Just hold that thought for a moment!" Cole grinned and ducked into his office.

"Cole, a courier envelope came while you were out." Hanna reached into her drawer.

"Thanks," Cole said taking the envelope. "Ah, I've been waiting for this. Cool."

Now, how would Kelly do this? Cole thought as he tore the zip tab on the envelope. He dumped the contents on the top of his desk as he sat down, and for a long moment stared at the two airline tickets. His mind drifted back to a hot, steamy Mexican restaurant in southern California. In his mind's eye, he could see Anthony "Whisper" Perez sitting across from him.

"I was thinking," Whisper said ages ago, "the extra money from the diamonds, what if we called it a scholarship? And named it after your lady, Ellie? Could we do that?"

Cole remembered staring at Whisper, emotion welling up. That day Anthony Perez was reborn. Cole felt pride and honor like he never knew before. This skinny little street hustler, who wanted out of gang life and to be a writer, wanted to pay tribute to Ellie. It was the best gift he was ever given. She would have been so proud.

"I think," Cole told the young man, "there could be no finer honor in this life than if that happened."

He reached up and brushed the tears from his eyes.

"Everything you do, everything you achieve, everything you accomplish in life will be Ellie living on in some way," Perez said. "It is a beautiful thing, my friend. A beautiful thing."

Anthony Perez, MA, had just received his first byline in the *Atlanta Journal Constitution* last month. He is a journalist, a man of honor, truthful, and hopefully part of the new generation of journalists who would stand up for what was right and give the people the kind of truth the First Amendment was written to protect.

Today, however, back in the Bay Area, two tickets lay on his desk purchased with the funds from Ellie's scholarship. Lindsey Frost hopefully, was going to fly across the country on wings paid for by Ellie's memory.

Cole swallowed hard and smiled at the memory. Ellie's memory was tucked in a very special place in his heart. It was his to keep. From time to time, less and less often now, he would go there and just bask in the glow of what was. Now his heart was filled with his daughter, Erin, and her family. Cole smiled at the picture of them on his desk. Then, there was Kelly. As much as he loved and cherished her, it was not like the love he felt for Ellie. Even so, he wouldn't dare to dream of asking for anything different. Kelly was now. Cole sighed deeply.

"Hanna?" Cole cleared the lump from his throat, "Can you come here a second?"

"Be right there."

He quickly tucked one of the tickets into an envelope in his desk drawer. Hanna appeared in the door a minute or so later.

"Do you remember me telling you about Erin's mom?" Cole asked.

"Of course."

"After she died I set up a scholarship in her name. Actually, it was Anthony's idea."

"Really?" Hanna was genuinely surprised.

"Yes. Now, It might be a little premature, but I've got a really good feeling about this test of Lindsey's."

"I don't follow," Hanna said.

"Lindsey and passing the test, I mean." Cole clarified. "I bought this with money from the scholarship for Lindsey." Cole handed Hanna the airline ticket.

"How wonderful!" Hanna squealed. "You really think she'll do well?"

"Yeah, if she doesn't totally blow it off. They're refundable if she does." Cole shrugged and gave Hanna a grin.

"I've been stewing about this since last Saturday: if she gets the scholarship I didn't know where the money would come from! She is going to be so thrilled. Cole, that is so amazing."

"And this," Cole reached in his desk drawer and took out an envelope, "is to help her out with stuff, for settling in and personal stuff, you know?" He took a check from the envelope and handed it to Hanna.

"You are too much, Mr. Sage! Why didn't you say something?"

"I like surprises." Cole grinned.

"I'll go call Lindsey," Hanna said excitedly, rushing back to her desk.

"How 'bout you wait until we see if she passed." Cole was almost wishing he had waited before springing this on Hanna.

"Yeah, you're probably right."

"Oh, one more thing…" Cole said, in his best back to business tone.

"What's that?" Hanna stepped back into the office,

Cole stood and rounded his desk to face Hanna. "We can't have a minor cross the country by herself. So, I got this for you." Cole handed Hanna the envelope.

"What's this?"

"I figured she needed a chaperone. So tag, you're it." Cole smiled and handed her the other ticket.

Hanna threw her hand over her mouth and tears ran down her cheeks. She pushed her glasses up on top of her head and wiped her eyes. "I am speechless. Thank you, thank you. Oh, Cole!" Hanna threw her arms around Cole's neck and gave him a tight squeeze.

"Alright, alright, none of that, Ms. Day. It's off to work you go," Cole said, more than a little embarrassed by the outburst of affection.

"Yes, sir," Hanna said sheepishly, knowing she crossed the invisible gulf between boss and secretary. "Sorry."

"Hanna, I don't know what I'd do without you," Cole said. "Thank you, for me, and for Lindsey."

For the next few minutes, Cole sat quietly, pleasantly digesting Hanna's reaction to his surprise.

* * *

"Alright, that's it for today! Remember, the question isn't who's going to let you, it's who is going to stop you! Go out and make a difference!" The instructor released the Tae Bo class.

Kelly wiped the sweat from her face with a terrycloth towel. It seemed the workouts she did three times a week weren't getting any easier. She questioned the level of class that she was hanging onto so tightly. The other women in the group were all at least twenty years younger than her. Maybe it's time to join the older group, Kelly thought.

"Wow, that was a butt burner," Claire puffed.

"Yeah. I think I may need to downshift to the older group. This doesn't feel good anymore. I think it is starting to affect my joints."

"Don't smoke so many then."

"Huh?" Kelly was too winded to get the humor in Claire's remark.

"Nothing."

As the class made their way out of the workout room, Claire stayed a couple of steps behind Kelly. Claire's eyes never left Kelly's long legs and taut backside.

"Why doesn't my ass look like yours?" Claire asked.

"Genetics, my whole family is long and lean," Kelly replied, wiping the back of her neck. "What's yours like?"

"I don't know. I was adopted."

"You'll have to tell me the story sometime." Kelly showed real interest in her friend's background.

Five minutes later, Kelly returned to her locker from the showers wrapped in an oversized, plush white towel. The class was gone, the locker room was silent. It wasn't unusual, on Fridays a lot of the women just grabbed their stuff and rushed for home. Claire sat on the bench in front of the lockers completely naked.

"There you are." Claire turned to face Kelly.

There was something strange in Claire's demeanor, and her nudity made Kelly uncomfortable. Kelly opened her locker and tried to shield herself with the door. She quickly pulled on her bra and panties.

"I've been waiting to talk to you," Claire said, a little above a whisper.

"Oh?" Kelly continued to dress.

"Did you like my poem?"

Kelly's ears seemed to burn with Claire's words. She felt like she was hit in the gut. As she reached for her blouse her hand trembled. Breathe, she thought, breathe.

"Well?" Claire pressed.

"I can't say that I did," Kelly said into her locker.

"Why not?" Claire's voice showed signs of repressed anger.

"Because I am a woman who likes men. I have no interest in women in a sexual context. I am, as they say, straight." Kelly steeled herself as she turned to look at Claire.

"Oh, I'm not a lesbian or anything like that! Heavens! I just love *you*."

"Excuse me if I don't see the distinction. I think we have different goals in life. Mine does not include anyone but my fiancé, my kids, and grandkids. So, I think it best if you and I part ways." The harshness of Kelly's answer surprised her, but it didn't have the same effect on Claire.

"Oh, don't be a fuddy-duddy," Claire continued. "I knew it the first time I saw you. You were the perfect partner for me. I will write my detective novels to support us. I know how to get inside the head of a killer, tell the story like they see it. My book will be bestsellers! We can have a wonderful life together." Claire did not seem to register Kelly's rejection.

"Let me put this another way…" Kelly slammed the locker door. "Get lost. Go away. Forget you know me because I fully intend to forget you as quickly as possible. The idea of a continued association with you repulses me. You, sitting there, naked, thinking that's attractive, or a turn-on, or whatever you're thinking, disgusts me. And, hey, I'm sorry it turned out like this. I liked you."

Kelly began stuffing her towel and workout clothes in her bag. Her movements were fast and angry.

"My turn," Claire began slowly like a dirge. "I won't go away. I was lost until I met you. I cannot forget you. It's impossible, and here's the thing: if I can't have you, no one will."

Kelly's eye's flashed with rage. "What is that supposed to mean!"

Claire lowered her voice. "That I will kill you."

"What did you say?" Kelly turned to face Claire who was pulling on a pair of sweat pants. She wasn't sure she heard Claire's threat correctly.

Claire muttered something Kelly couldn't understand. Claire reached for a 49er sweatshirt and pulled it over her head. Again, her words were inaudible.

"I think you are getting all worked up over nothing, Kelly," Claire said suddenly complacent. "Please sit down. Let's talk about this. I have money saved, quite a bit of it, I have a great apartment and you can see the Golden Gate from the deck. I have everything you could ever want."

"Except a rational mind. Claire, you need help. I have a wonderful life and a wonderful family. You have been a nice friend up until now. I guess I should be flattered, but I'm not. Cole told me if one of the girls made advances toward me to politely refuse, say 'I'm straight' and that would be the end of it. You…you are something else. I don't know what, but I want none of it. Goodbye."

Kelly picked up her bag, made a beeline for the exit and didn't look back.

***

"Hey, what are you doing here? I thought you had a big day planned." Cole smiled and stood up, surprised by Kelly Mitchell's appearance in his doorway.

"I just needed to see you." Kelly's voice betrayed her emotions.

"Whoa, whoa, whoa, what's all this?" Cole rounded the desk and closed the door behind Kelly. He took her shoulders and turned her toward him. Her chin trembled, and tears streamed down her face. "What's wrong, sweetheart?"

"Just hold me for a minute." Kelly pressed her face into Cole's broad shoulder.

They stood quietly. Kelly cried softly. Cole stood arms around her, worrying in silence. When Kelly moved away from Cole's embrace several minutes later, she smiled up at him in embarrassment.

"I'm sorry."

"No need to be sorry, but what in the world has happened?" Cole asked, reassuringly.

"You know my friend, Claire?"

"I think so. The gal from the gym?"

"Yes. She told me she loved me and wanted us to be together forever."

"Well, that's a little awkward."

"I reacted badly. I was so shocked that I said mean things. I…I was so shocked. Claire wrote the poem, she took the picture, she put the rose in my locker. It's like I have a stalker! She said she wasn't, you know, a lesbian. She said she just loved me. I freaked out, Cole."

"So how did you leave it with her? You didn't punch her out, did you?" Cole tried his best to lighten the mood a bit.

"Don't be ridiculous. Of course not!" Kelly took another step back. "Your advice didn't work. She just wouldn't let up. So, I shoved my stuff in my bag and ran. I'm never going back there again, Cole, never."

"Look, as strong and straight forward as I'm sure you were, I doubt if you'll ever hear from her again." Cole stepped forward, kissed Kelly on the cheek and embraced her again.

"I've never encountered anything like that in my life. She was so creepy. Not like you said it would be. I said I wasn't interested, and she just got more persistent. I was so uncomfortable. Then, she said something about 'if she couldn't have me no one could'. It was so scary, Cole. She said she'd kill me."

"I'm so sorry. Are you sure she threatened you? I mean, are you certain that's what she said?" Cole pressed.

"A lot of it was mumbling but, yes, that was what she said." Kelly's eyes were full of fear.

"We should call the police. This needs to be reported." Cole was concerned with the strange turn of events.

"No, that's silly. She was angry. She has a real temper. I saw her go off on a poor girl in the coffee shop the other day. I'm sure it was just rejection talking, but it was so weird. The whole thing was like nothing I had ever experienced, ever."

They both stood silently for a long moment. Cole reached out and took Kelly's hand. He felt helpless and tried to find the right words.

"Carlos was gay," Kelly began. "We were friends. You were friends with him. You know lots of gay people. Do they hit on you?"

"Nope. Never. I think Claire might have other issues. If she wasn't attracted to the same sex in general, just you in particular, that strikes me as kind of, I don't know...." Cole's voice trailed off into thought.

"Was I wrong to do what I did?" Kelly looked directly into Cole's eyes.

"If you felt harassed, pressured, or threatened in some way, no. Advances from anyone, male or female, gay or straight, should end once they are rejected. If they continue, especially from a superior, then that is what sexual harassment is. I think you did what you felt was necessary. I'm good with that." Cole ached to see Kelly so upset.

Cole pulled out the chair in front of his desk and motioned for Kelly to sit down.

"How 'bout you spend the rest of the day here with me? Maybe I can steal a kiss or two along the way." Cole smiled broadly.

"Won't I be in the way?" Kelly said softly.

"I hope so." Cole grinned. "I'm supposed to help Lindsey with her homework and give her some writing tutoring. You can sit with us. You can be a great help if she has math homework."

"I'd like that."

"Good. I hate math. Hanna will go and pick her up in a few minutes."

Chapter Eleven

Cole really didn't get much work done. He chatted with Kelly, talked about going to dinner, and defended his messy office. Kelly, for the most part, sat quietly and watched Cole shuffle through his notes, type, and take a few calls.

"Is this what you do all day?" Kelly asked after about an hour.

"No. When I don't have a beautiful distraction, I do nothing but think about her," Cole teased.

"When will Hanna be back?"

"She should have been back about thirty minutes ago," Cole said, looking at the clock on the wall.

It was another fifteen minutes before Hanna returned.

"She stood me up." Hanna's voice came from the doorway.

"What?"

"She was nowhere to be found." Hanna was obviously peeved.

"That's not good," Cole offered.

"No. Now, that's twice. I've about had it."

"Why haven't you said anything?"

"I kept thinking it was me. I know nothing about teenagers. Lindsey has been a royal pain in the ass all week. She snaps at me, slams doors, and disappears. Arrgh!" Hanna threw her hands in the air.

"I had no idea," Cole replied.

"You wouldn't, would you! She's a Disney princess when she's around you." Hanna turned and went to her desk.

"Is *this* what you do all day?" Kelly asked with a giggle.

"Funny." Cole shook his head. "Lindsey is *not* a Disney princess around me. She's a little snot. I warned Hanna. Sometimes I feel like an old Barry Manilow record: Nobody ever listens to me."

"I do. Well…most of the time…sometimes." Kelly's mood was brightening.

At a quarter to five, Cole stood and pronounced that the day was over. He gathered the notes strewn over his desk into a neat pile and put a brass see-no-evil, hear-no-evil, speak-no-evil paperweight—three monkeys joined at the hips—on top of the papers.

"What do you say we get out of here?"

"Sounds good to me," Kelly said, checking the clock.

Cole knocked gently on the front of Hanna's desk. "Tomorrow we'll talk about what to do with "the kid," that is after I get all my ideas rejected by my life coach." Cole jerked his head in Kelly's direction.

"I'll pray for you. It's going to work out the way it should. Don't worry." Kelly went around and gave Hanna a hug.

"Sorry for the outburst," Hanna said, self-consciously.

"It could have been way worse!" Cole smiled. "We'll hash this all out later. When do we get to hear about Lindsey's test results? I sure hope she scored high enough to get her out of your hair."

"I don't know, but they said it shouldn't take too long. But they won't put up with this disappearing act of hers. She could lose a scholarship." Hanna was bristling. "If she blows it, I'm through…that is if she even gets it. Who knows? She might have flunked it on purpose."

"We have got to stay positive. Either way, I'm with you all the way. You want to come with us to dinner?" Cole tried to console Hanna.

"Thanks, but if Lindsey shows up, I need to be home. Geez, I'm beginning to feel like *I'm* the prisoner and *she's* the warden."

Kelly stood quietly trying to think of something to say that wouldn't sound hollow and trite. She couldn't think of anything, but she didn't want to just walk away. Hanna was hurting and needed support.

"Cole Sage's office." Hanna raised her index finger motioning Cole not to leave. "Yes, sir, he's right here. No sir, we all work until five. Here he is." Far-a-day, Hanna mouthed silently.

Cole took the phone, "Sage. Alright, …alright…I'll be right up." Cole turned to Kelly, "Can you keep Hanna company? It seems the new editor has a thing or two to say about my column for Sunday."

Faraday's secretary scowled at Cole as he approached her desk. "Don't speak to me," she snarled. "Just go in."

Cole didn't knock. He just went directly into the editor's office.

"What the hell is this?"

"To answer that, I'll need a little more information," Cole said flatly.

"It's your so-called column for Sunday." Faraday was seething.

"The one I gave you last week?"

"I told you I wanted a story on Father Thomas Melo and his fight to keep San Francisco a sanctuary city. This…this is an indictment of the way the Child Protective Agency is being run." Spit flew from Faraday's mouth as he fought to keep from screaming.

"And I told you, I don't do puff pieces, especially on topics that I disagree with. I made that very clear the first time we met. I was hired to do what I did there," Cole pointed at the papers in Faraday's hand. "Bring to the light the wrongs, inadequacies, and failures of the government and its agencies, officials and policies. I was also hired because my reputation preceded me as a fighter for the underdog, downtrodden, and abused. This, Mr. Faraday, fits all those criteria in spades."

"Your holier-than-thou bullshit may work on the artsy-fartsy, know-it-all, first amendment worshippers of the journalism world, but I assure you, my only interest in you is filling column inches with what I see fit and necessary for the profitability of this newspaper."

"Any kid fresh out of college could, and should, write the kind of propaganda you want written. They could because it isn't journalism. They should because they would be afraid to lose their job. If they, the paper, and you were worth a damn they would refuse. Either way, it is a sellout to the very foundation of what a free press represents." Suddenly the world seemed to come into focus for Cole.

As Faraday went into a lengthy tirade about politics and power structures (and a subordinate's place in it), Cole for a fleeting moment went back to a place and time long buried in his memory.

He could almost feel the cold, hard, concrete bench in the Cook County jail cell the night he spent a night behind bars so many years ago. The Honorable Judge Irwin Fields Blumenthal cited the young *Chicago Sentinel* reporter, Cole Sage, for contempt of court for refusing to reveal the name of a source. Cole wrote a scathing piece on the influence of organized crime on—and the lack of oversight in—building permits, as well as, inspections in the Wards of the south side of the city.

Against the advice of counsel, Cole decided to stand his ground. He feared for the safety of his source, and that of the man's family. His decision to protect his source Cole believed, would be covered by Illinois "Shield Law" that protects journalists and their sources. The judge, so angered by Cole stance, ignored the statute and found him in contempt.

The holding tank he was confined to contained men of various ages, races, and dispositions. Twenty-eight-year-old Cole Sage went to the far corner of the cell and waited to be processed. He felt out of place in a suit that actually fit, and a shirt that was starched and pressed.

A small, frail-looking man with a new shave and hair-cut looked oddly out of place in the group. He never looked above the floor. His hands trembled badly when he wasn't holding them tight to his chest. Cole wondered what his offense could possibly be, as he watched the man bounce one foot nervously up and down.

"Killer." The black man sitting to Cole's right said.

"What's that? Cole asked.

"I saw you staring at ol' Jimmy over there."

"It was that obvious?"

"You never been locked up before, have you?"

"First time. So what's the story on Jimmy?" Cole asked, wanting to change the focus away from him.

"Got in an argument with another homeless guy. Jimmy said the guy stole his bedroll. One thing led to another and Jimmy broke a wine bottle, and gouged the guy in the throat with it. The guy bled out like a stuck pig. You want to hear the funny part? Jimmy was so drunk he didn't know he was sittin' on his own bedroll!" The man laughed exposing a mouthful of rotten, broken teeth.

"So what are you in here for, if you don't mind me asking?

"Public drunkenness, peein' in public, resistin' arrest, and assault on a police officer. The usual. You?"

"Refusing to give the name of a source on a story I wrote for the newspaper."

"You a writer?"

"Yes, sir. At least I was. We'll see how well the *Sentinel* likes me going to jail for contempt of court."

"So...they put you in here because you wouldn't snitch?"

"Basically, yeah, I guess so. It's a little more complicated than that. But yeah, I wouldn't rat on the guy who gave me the information that led to the arrest of some mobsters."

"Baby Jesus and Mary, you a pretty brave fella. Either that or pretty damn dumb!" The black man threw back his head and laughed loudly. "What's your name?"

"Cole Sage." Cole extended his hand.

"Tyrone Partridge," the man said, shaking Cole's hand.

"How long you in for, Mr. Sage?"

"We'll see in the morning, Tyrone, we'll see in the morning."

* * *

At nine o'clock the next morning, Cole was returned to a holding cell to wait his turn before the judge. There was no sign of Tyrone or Jimmy. About ten-thirty Cole was escorted before Judge Blumenthal for round two.

"Mr. Sage, have you changed your position since we last met?" the judge asked.

"No, your honor, I have not."

Cole could see the judge shudder with anger.

"And why might that be...if I may ask such a distinguished member of the press?"

The judge smirked at his own sarcasm.

"Section 8-901 of the Illinois code regarding Shield Law states, *No court may compel any person to disclose the source of any information obtained by a reporter except as provided in provisions of the Shield Law.*"

"Are you quoting the law to me in my own courtroom, Mr. Sage?" The judge's face turned almost a burgundy as his anger grew.

"It does appear that way, your honor. I believe I am protected, shielded if you will, from disclosing the identity of my source, by the laws of the State of Illinois." Cole looked directly into the judge's eyes.

"Damn stupid law, if you ask me," the judge mumbled. "The court recorder will strike any mention of Mr. Sage's appearance before this court."

The lead defense attorney stood and loudly said, "Your honor, I must object. This is most irregular."

"Counselor, you picked the wrong day to try my patience. I suggest you take advantage of my willingness to let your objection go unnoticed. Sit down."

The lawyer sat.

"Mr. Sage, I want you out of my courtroom, and I suggest in the future if you see my nameplate on the wall outside, that you steer clear."

"Thank you, your honor." Cole turned and walked briskly out of the courtroom.

"You're not leaving just yet, Mr. Sage!"

Cole stopped short of the door.

"I don't think you're listening to me!" Faraday shouted.

"No, your honor. I mean, yes I'm listening," Cole stammered, caught in his memories.

"I am writing you up for gross insubordination. I will be putting the citation in your personnel file, and I guarantee the next time you cross me I will have you removed from the employment rolls of this newspaper. Is that clear?" Little white balls of sticky white froth were collecting in the corners of Faraday's mouth.

"So, you are printing my article as is?" Cole said, further pressing his luck.

"I have no choice. It is too much space to fill. Next week, by God, you will write the Sanctuary City piece or you will find yourself *selling* newspapers, not writing for one. Now, get the hell out of my office!"

Cole stood and walked out the door. "Have a nice evening."

The sound of papers and something heavy hitting the floor came from behind him as Cole closed the door.

"Have a wonderful evening, Beautiful. Try and get some rest. You're looking a bit drawn.

The secretary cursed Cole profusely as he made his way to the elevator.

Kelly and Hanna were deep in conversation and didn't notice Cole until he was nearly upon them.

"It is now after five o'clock, Ms. Day, you are no longer being compensated for your presence here. I suggest you retreat and begin your evening."

"What did Mr. Faraday want, Cole?" Kelly asked.

"Yeah, what did he say?" Hanna added.

"To tell you the truth, I wasn't listening. I believe he threatened to fire me if I didn't write the Sanctuary City piece for next week's column."

"What did you say?" Both women said at almost in unison.

"I told him to have a nice evening. And that, my dear, is exactly what we are going to do." Cole took Kelly by the arm and started for the elevator.

"Good night. Hanna! Go home!"

"Be nice," Kelly whispered. "She is really upset about Lindsey."

"I wish I'd never met that kid."

Even with Kelly's pep talk, Hanna left work in a foul mood. She sputtered and cursed all the way home, rehearsing what she was going to say to Lindsey. Her self-talk took the form of regret, seasoned with anger and accusation.

"How could I be so stupid!" she shouted above the blaring radio.

Her usual speeding bordered on suicidal as she flew down side streets and alleys she used as short cuts home. A poor homeless woman dove for cover behind a dumpster as Hanna flew by, missing her by inches.

As she parked the car, she tried what Kelly suggested.

"OK, God, you know I'm pretty much an unbeliever. Kelly says prayer in a time of extremity really helps: God's opportunity. I need help. This kid is driving me crazy. She is throwing away a future I would have killed for. Sorry, not killed, would have really liked. Please, please, please help me to say the right things. And please put some sense in that brat's head. I'm sorry, I know she's had a rough life. But so have I, and I've always tried to do the right thing, and try my hardest to get ahead. That's all." Hanna suddenly recalled the end of prayer from Hebrew school and added, "Amein. Y'hay sh'may raba m'vorach l'ola-mul'ol'may ol'ma-yuh yis-buh-raych." She then crossed herself. (Even though Kelly was a protestant and didn't cross herself, Hanna wanted to cover all her bases.)

As much as she hoped the prayer worked, Hanna had a sinking feeling there would be no sign of Lindsey when she got upstairs.

* * *

Claire left her office still feeling the hurt, depression, and anger of Kelly's rejection. Her scorn burned crimson. She fantasized about choking Kelly with one of her expensive silk scarves or driving her off the road and over a cliff. The image Claire enjoyed the most though, was putting poison in Kelly's water bottle and watching her convulse, and writhe on the floor during Pilates class.

Claire's fantasies and rage soon slipped into a silent, oppressive depression. Rejection was Claire's greatest fear and most frequent companion. Her single, teen mother who gave her up for adoption as an infant; her adoptive family, who returned her to social services at three, stating "She wasn't pretty enough"; the aging couple who adopted her at six were harsh and uncaring—most of the foster families she found herself with were kinder than the Hennings. They just wanted someone to fetch things from the refrigerator, fold clothes, and vacuum the house. As she got older they demanded more and more, and as they aged, the Hennings could do less and less. Claire just cooked, cleaned, and ran errands on her bike.

When "Father Hennings"—as he insisted Claire address him—passed away, old Mrs. Hennings became nearly chair bound. She ate, slept, and watched endless hours of television from her moth-eaten, forest green recliner. The day she asked Claire to take her to the bathroom and demanded she clean her when she finished, was the day Claire ran away.

For the last two years of high school, Claire stayed in the basement at the home of a friend from school. She worked at McDonald's after school and paid two hundred dollars a month to the family for room and board. It was the best two years of her life. The night of her graduation the family threw a party for Claire and her friend. Claire finally felt like she was in a place where she belonged. At the end of the evening, the mother and father came to Claire with a card. In the card was a hundred dollar bill…and a note saying she must vacate the premises by the end of the week.

In college, Claire faired a bit better. Being a ward of the state had its rewards. She could attend any state college or university she qualified for...for free. She chose California State University, Hayward.

For the first time, she could eat whatever she wanted, and the dining hall provided the infamous "freshman fifteen" weight gain. She went where she wanted, and the parties on the weekends introduced her to beer and pot. She found comfort in the arms of college boys, one after another, and even a few of the girls. For a short time, they all made her feel wanted and cared for. In the end, they all rejected her because, as they said, "she was just too clingy."

Claire left Hayward with a degree in marketing and an "easy" reputation. Now, ten years later, there has been a string of short and long-term relationships, several job changes, a great apartment, and another sexual rejection. Her life seems to have come full circle. Perhaps, she thought, she would someday, some way meet a nice guy, perhaps if she went to a gym that admitted men. Everyone would be sorry when Claire was a famous mystery writer, married to a handsome hunk.

As Claire approached her car, a lanky figure stepped from behind a concrete pillar.

"What do *you* want?" Claire snapped.

"Do you work here?"

"You know I do."

The figure moved from the shadows and closer to Claire. The parking garage was quiet. There were few cars left this time of the evening.

"I was hoping you might give me a ride home."

"Why would I do that?" Claire fumbled in her purse for her keys.

"Because we're friends."

"Is that what we are?"

"I thought so."

Claire toyed with her keys, then clicked the locks open. "Well, I don't. I'm not going that direction anyway."

"Which way is that?"

"Whatever direction you're going." Claire turned and opened her car door.

Faster than Claire could turn around, there was the flash of oncoming fury, an ice pick was shoved deep into the base of her skull. Her hands shot skyward, and her fingernails clawed the air desperately.

Three quick twists of the ice pick and Claire's body went limp. Before she could drop to the ground, her attacker gave her body a hard shove. Claire fell across the seats of her BMW, her head lying at a perverse angle in the passenger seat. This time rejection was fatal.

"You're right, we're not friends."

* * *

The knock on the front door stopped Hanna's pacing. She was angry, frustrated, and hurt, that all the promises Lindsey made were turning out to be meaningless.

"Sorry I'm late," but Lindsey's tone and demeanor screamed, "No I'm not".

"Where have you been? It's after nine o'clock. School was out at two. You are supposed to be at the paper by two-thirty. I waited for forty-five minutes at the school. My job is on the line here, Lindsey. I could be fired for disappearing in the middle of the day. It's a good thing Cole is connected to all this." Hanna released all her thoughts out at once. Though she tried desperately to not raise her voice, her anger was starting to get the better of her.

"I said I was sorry," Lindsey snapped.

"Look, I know I'm not like your mother. I am just the lady helping you out of a mess. However, I think I am due some respect, and a tiny bit of courtesy. What is the matter with you?"

"I don't like to be told what to do. I really don't like to be shouted at! And you're right; you're not my mother, so stop acting like it. I'm going to bed."

"Stop right there, young lady!"

"Lindsey turned and glared. "What?" she demanded.

"You don't *have* to stay here, you know. I am trying to do my best, but if you would be happier somewhere else…." Hanna lowered her voice.

"I don't have to *stay* anywhere!" Lindsey interrupted, then spun around and stomped to her room and slammed the door.

Hanna threw her hands up to her burning cheeks and sobbed.

* * *

"Hello."
"Cole, its Hanna."

"What time is it?" Cole said groggily.

"A little after eleven. Did I wake you?"

"Doesn't matter. Is something wrong?"

Hanna knew what she wanted, and needed to say, but she was suddenly overwhelmed with emotion. "Oh, Cole I think I've made a big mistake. There's a reason I'm not a mother. I don't have the temperament to deal with a teenager. I have lived alone far too long. I hate defiance, and I am starting to hate Lindsey."

"What's happened now?" Cole was now fully awake.

"She didn't get home until after nine o'clock. I was worried sick. I went from mad, to worried, to resentful, to fed up." Hanna blew her nose into the tenth tissue of the night. "Sorry, I don't want to do this anymore. There's a nasty side to this kid. You've never seen it, but she is like a little Miss Jekyll and Hyde."

"So what are you saying? You want to turn her over to CPS?"

"Could you talk to her before I do anything final?

"Sure, I can talk to her, but my daughter came to me full grown, married, and with a daughter of her own. I don't think I'm the best resource for child counseling." Cole was trying to wrap his head around this sudden turn of events. "So, how long has this been going on? I mean she's only been with you, what, ten or twelve days?"

"She nearly bit my head off at breakfast. All I did was ask her about a call I got from the school. It seems she ditched halfway through the day. I don't even know if she went to school today. I am so upset. I don't know what to do."

"I tell you what: try to get some sleep, tread lightly in the morning, and I'll talk to Lindsey after school tomorrow." Cole tried to put a positive spin on a bad situation. "How's that sound?"

"Like two-thirty can't come soon enough."

"How many glasses of wine have you had?"

"What's that supposed to mean?" Hanna snapped.

"Come on...."

"One," Hanna lied.

"Well, have another and go to bed. See you in the morning."

"OK. Thank you. Really, Cole, thank you."

"It's gonna be alright. Good night."

* * *

Cole shook his head trying to clear the cobwebs. Why must the day always start with morning? he thought. He showered, dressed, and made his way to the kitchen. After popping the last bagel into the toaster and hitting the start button on the coffee maker, Cole went to the front porch to get the paper.

The plastic screeched as he attempted to free the paper from its cocoon. Cole flopped the paper open on the kitchen table. He froze when he saw the face of another woman above the fold. He quickly read the caption and then the story. "Found in her car, stabbed in the back of the head, one more in a rash of unexplained ice pick murders," Cole scanned the article frantically. Then he saw it, and at first, it didn't register: Claire Muir.

"Why do I know that name?" Cole said, aloud. Claire! That's the name of Kelly's not-so-secret-any-longer admirer, that's why. Cole smiled at the irony of him not knowing where he heard the name.

As he rushed around the kitchen cleaning up, Cole made a mental note to call Leonard Chin when he got to the office. He folded the paper, tucked it under his arm, and made his way to the door. Just as he closed the door behind him, he heard the phone ring. For a moment he thought, let the machine get it, but something told him to answer it.

"Cole! Have you seen the paper? Claire is dead! Murdered! I can't believe it!" Kelly was frantic.

"Yeah, I saw it. That's your Claire?" Cole asked.

"She's not *my* Claire, but yes, that is the one I know. It's horrible. Hours after she, I mean while we ate dinner. The article says a security guard found her at 7:30. Oh my heavens, Cole, that poor girl." Kelly sounded breathless. "I just can't believe it. Who would want to hurt her?"

"I don't know, Kelly. I'm really sorry," Cole offered.

"She had no one, she was adopted, she ran away at sixteen—seems like she never had a chance."

"Claire had the same chances we all do, Kelly. These murders are random. Don't go there." Cole sighed. "Look, I know this hits really close to home. I'm sorry the woman is dead. It is horrible, no question, but it has nothing to do with you rejecting her. It has nothing to do with you knowing her. It is a senseless act of violence. Please don't make any more of it than that. Please."

"How can you be so cold?"

"I'm not being cold. This is like the seventh of these puncture murders. Look at yesterday's paper, the day before, the week before, the month before—people are killed every day, Kelly, in meaningless, senseless acts of brutality. It's a fact. Innocent, guilty—violence is no respecter of age, sex, race, or anything else. Violence makes no sense because it makes no sense. I have been reporting the news for a long time and it is just the cold, hard truth. I hate it, but that is just the way it is."

"I need to go."

"Kelly. Kelly!"

The line was as dead as Claire Muir.

* * *

"Good morning," Cole said as he approached Hanna's desk.

"Says who?"

"Yikes, you look like I feel. You alright?"

"Apart from not sleeping, getting the silent treatment and dirty looks all the way through breakfast and the drive to school, my morning is unicorns, butterflies, and daisies." Hanna gave Cole a wide, sarcastic, very forced grin.

"I managed to get in my first fight with Kelly!" Cole announced. "She hung up on me!"

"Why?"

"You haven't seen the morning edition yet."

"Not yet." Hanna flipped over the paper on her desk. "Oh, my God! It's Claire, the woman at…. What happened?"

"Another victim of these puncture killings, stabbed on the way to her car." Cole shrugged. "I tried to tell Kelly people are killed every day and this is just another senseless act of brutality…"

"That is really harsh, Cole!" Hanna interrupted. "Claire was her friend."

"You don't know the half of it" Cole interjected. "Hold my calls, I'm phoning Chin." Cole shook his head and went to his office.

Cole got a recording and left a short call-me-back message. In less than a minute his phone rang.

"Sorry. I was in the john." Chin spoke before Cole was able to say "Hello."

"Since yesterday?" Cole quipped.

"Some of us actually work for a living."

"Aren't we touchy today?"

"What's up?" Chin ignored Cole's remark.

"These puncture murders."

"Ice pick. We figure the killer is using *The Iceman's* old trick. Handle deep, with a twist!"

"That's rough."

"The woman last night was lucky number seven. This is crazy. It's like every other day. No connections, no relationships, different neighborhoods, from poor to pretty well-off. We have absolutely nothing linking any of the victims. Black, white, male, female—it is totally random, murder for sport."

"I have to tell you, Kelly knew Claire Muir. They went to the same gym. Friends of sorts, until she hit on Kelly, that is."

"Kelly? Geez, she must have freaked."

"Even worse was when I said the same thing you did, about it being just random acts of violence, and they happen every day."

"That's pretty rough. The victim was her friend. You are really a jerk sometimes, Sage."

"Gimme a break. So, what's next?"

"You better apologize right away," Chin offered.

"No, not with Kelly, with the murders."

"For print? But we got nothin'. This is a tough one. We keep waiting for a slip up of some kind, but it is all so random.

"All to the head?"

"No. Two were to the chest, square in the heart."

"That is really in-your-face killing. That takes a special kind of hate...."

"Or training," Chin cut in.

"So you're thinking military, then?"

"We're thinking everything. The mayor is threatening heads will roll, *again*, if we don't catch him quick."

"What if it were a woman? You said 'him'. What if it isn't a man? Maybe a 'she' could gain the target's confidence easier," Cole pined, more out loud to himself than to his friend, the detective.

"Yeah, could be…but it would be very unusual for a woman to commit this kind of killing."

"But not unheard of. Four of the seven victims have been women," Cole suggested.

"I hate to swell your head up, but you might just be on to something. We hit on that idea at first, but it was dismissed pretty quickly. I'll run it through again. Many more of these and we'll start seeing empty streets. Anyway, what was it you needed?" Chin asked.

"Yesterday I was looking into filing a complaint on someone taking a person's photo in the shower at a gym and emailing it to them."

"Kelly?"

"No need now. It was Claire who was stalking Kelly, leaving creepy poems in her windshield, a rose in her locker. The topper was a full-length shot in the shower, from behind. She e-mailed it to Kelly."

"She won't send any more," Chin quipped.

"Now who's cold?"

"Claire."

Chapter Twelve

The weekend turned out to be just what Hanna needed. She and Lindsey talked, baked cookies, laughed and joked, did their nails, and ate tons of junk food. They binge-watched the *Gilmore Girls* on Netflix and went to bed around twelve.

It seemed Lindsey turned a corner. She and Jake got along fine, by Sunday night they were joking and teasing each other, and at one point when the movie got to be too scary, Lindsey actually snuggled up next to him on the couch.

The tough love Hanna applied when Lindsey showed up at nine o'clock after standing her up after school seemed to have really fired Lindsey up. Around midnight she came out of her room. Hanna felt Lindsey's embarrassment was a good sign. After a late snack of milk and cookies, Lindsey seemed to "normalize." Hanna really felt she was making headway. They both went to bed with apologies and promises to do better.

Wednesday morning, Hanna felt better than she had in days when the alarm went off. She showered and dressed, woke Lindsey, and was in the kitchen ahead of schedule.

"Hello?" Hanna said, answering the phone with a glance at the Felix-the-Cat wall clock. Seven o'clock! Who would be calling at this hour, she thought.

"Ms. Day?"

"Yes?"

"Good morning! Penny Crawford, from Wallenberg."

"Good morning," Hanna said hesitantly.

"Good news!" the counselor nearly squealed with excitement." We got Lindsey's test scores!"

"Wonderful." Hanna's stomach flipped over.

"It's kind of a good news-bad news report. Her math and science scores weren't the best. No matter…her writing and verbal skills scores were off the chart. Wellsburg Academy is offering her a "disadvantaged student scholarship" set up by a wealthy alumnus. She's in!"

Hanna laughed. "I can't believe it!" Her problems with Lindsey all seemed to disappear. She felt a tinge of guilt but was thrilled with the idea of her not being responsible for Lindsey much longer. "Have you told her? When would she start?"

"I was leaving that honor to you. I think it's only fair. As far as the time frame goes, she could start as early as the Summer Session. That would help her get caught up a bit by fall. That said, Lindsey really must pass all of her classes this semester. Wellsburg Academy is willing to bend, but if she gets further behind, I don't think they will be willing to gamble."

"I understand."

"I'm here to help or encourage any way I can. Lindsey's a tricky case. I'm never quite sure how she will react to things," the counselor said.

"You and me both," Hanna agreed.

"We'll just stay positive and get her through."

"Yes, we will."

"Have a wonderful day!" With that, the counselor was gone.

"Good Morning," Hanna said cheerfully as Lindsey came into the kitchen. "Hungry?"

"Kinda."

"There's yogurt and some blueberries in the fridge. There are bagels and I got some amazing strawberry cream cheese. I can cook up some eggs if you want."

"A bagel sounds good." Lindsey opened the bag on the counter and put a bagel in the toaster.

"I have some wonderful news," Hanna began. "Your test scores came back."

Lindsey didn't respond.

"You did really well. Matter of fact, they said you were 'off the chart' in English and verbal skills."

Still no response.

"The area you didn't do so well in was math and science. Surprised?"

"No. I hate math," Lindsey finally replied.

"Here's the best part: Wellsburg Academy has offered you a full scholarship: room, food, tuition, everything!" Hanna said excitedly.

Lindsey didn't make a sound. She opened the refrigerator and stood a moment looking for the cream cheese. Finding it, she closed the door and went to the counter.

"The thing is—and this is important. Are you listening?" Hanna turned around and Lindsey's back was to her.

"Yeah, I'm listening."

"You *have* to pass all your high school classes this semester. And no matter what, you cannot miss any more school," Hanna said firmly. "If you screw up, you'll lose the greatest opportunity of your life. Sometimes I don't think you realize how cool this is. It's an unbelievable opportunity." Hanna turned back to her cup of tea.

"An opportunity for you to get rid of me," Lindsey snapped, not turning.

"That's not true. I just want you to have an amazing future, a brilliant career as a writer. This school will open new doors for you. From there you can get into any college you want. I never had a chance at anything like this. You've won the lottery, kid!" Hanna was almost pleading with the girl.

"I have to leave San Francisco? I love this city. It's my life. Everything I know is here."

"You can come back and stay all summer. I'll come and visit you. Maybe we can arrange for you to come home at Christmas and Spring break."

The bagel popped up out of the toaster. Lindsey looked at the brown mass and pushed it down again.

"Lindsey, there are people who really care about you, like Mrs. Crawford, the counselor. Pam in the attendance office really likes you, and worries when you're not in school. Cole has done something very special for you that I haven't even told you about. And I'm behind you all the way." Hanna steeled herself, knowing she was entering difficult territory. "I know your life so far has been crap. I understand how much you love San Francisco. Truly I do. You are a *very* talented girl. But you have to learn some discipline. You really need to allow people who are older and have more experience in the world to help guide you. Otherwise, where are you going to end up?"

"Like my mom again! Is that all what you want to say? A whore, a druggie, an old lady beater? That it?" Lindsey's voice rose with anger.

"That's not what I'm saying at all."

"Yes, it is! You're just like my mom. My way or no way. All or nothing. Always giving orders. I have choices in life! I am a writer and a good one. Cole said so! Yeah, yeah. Who are you to tell me what to do?"

Hanna clinched her teeth. She was determined to stay calm and choose her words wisely. "Let's have a nice breakfast and talk this out. We don't have to fight and argue. Please, Lindsey. Let's go back to being friends. I'm *not* like your mom. I need you to understand that. I have not had a happy life either. My mother was abusive and an alcoholic. Believe me, I get it. I don't want you hurt anymore."

"But you want me to leave San Francisco." Lindsey's tone softened.

"Yes, for a while. Once you get your education you can live here for the rest of your life if you want. In fact, you can come back here for college. We're just talking about a couple of years."

Lindsey didn't answer. The bagel popped up again, and she opened the drawer to get a knife to spread the cream cheese. Laying along the edge of the drawer was a wooden handled ice pick.

"And what happens if I refuse to go to this fancy school in Virginia?" Lindsey slowly reached out and picked up the ice pick.

Hanna felt a chill of panic come over her. She knew what she needed to say, but was terrified at what Lindsey's response might be. "Then, you wouldn't be able to live with me anymore."

Hanna took a sip of her tea and waited for Lindsey to respond.

"You *are* my mom." Lindsey's voice took on a strange, almost tender tone. "I understand what you are saying. You help me best by getting rid of me. It's for my own good. You'll be much happier. I've heard it all before. She sold me off to all kinds of whores, junkies, and even strangers. I was in the way. I'm in the way now. Well, no more."

She turned and stepped up behind Hanna. In a heartbeat, she grabbed Hanna's forehead and shoved the icepick into the base of her skull. The teacup dropped to the floor. Hanna's arms flailed and her legs jerked convulsively. Lindsey withdrew the shaft and thrust it again into Hanna's brain, this time giving the ice pick three hard, circular twists. Hanna's body went limp.

"I am *not* leaving San Francisco. Not for two years, two days, or two hours. I don't need you. I don't need anybody! I'm a writer, I work alone."

Lindsey threw the ice pick on the table. Hanna's lifeless body slumped to the floor. Without emotion or concern, the girl turned and spread the strawberry cream cheese on half of her bagel.

Bagel in hand she returned to her room. She took three pairs of fresh panties from the dresser drawer and shoved them to the bottom of her backpack. She took the new jacket Hanna bought her and put it on. She glanced around the room. Deciding there was nothing else she needed, she returned to the kitchen.

Hanna's purse was hanging on one of the chairs at the small table. Lindsey opened it, took out Hanna's keys. She opened the wallet and plucked out whatever money there was. There were several plastic cards: Visa, insurance, library card, a Safeway grocery card. She threw all but the Visa on the table. She overlooked the envelope with the airline tickets and check from Cole.

Stepping over Hanna's motionless body, Lindsey grabbed the other half of her bagel and stepped back over Hanna.

"See ya', *Mom*," she said sarcastically.

Lindsey headed to the front door, putting her backpack on as she walked. Almost as an afterthought, she turned and tossed the keys back into the apartment.

"Later," she said cheerfully as she closed the door.

* * *

At nine-thirty, Cole was genuinely concerned. He had called Hanna's cell phone at eight-thirty, but she didn't answer. Since she now took Lindsey to school each morning, it wasn't that uncommon for Hanna to be a few minutes late. He called again fifteen minutes later. Still no answer. At nine, he had decided to call Lindsey. Her phone went to voice mail. Cole figured it was class time and he hoped she would call when she saw his message.

Cole busied himself online, searching for houses in the Palo Alto area. Around five to ten o'clock, he took a break and went to the coffee station for a mocha.

"Gee, Hanna on strike?" said a petite young woman in a floral dress.

"Why?" Cole asked.

"I can't remember the last time I saw you get your own coffee. Good to know you can still do it." The woman teased.

"She hasn't come in yet."

"It's ten. Is she sick?"

"That's the weird thing, She hasn't called. She's never just not shown up before," Cole stated awkwardly.

"That's not like Hanna. At least, I mean, I don't know her well, but it seems out of character."

"Have you called her?"

"No answer."

"Worried?"

"Yeah, I'm getting there."

"I am, too." Cole didn't mention Lindsey. Not a lot of people knew of Hanna's new house guest. He respected her privacy, so he let it go.

On his way to his office, Cole checked Hanna's desk calendar. There were notes about making Lindsey's doctor and dentist appointments, a hair appointment for Hanna and a date with Jake. Nothing for the current date.

At ten-thirty after calling Hanna three more times and Lindsey twice, Cole was now officially worried. Something was wrong. He could feel it: a heavy, sick feeling in his stomach.

Cole went back to Hanna's desk until he found a business card for Jake Salem.

"Jake? Cole Sage," Cole said when the detective answered his cell.

"Hey, how ya doin'?" Jake said, cheerfully.

"I'm not sure. Have you talked to Hanna today?"

"No, why?"

"She didn't show up for work. She didn't call, and I can't reach her. I called Lindsey, no answer there either."

"Did you call the school to see if the kid showed up?" Jake asked.

"After the hard time they gave Hanna, I figured there would be no way they'd talk to me."

"I tell you what. Let me call. I'll get back to you."

"Sounds good, thanks." Cole didn't like the investigative tone Jake took. He'd heard it a thousand times. It wasn't personal anymore, he was full-on cop.

When he dialed the school, Jake was connected with Pamela in attendance.

"This is detective Winston Salem, SFPD. I need to know if a student is in attendance today."

"Certainly. Is there a problem?"

"Not yet," Jake said trying to sound friendly. It didn't work.

"Students Name?" Pamela asked.

"Lindsey,"

"Frost? The attendance clerk interrupted.

"Yeah, how did you know?"

"She's my special project. I have to say I'm not doing my job really well. Let's see here…so far she's missed first, second, and third. Fourth period is lunch. Do you want a campus supervisor to try and spot her?"

"Sounds like that would be a waste of time," Jake said flatly.

"Probably. She's not in trouble, is she? I hope not. She is so bright. Have you called her guardian Ms. Day? Maybe Lindsey stayed home sick. She was out last week. Her guardian called that in though. Sorry, but that's all I have."

"Thanks, that's all I needed." Jake terminated the conversation.

Without regard for Cole's story of having called several times, Jake punched in Hanna's number. He memorized it because he was always thinking about her and wanting to call.

After several rings, the number went to voice mail. From his location, Jake figured he was about fifteen minutes from Hanna's apartment. He did a U-turn and started for her place.

As he pulled into the apartment complex, Jake immediately spotted Hanna's Volkswagen.

"Dummy forgot to turn on her phone." Jake smiled in relief.

He quickly climbed the outside stairs. Panic set in for a moment: what was his excuse for showing up unannounced in the middle of the morning when they both were supposed to be at work?

He decided the best excuse was the truth. Trying to be as jovial as possible, Jake rapped out shave-and-a-haircut. The knock on the door was not firm; it took a moment for Jake to realize it was not fully closed. He knocked again, pushing slightly with each contact with the door. It moved inward.

"Hanna!" Jake called out as he opened the door. "Hanna? It's Jake!"

There was no answer. The detective unclipped his pistol and slipped it from the holster.

The apartment was still. He moved slowly across the entry into the small living room. Nothing seemed out of order. He moved toward the kitchen.

The first thing he saw was the ice pick on the table next to a bowl. The sinister purpose of the oddly out of place item didn't register. His eyes flashed around the room. Then he saw the body lying behind the table. He moved across the room to where Hanna lay motionless. Jake put his index and middle finger on her neck looking for a pulse. Nothing.

"Lindsey!" Jake shouted, fearing there would be no response.

The cold concentration of years of training and police work, murder scenes, and confronting active shooters, steeled Detective Winston Salem as he rose and walked to the hall. His mind raced with each step he took, trying to process what he had just found. He ran through numerous scenarios as he made his way down the hall.

The bathroom door stood open, the room was empty. He went to Hanna's room. The bed was neatly made and the toss pillows were in place. He turned, gun at shoulder level, and entered Lindsey's room. The bed was not made, the top drawer of the dresser was out. A pair of powder blue panties hung from the top of the drawer. At that moment, Jake's nightmare scenario became a reality. Lindsey killed Hanna and was on the run.

"4180," Jake said into his radio.

"4180 copy."

"I am on scene at a 187. I need CSI ASAP.

Jake made his way down the hall to the kitchen. He went to Hanna's body. This time not as a cop, but as a friend and suitor. Slipping his large frame between the table and the counter, he collapsed back on his bended knees. The detective broke protocol without hesitation and gently turned Hanna and put her head on his lap. As he stroked her hair, his broad shoulders began to shake. Tears streamed down his tanned unshaven cheeks.

"Hanna, oh Hanna," Jake repeated, gently rocking and stroking the cheek of the woman he fell in love with.

He gazed at the ceiling and closed his eyes. Stop it, he told himself. "Stop it!" The black and whites will roll up soon. Get it together!

As he opened his eyes he was looking eye level at the table. The blood on the steel shaft of the ice pick lay right in front of him.

He gently laid Hanna back on the floor. In the distance, he could hear the approaching sirens.

Reaching in his pocket he removed his phone and punched in a number.

"Leonard. I found the ice pick killer."

Within minutes the small apartment was swarming with crime scene investigators, a photographer, videographer, and Leonard Chin.

"What are you doing here?" Chin asked.

"Cole called and said Hanna hadn't shown up for work. He called her and Lindsey a bunch of times. He called me to see if I had talked to her. I wasn't far away and thought I would drop by and see what was up."

"I am so sorry." Chin reached out and squeezed Jake's arm.

"We need to tell Cole," Jake said softly.

"He doesn't know? Oh man. Oh my, oh God." Chin shook his head as if to say "I can't do it."

"Do you want me to go?" Jake asked.

"Can you? I mean, are you..." Chin paused, "are you able to?"

"We both love her. I need to do it. He deserves that much. I know you are close, but I think it will be better if I do it. Then, I'll be back on the street."

"Look, you know you can't work this."

"I have to find her."

"Then what? The state you're in you'd shoot her."

Jake didn't respond.

"Badge and service weapon." Chin held his hand out.

"Are you serious?" Jake demanded.

"You know the rules. I am your closest superior and it is my responsibility. Besides, you're a witness. You're already in deep enough trouble for moving the body. I understand. I would have probably done the same. Just the same, it is my responsibility. Don't make this any harder than it is." Chin again put his open palm in front of Jake.

"I'm still going to look!" Jake handed Chin his pistol and badge.

"I can't stop you. But, you will call it in. Under no circumstances are you to make contact with that girl. Do you understand me, Lieutenant?"

"Yes."

"Yes, what?" Chin's tone was no-nonsense.

"Yes, sir."

Leonard Chin and Jake Salem had worked together from more than a decade, and in all that time Chin never pulled rank. There was no doubt that Jake was under direct orders to not interfere with the investigation. No matter, Jake swore he would be the one to find Lindsey Frost.

* * *

Cole Sage knew the look. He'd seen it more times than he could possibly begin to count. When Jake Salem stepped up to his open door, Cole knew something was terribly wrong.

"What is it, Jake?" Cole's question left no room for doubt. He expected bad news.

"Can I sit down?"

"Of course."

The handsome detective now seemed diminished in size, and he seemed to have aged in years since their first meeting a few days before.

"I'm here as a friend, not a cop, Cole. I have some very bad news. Try and brace yourself for the worst." Jake's voice quavered slightly.

Cole didn't answer. His eyes narrowed as he stared at the man across his desk.

"It's Hanna. She's been killed."

Cole gave a slightly nervous chuckle, he didn't mean to, and he found nothing funny in the statement. His complete shock, denial, and disbelief wouldn't allow him to process the words still hanging in the air.

"Wh…what?" Cole finally said.

"She's been murdered. She's dead. Lindsey stabbed her. Lindsey is the icepick killer."

"She's a child."

"No matter."

"Hanna's dead? Who told you? Are you sure?" Cole refused to believe.

"I found her myself. I took her pulse. I held her in my arms."

As if drawn by some great magnetic force, Cole's chair spun and faced the wall behind his desk. He heaved great sighs trying to get a breath.

"I found the ice pick on the table," Jake continued. "The wound was the same. I have no doubt that Lindsey killed Hanna as well as all those other people who died of puncture wounds."

"So, it was instant?" Cole asked softly.

"I believe so."

"What now, I mean, how will they find her?" Cole blinked hard.

"I'm off the case. Chin took my badge and gun. I understand. I'm too close. But I'm not sitting still. I just wanted to be the one to tell you. Not some snot-nosed rookie patrolman." Jake approached Cole's desk. "I know that whatever I'm feeling you are feeling a hundred times worse. It hurts like hell. Down to my marrow, I am aching. I will find her, Cole."

Cole stood. "I'll go with you."

"Can't do it. Chin would blow a fuse. Call 'im. I'm sure he'll let **you** ride along with him. You know better than anyone what Lindsey looks like. Really looks like, not just a school picture."

The two men stood silently for a long moment.

"I really thought I found…the one." Jake's voice was quaking.

"You have no idea what you found. She was one of a kind." Cole rounded the desk. "I don't usually do this." Cole reached out and they hugged.

"God knows I needed that. Thanks, buddy." Jake turned and left the office.

As Cole closed the door behind Jake, he could no longer contain his emotions. Collapsing into his chair he folded his arms across his desk and wept.

It took a while for Cole to process the news. He sat staring and holding his hands over his eyes for a long while. Finally, he sniffed hard and reached for the phone.

"Leonard? Cole."

"I'm so sorry, my friend. I just don't know what to say."

"Say I can ride along with you."

Chin didn't respond.

"Look, I can ID her from a distance, I know her, I can...."

"OK, I get it. I took Jake off the case because he's too close. You're even closer. The first misstep, friends or not, I will drop you at the curb. Understood?"

"You have my word."

"I'll pick you up in a half hour." Chin paused. "We'll get her Cole, I swear to you, we'll get her."

Cole paced on the sidewalk in front of the *Chronicle*. His thoughts raced from anger to sorrow, from hatred to guilt. The sight of Chin's dark blue sedan and a deep breath cleared Cole's head and prepared him to face his friend.

"Thank you for this," Cole said getting in the car.

"I have to tell you: the odds are we won't be the ones to spot her. If and when we get the call, you have to stay out of the way, you must do as I tell you.

Unless I specifically ask for help, you are just a silent observer. Clear?"

"Yes."

"Where do you suggest we start?"

"Palace of Fine Arts. She loves to go there and write."

The friends rode mostly in silence. Cole looked out the window and scanned the sidewalks, alleys, and side streets for a glimpse of Lindsey. The radio occasional squawked out calls.

As they turned onto Baker Street, Chin turned to Cole, "So, we can circle the whole park in a matter of minutes. You up for it?"

"You bet."

Near the corner of Beach and Baker, Chin spotted a parking place and pulled over.

"OK, How about you go right and I go left. We'll meet on the other side. *If* you spot her, lay low until I get around to you. Do not make contact. We'll do it together. Agreed?" Chin opened his door and waited for a response.

"Absolutely."

The warmth of a clear day brought people outside and into the park. Lots of tourists, cameras around their necks, strolled the sidewalk that circles the magnificent exposition structure.

The benches and few tables on the grounds were empty. Cole tried to look fifty or more yards ahead to make sure if Lindsey was there, he would spot her long before she saw him. He walked slowly and tried to calm his nerves by counting his steps.

Anything to keep his mind off the reason for his search.

It only took a few minutes for Cole and Chin to meet on the walk across from where they started. Cole shook his head.

"Possible sighting of Female Juvenile matching the description of Lindsey Frost. Southside Union Square. Officers approaching. Will detain. Please advise."

"On our way." Chin slammed the radio back on its base. "Hold on!"

Lights and siren cut through the peaceful setting as they spun a U-turn and roared up the street.

"Wouldn't Franklin be faster?" Cole asked as they turned onto Scott Street.

"I don't want to chance the traffic."

Chin's agility driving through traffic running red lights was a mix of passive-aggressive bobbing and weaving, full-out manic abandon. The normal twenty to thirty minute trip across town was cut to fifteen.

Three black and whites were parked at the curb and in the street as they approached Union Square.

"Hang back a minute," Chin instructed as they exited the car.

Cole watched as Chin approached a police cruiser with the back door standing open.

"What have we got?"

"She won't give us her name and has no ID."

"What's your name?" Chin demanded leaning down at the silhouette in the back of the car. Cole watched and strained to hear.

"I ain't done nothin'."

"What's your name?" Chin barked.

"Bite me. I'm not saying nothin' 'til you let me out of here and get these cuffs off."

Chin stood and waved Cole forward.

Cole quickly moved to the door. His heart sank as he spotted the pimple faced girl in the back seat, right age, right size and build, right hair…but it wasn't Lindsey.

Cole shook his head.

"Take her to Juvenile Hall until she remembers her name. See what we have on her." Chin walked toward the idling car. "Thanks, guys! Keep looking," Chin shouted over his shoulder.

"Close, but no…."

"Get ready for a lot of that." Chin opened the door of his car. "If she hangs around the Palace of Fine Arts, what do you say we scour that area?"

"Works for me," Cole responded.

For the next two hours, they worked a grid of Franklin on the east, Divisadero on the west, Lombard on the north and Turk on the south. Up and back, side to side, down alleys and up side streets, mile after mile. They stopped once for coffee and once for a bathroom break and to stretch their legs.

The excitement of the search gave way to the monotony of block after block of empty streets, neighborhood traffic, street people, and lost tourists. Chin deflected calls and reassigned his department's manpower to cover a variety of calls.

"So, how do you like being the head man?" Cole inquired after a lengthy call.

"Temporary. Just until they transfer somebody in."

"Why not you?"

"Combination of politics and the fact I said I didn't want the job."

"Really?"

"I liked what I did. I don't want to be anybody's boss. I want to work my cases and go home, it's worked real well for this long, why shake things up?" Chin signaled and turned another corner. "Getting dizzy yet?"

"Not yet."

The radio squawked and screeched. "Possible sighting on FJS."

"Location?"

There was a long pause. "South of Market on 5th." After a short pause: "ID doesn't match. False alarm."

"Alright, no problem. Thanks for the alert."

"Roger that."

As daylight began to fade, Chin turned onto Hyde and headed for the Embarcadero. "I tell you what: let's end the day at least with some pretty scenery. Let's sweep the Embarcadero, then I'll take you back."

"Sounds good. You can just drop me at home. That way you can get home without a bunch of backtracking."

"You sure?"

"Yeah. Let's do that."

After cruising the Embarcadero north and south, they called it a day.

"I really appreciate your letting me be part of this. I think I would have gone nuts otherwise."

"That I can understand. You up for more tomorrow? More of the same, I mean. I may not be able to dedicate the whole day, but as long as I can we'll run support and back up for any and all leads. You in?"

"That would be great."

"OK see you at nine."

Cole watched the cruiser disappear into the violet hues of the last vestiges of day. At his front porch, Cole turned and sat down. The air was cool and the breeze of nightfall blew his pant legs.

The day had drained Cole. His spirits were lower than he had faced in a long time. Now, alone and sitting quietly, the street motionless in front of him, his mind ached in sorrow, his body ached from lack of movement. He wanted to sleep, close his eyes and pray it would all be a dream when he awoke.

The reality was that it wasn't a dream. The days to come would be filled with the excitement of marriage, Stanford, and all the changes that will come with it. The move will be dulled with the pain of losing Hanna, the capture and trial of Lindsey, and the emptiness of life without his buddy, his helper, confidant, "partner in crime", aide-de-camp and dear, dear, friend.

Cole had no more tears, just a dull aching in his heart.

Chapter Thirteen

"Cole, we are going to have to stop for something to eat. It's nearly one. I've only had the cup of coffee I grabbed when I left the house," Chin said as they turned onto Post from Webster Street. It was the first time either spoke in nearly an hour.

"Yeah, no problem. I probably need something, too."

"Here we go. How about the New Korea House? There is a spot right in front."

"Sure, that's fine."

Once seated, Chin sighed deeply. Cole rubbed his face and took a sip of water.

"I have to tell you something. You might not like it." Chin placed his radio on the side of the table.

"That wouldn't be new."

"Funny. We may be just spinning our wheels. That kid could be anywhere. San Francisco may seem like a small city geographically, but it is a huge haystack to look for a needle. This kid is street smart and has roamed this city for years. She has places she's probably spent the night, hid out, and where she's just another street kid."

"I have been thinking the same thing. You think we should give up?" Cole asked.

"I'm not saying that. I'm saying it is going to take a hell of a lucky break to find her. The entire force has her picture and description. Every patrolman, beat cop, and safety volunteer has their eyes peeled for her. We will catch her. I just don't want you thinking we'll just roll up on her."

"I know that. But as long as you're willing, and don't get another call, I'd sure rather be out looking than sitting at my desk. Is that stupid?"

"Not at all. I'd feel the same way. But," Chin paused, and reflected a moment before addressing the real issue bothering him, "don't you need some time alone, or with Kelly to process, grieve, and really get your head around your loss?"

"I keep thinking all this started with my interest in Lindsey's writing. There were signs, then Hanna cried out for help, I told her to bail on keeping Lindsey, she thought she was making headway…then poor Jake."

"He has taken three days off. But I know without a doubt he is doing the same thing we are."

The friends fell back into silence. They ordered and sat quietly waiting for their food. The radio, though turned down, squelched. Occasionally, Chin would catch something and turn the radio up. He wouldn't comment, just turn the volume back down.

"You know, you are one of my oldest friends here in the city," Cole said, breaking the silence. "We have been through some crazy stuff together."

"And some great lunches." Leonard Chin interjected reaching for the Kim Chee.

"And great lunches. I've been meaning to tell you something and the time just hasn't been right. I'm leaving the paper."

Chin stopped his next bite halfway to his mouth. "I beg your pardon."

"I've been offered a teaching position at Stanford, teaching writing and journalism."

"When would you start?" Chin was clearly surprised.

"Summer session. In about three months."

"Wow. *That* is something."

"A lot has led to my decision. The new editor, well, I already told you about him. Now, it seems like Stanford would give me a clean break. Now with Hanna gone...." Cole's words faded as he took a spoonful of soup. "The offer came from out of the blue. But, you know, I think it might have been God's way of preparing me for Hanna's death."

"Really? You believe that?" Chin asked a bit mystified.

"I believe God has a plan for our lives. His ways are not our ways, but the master plan in hindsight always has meaning."

"We believe that what happens to one is a consequence of the choices we've made as well as events in the world over which one has no control—voluntary versus involuntary. In Buddhism," Chin went on, "we believe that it may take several lifetimes for our choices to catch up to us. Many events in our lives can change our destinies. For some, their lives are changed because of a certain person or event—any one of which can bring very different change to your destiny."

"Karma," Cole responded.

"If you wish. That is what we call it, but it has been so trivialized by people with little understanding."

"Enlightenment," Cole said.

"Are you sure you're not a Buddhist?" Chin laughed.

"Who can tell?"

The radio squawked again. Chin turned up the volume quickly this time.

"Lt. Chin. We may have spotted your girl," the voice sputtered through the crackle.

"Identify, what is your 20?" Chin asked.

"Tomlinson, Bridge security, Golden Gate." The voice reasoned.

"This is Chin, Salem, are you 10-8?" Chin rolled his eyes and said to Cole, "I knew he was out there."

"I heard. En route." Jake Salem's voice came through loud and clear.

"Rendezvous at the Bridge Security Office. Jake, wait for us. Understood?"

"Roger that."

"What's your 20?"

"Ten minutes out."

"10-4.

"Let's roll." Chin threw a twenty on the table and rushed for the door.

Cole was sprinting several steps behind Chin, and the car was already running when Cole got in. Chin turned on the lights and siren and shot away from the curb. In less than ten minutes they were at the Bridge office.

"Who's Tomlinson?" Chin shouted as they ran through the doors into the building.

"Here, sir!"

Chin and Cole were guided through the security door and into the control room. In front of them were at least twenty monitors, showing various vantage points on the bridge. In the center was a large monitor screen.

"Bring up twelve," Tomlinson said.

The large monitor went from black to a shot of a girl on the rail of the bridge.

"That's her," Cole said excitedly.

"What the hell is she doing?"

From the angle of the camera, Lindsey could be seen throwing something over the rail.

"Watch," Cole said. "She's wadding up paper. She's tearing out pages of her notebook. I have to get out there."

"She a jump risk?" Tomlinson asked.

"Could be," Chin replied. "Depends on who approaches her." Chin and Cole locked eyes. "Do you think she'd jump, Cole?"

"Dear God, I hope not."

"Are you up for this?"

"I hope so."

"Not good enough. I can't have civilians…" Tomlinson bristled.

Chin cut Tomlinson off. "She doesn't know me. I'll position to the north of her."

"Where are we?" Jake Salem entered the room.

"It's her," Cole said.

"What's the plan?"

"Cole will take her in. I'm going to pass and position just to her left."

"And me?" Jake pleaded.

"Go with Cole. Support, back-up—you make the collar."

"Sage, you good with that?" Chin asked.

"I don't know. What do you think, Jake? Can you allow me to deal with her?"

"You think she'll jump?" Jake asked.

"It hadn't entered my mind. Now, I'm not so sure." Cole looked back at the large televised image of Lindsey standing at the rail. "Let see what we can do."

"We'll be back," Chin said turning for the door.

Chin changed his sport coat for a red 49er's sweatshirt he kept in his trunk. The three men crossed at the toll booth and began the near mile walk to the center span where Lindsey stood. Traffic on the Golden Gate was brisk and heavy. Bicyclers and pedestrians share the east side of the Bridge's only walkway. Cole thought of the many times he rode the bridge heading for Kelly's Sausalito houseboat.

One hundred yards from the center of the bridge, Chin broke away.

"Good luck. See you on the other side." Chin quickened his pace.

"Have you thought of what you're going to say to her?" Jake asked as soon as they could see Lindsey.

"To tell you the truth, I've been praying so hard, I haven't given it a thought."

"Let's hope He's listening."

"Oh, He's listening all right, but I can't help thinking what Garth Brooks said."

"There's a real theologian," Jake said nervously. "What'd he say?"

"Some of God's greatest gifts are unanswered prayers."

At that moment, Lindsey turned and saw Cole, then Jake.

"She's spotted us," Jake said softly.

"Yep."

The two men continued toward the girl.

"Stay here," Cole cautioned.

Jake stopped and Cole proceeded. He could see now that Lindsey's backpack sat open at her feet. In her hand was one of her notebooks. Cole was now less than twenty feet away.

"Don't come any closer!" Lindsey yelled into the wind.

"OK," Cole called back. "What are you doing?"

"Cleaning house!"

"Your notebooks? Why?" Cole said inching forward.

"It's all over now. I don't need them. Where I'm going I can't keep them."

"That's not true. Please don't tear any more up. They are wonderful. They are part of your soul."

"I have no soul, or haven't you read your own paper?"

"Do you want to talk about what you've done?"

"What? You want to interview me?" Lindsey's anger reared its head.

"No, no, nothing like that." Cole was now about fifteen feet away."

"I hate people who complain. They have nothing to complain about." Lindsey tore out several more pages from the notebook she held, wadded them up, and threw them over the rail.

"Please don't rip out any more," Cole pleaded. "You killed Hanna because she complained?"

"She was going to send me away. Throw *me* away, just like my mother did."

"She thought the academy was a wonderful chance for you."

"No, she didn't. She just wanted me gone. I could see it in her eyes. She made a mistake, and she knew it."

"The others?"

"The guy in the park wanted sex. That was self-defense. The women all sniveled about how awful their lives were. Same with the drunk at the movies."

"And Claire?"

"I did her for your girlfriend."

"Kelly? But why?"

"I was sitting outside your door when she told you about the Lesbo hitting on her. I was there. I could hear you. Too much for you to handle?"

Cole stood staring at Lindsey. He couldn't think of what to say next, where to take the conversation.

"You're OK, though" Lindsey admitted. "You kind of understand me. Here's one for your story. You can't help but write this story. It's too good. I know, I wrote about it this morning already." Lindsey tossed the whole notebook over the rail. "My mom used to loan me out, rent me...for money, you know. When I was ten she sold me to this guy who made movies of me. I bled for three days. I ruined his big movie, his big break, so he threw me back. He wanted his money back! Funny huh? He tears me open and he wants money. Of course, the money was long gone. He beat the shit out of my mom. How's that for your story?"

"Lindsey, let's go get you some help. I understand your anger now, really I do. Please don't do anything foolish."

"You mean turn myself in! Hell, no! I want to stay here where I can see my city. Smell the air. I figured out after Hanna, the only way I can become immortal isn't by writing; it is by becoming a legend. I can see it now. Headline: 'Eight Ice Pick Murders – Killer Jumps from Golden Gate'!"

I must distract her, Cole thought. He could see Leonard Chin over Lindsey's shoulder approaching slowly, twenty yards away.

"Why an ice pick?" Cole blurted out.

"Don't get any closer! You don't think I feel you getting closer!"

"OK, OK."

"That's better! The ice pick idea? I read about it in the library. A killer for the mob in Chicago used an ice pick. I thought that was cool, frigid in fact. Besides, they're easy to steal."

Chin was now trotting toward Lindsey. Cole glanced at him. Lindsey turned and made eye contact. She grabbed her backpack and tossed it over the rail. In a smooth, graceful move her long legs projected her up to the rail, a graceful balance beam.

"Lindsey! No!" Jake screamed as he reached Cole.

Cole stood motionless as the girl weaved back and forth, flailing her arms out for balance.

"Write a good story!" Lindsey cried as she disappeared over the side of the Golden Gate Bridge.

Cole turned away. Jake and Leonard Chin ran to the rail and gazed down at the water. A cluster of colorful notebooks floated on the waves. There was no sign of the girl. After a few moments, there was a brief splotch of white water and a couple of seconds after that, a muffled splash.

"We need search and rescue! Jumper midspan," Chin called into the radio.

"Roger. On their way." A voice on the other end of the radio replied.

Cole stood with his hands on his knees, looking down at the pavement.

"You did all you could, Cole. She knew what she was going to do before we got here." Jake put his hand on Cole's shoulder. "Let's go."

"That's it? We walk away?" Cole asked.

"Justice is duly served. I'm glad she's dead. Jail was too good for her. I hope she rots in hell." Jake turned and walked back the way he came.

Cole stood and faced Leonard Chin. "So?"

"So…a mentally unstable kid who murdered eight people took a nose dive off the bridge. Given her mental state she would have spent several years in a psych unit somewhere and they would eventually let her go. Hey, she saved us all a lot of trouble."

"That's how you really feel?" Cole asked.

"No. That's the cleaned up, sensitive version for my buddy who just lost his wonderful friend and protégée, Hanna Day, murdered by the piece of shit that just went over the rail. You don't want to hear what I really feel." Chin walked around Cole and started for the toll booth and security office.

Cole watched the tourists gathering at the rail. They talked, shouted, pointed down to the water, took pictures. He refused to look. Overhead, he heard the beating blades of the search helicopter. Below, the roar of the approaching rescue boats titillated the crowd even further.

Cars whizzed by unaware of the events of the last few minutes. They would go about their lives untouched by the girl who loved to write, or the lives she so hatefully took. Cole wanted to talk to Hanna one more time. He wanted her to give him that magic smile after a smart remark. He loved the little pixie of a woman that kept him on task, cheered up, and laughing on days he'd have rather not.

Who was going to mourn Hanna's passing? She claimed she had no family, and there was no reason to doubt her. Cole thought of the delight in her eyes when Jake told him that he had come to take Hanna to lunch. She had found someone to love. Granted, tempered by the madness that was Lindsey, Jake was someone who was going to see Hanna through the turbulence.

In a moment of reflection, Cole thought of going to Stanford without Hanna. What an adventure for the two of them it would have been. He was so anxious to see her blossom in the heady world of academia. His plan for an Administrative Assistant desk plaque, the dinner at which he and Kelly planned to celebrate, even the excitement of Hanna finding an apartment on her new higher salary—these weren't the thoughts of a boss, but of a friend. He would miss her so.

What of Jake? Cole barely knew him, yet at this moment he couldn't help but ache for him in his grief.

The sound of a siren's short blast shook Cole from his thoughts. At the curb, lights rotating, sat Leonard Chin in his car.

"Get in!" Chin shouted.

Cole climbed in the car and with another short blast of the siren, they sped into the bridge traffic.

A half-hour later Chin let Cole out in front of his house.

Cole went to the living room and sank deep into the familiar caress of his overstuffed leather couch. He closed his eyes. What to do next? He must call Kelly.

"Hey, big guy! What's goin' on?" Kelly asked cheerfully.

"I have some bad news," Cole began. "It's Hanna."

"What is it?"

"She's dead, Kell."

"Oh, sweet Jesus. What? Oh Cole, how?" Kelly was crying.

"She was killed by Lindsey. Stabbed in the back of the head with an ice pick. Lindsey, if you believe it, was the Ice pick killer." Cole choked up and couldn't go on.

He could hear Kelly softly sobbing through the line and caught fragments of what must be a prayer. They sat, each holding a phone, neither moving, neither talking—just aware of the other's presence.

After several minutes Kelly said, "My darling, I am so sorry. I know what she meant to you."

Cole didn't respond, just sat with his eyes closed.

"Let me pray for you."

Again, Cole was silent.

"Heavenly Father, we come unto you with broken hearts. Our grief is beyond words and understanding. Please comfort my sweet Cole at the loss of his friend. Help us understand how such a cruel death could serve your master plan. We are so frail and death is so consuming. Soften this dreadful blow to our hearts and somehow draw us closer to you in the hour of our mourning. In Jesus name, I pray, Amen."

"Amen," Cole added.

"Do you want to talk about what happened?" Kelly asked softly.

"Not really, but I think I need to. Maybe it will help."

Cole took Kelly through the events of the morning. As he spoke the pain seemed to lessen. He stuck to the facts, almost as if he was writing a news story. Kelly only interrupted with questions twice.

He was glad when he came to the part of the story where Lindsey jumped, that he hadn't looked over the rail into the water. He stopped at that point and gathered his thoughts.

"You know, as angry and hurt as I am at Hanna's death. I can't hate Lindsey. I mean she had no right, no excuse, no justification for killing all those people." He paused. "Especially Hanna, but it's kind of like a crazy, mean, dog biting people. You don't hate the dog, you hate what it did. She was sick, deeply, mentally scarred and wounded, twisted by her circumstances and years of abuse. I feel sorry for her. I can't find a place in my soul to hate her. Does that make sense? Even on the bridge, I didn't want her to die."

"Your heart is in a good place if you can do that," Kelly said. "It makes perfect sense. I love you, Cole Sage. I am so sorry for your loss. So very sorry. Any chance we can get together?"

"Do you mind coming over here?"

"Of course not."

"I'll see you in a bit."

Cole turned and stretched out on the couch after Kelly's call. He closed his eyes and drifted off. He floated in that peaceful space between waking and sleeping. His lucid thoughts were of Kelly and her place in Sausalito. He pictured the deck, and the evening lights coming on in the city across the bay.

The sound of the phone broke his peace.

"Hello."

"Mr. Sage?"

"Yes."

"This is Marc Gromyko. I'm from the coroner's office."

"How can I help you?" Cole didn't want to deal with this call.

"It's regarding Hanna Day, sir. Lieutenant Chin informed me that you were listed as next of kin in Ms. Day's things they found in her apartment. Were you aware of that sir?"

"No, but it doesn't surprise me." Cole smiled. The thought was a comfort.

"The reason I'm calling sir is to find out if you will be making the arrangements for the body. It is my understanding Ms. Day is Jewish. If she was observant, that shortens our time for funeral arrangements significantly."

"It does indeed," Cole replied, not sure what to say.

"Then you will be making the arrangements, Mr. Sage?"

"I believe I am."

"That's good news. Please let me know as soon as possible which funeral home will be doing the service and I will do all I can on my end to assure a smooth transfer of your loved one. Thank you, Mr. Sage. And I'm truly sorry for your loss."

"Thank you," Cole said to an empty line.

When Kelly arrived and after more condolences and some much-needed cuddling on the couch, the subject turned to Hanna's funeral.

Who does a person call for a Jewish funeral?"

"A Jewish Funeral Parlor, I would imagine," Kelly replied.

Cole went to the other room and got his laptop. A Google search gave the names of Bay Area Jewish cemeteries and funeral homes.

Cole dialed the first on the list.

The man who answered spoke in soft, deep tones.

"My name is Cole Sage, I am not Jewish. I am, however, listed as a dear friend's next of kin. She was Jewish."

"My name is David Howitz, How may I be of assistance?"

"I understand that it is necessary to have the burial within twenty-four hours of death. Is that correct?"

"That is our belief, but it is an impractical consideration today. We try to hold to a three-day schedule. When was her passing?" Howitz inquired.

"Yesterday morning. It should be a very small affair. She has no family and only a few friends. I think the reasonable thing to do would be to have a graveside service only."

"Our people are a family, Mr. Sage." Howitz was almost condescending in his reply but Cole let it go by. "The service will need to be tomorrow then? I believe we can accommodate your request."

"Closed casket," Cole said firmly.

"That is all that is possible graveside."

"Good," Cole said.

"When will you come to select a casket?" Howitz asked.

"Tomorrow morning," Cole replied.

"How about tonight before eight o'clock?" The question was more of a command.

"If that's what's necessary."

"It is," Howitz confirmed.

"Then I will see you in a couple of hours."

"Tomorrow will be the service," Cole said turning to Kelly. "I will pick out the coffin tonight. Will you come?"

"Of course."

David Howitz was much more personable face to face. He was very gracious when he realized that Cole would bear the expense of the funeral. He volunteered the community Jewish organization that provided plots at no charge in the Jewish cemetery. Cole was relieved that the process was as pleasant as it turned out to be. Howitz assured Cole that everything would be attended to by three o'clock the next day. Cole signed the paperwork, guaranteeing payment. Howitz called the coroner, assuring the timely release of Hanna's body.

Cole and Kelly left the funeral home in just over an hour. On the way home, they stopped for Thai take-out. Cole spent the next hour calling Jake Salem, Leonard Chin, and Randy Callen, to tell them of the arrangements. He started to send an email to the staff of the *Chronicle*, but then changed his mind when he realized he didn't want anyone at Hanna's funeral except "family."

Kelly went home around ten that evening. Cole retreated to his couch. Even though he was emotionally drained he found it difficult to relax. He found it even more difficult to get comfortable. After a few minutes, he grabbed the pillow he rested on and rolled onto the floor. Wiggling and scooting he managed to rest his back against the front of the couch. He rolled the pillow and gave a great, heavy exhalation.

Thoughts and memories swirled round and round as Cole began to finally relax. In front of him, as clear as if she were standing there, he saw his soul mate, Ellie, at her funeral. Instead of his daughter, Erin, standing beside him, Kelly held his hand. As dreams will, time and events shifted before him. He was at Hanna's service. Instead of the rabbi, Ellie herself stood before the casket.

"My heart goes out to my beloved Cole," she began. "As he stands once again before the casket of someone dear to him. I loved Cole my entire life and to see his pain again is almost more than I can bear. Kelly, I know you will hold him near and comfort his aching heart. Be strong my beloved." The scene once again was Ellie's funeral and she seemed to fade into a sea of yellow daisies around her casket.

Cole slipped off into a deep sleep. Around dawn, he awoke with a start and made his way to his bedroom where he collapsed across the bed.

* * *

A sharp knock on the door and a series of rings from the bell brought Cole from the kitchen.

"Leonard," Cole said in genuine surprise.

"I didn't want to go alone. You mind?" Chin said hesitantly.

"Of course not. Come in."

"Cup of coffee?"

"I'd ask for something stronger but I know better," Chin teased.

"Cooking sherry?" Cole suggested.

"Coffee's good," Chin replied. "Heard from Jake?"

"Not today."

"I feel like such a jerk taking his gun and badge. But honestly, he was in such a dark place I could see him actually shooting that girl."

"Lindsey," Cole said.

"Lindsey," Chin repeated.

"I don't imagine they have found her body." Cole knew the answer but needed to hear it.

"No, and they probably never will. You know that. The tide is so strong that she was probably out beyond the Farallones by nightfall."

"Has anyone notified the mother or grandmother?" Cole was curious about how the notification would be handled.

"Grandma is so out of it, they didn't bother. The mother...now that was a different story. You really don't want to hear about that today. We'll save it for a later date." Chin smiled and Cole knew to change the subject.

"There you are, one coffee, black. Want to stay in here or go in the living room?"

"This is good." Chin took a seat. "I need to do something, and I don't want you arguing with me. I talked to May, my better half, and she agreed."

"What's that?" Cole asked.

"Here." Chin reached in his pocket and took out a small square of paper.

"What's this?" Cole could see it was a check. He looked at it for a long moment.

"Leonard, you didn't have to do this."

"It is an old Chinese custom that the village buries the dead, not the family. In old times the village men would take turns pulling the cart that carried the bodies to the place of burial. They believed during the ceremony the soul of the deceased is still present and would show their respect by putting money on the coffin or body if they were really poor." Chin cleared his throat. "We like to carry on traditions. You remember that when I take a bullet." Chin chuckled at his forced attempt to make Cole more at ease.

"This is most generous. And if Hanna were still with us I'm sure she would give you a huge hug."

"A hug from a ghost is bad luck."

Cole smiled and put the check in his shirt pocket. "Please tell May how grateful I am."

There was a rat-a-tat-tat on the front door.

"That will be Kelly."

The drive to the cemetery took longer than they anticipated. Traffic was heavy and there was a downed power line making matters worse. As they entered the huge cemetery there were several groups of people gathered for services.

They circled a large area with far fewer headstones and saw a black hearse, a small green tent, and a flower-draped coffin. Next to the casket stood a man in a dark suit with a beard and fedora, and across from him stood Jake and Randy Callen.

As they approached, the Rabbi said something to Jake and he nodded. Randy turned and gave the group a wave of greeting. Jake didn't turn around.

"So sorry we are late Rabbi, we…"

"Hanna is not going anywhere." The heavyset Rabbi smiled. "Shall we begin?"

Everyone in attendance nodded.

"I am not going to talk about 'tragedies like this' because as I understand, you are a group of policeman and journalists. So, you understand the evil mankind is capable of and you live with it on a daily basis. I am not going to talk about Hanna's faith because it seems she didn't really ascribe to any tenets of her upbringing."

The Rabbi stepped closer and took five carnations from the spray of flowers atop the casket. He came around the casket and handed one to Randy, Jake, Cole, Leonard, and Kelly. He moved back to his position before the casket.

"I want to talk to you today, instead, about yourselves. We have never met so I can speak with the candor of a stranger or as a man of faith. I will not describe the tenets of Judaism, as great and marvelous as they are. So…you can relax, I don't intend to convert you." The Rabbi smiled broadly.

"Today, I want to talk about your pain. In speaking with Jake and Randy before we began they told me about your friend, Hanna. It grieves me that I never met her because she was my kind of girl, bright, sassy, fun, a hard worker, full of energy, and caring. Isn't it ironic that the thing that killed her was her willingness to share her life, home, and love with the person who would take that life?

"This kind of death makes me angry. I feel a rage well up in me that makes me want to strike out. It is unfair, that your loved one has been stolen away from you. It is unfair that the woman who touched all your lives is never going to smile at you, joke with you, love you, again.

"I understand your grief. I lost my son to such a wanton act of hate. For a long while, I hated everyone and everything in this world. It nearly ruined my marriage, my relationship with my daughter, my congregation. Most terrifying was my faith, or lack of it, in the Creator.

"So you see, I have walked where you are. So, believe me when I tell you, the one that your anger hurts the most, is you. So, you ask, how does one let it go? By seeing this for what it was. Senseless. If you try to attach the reason of Man to it, you will come up short. We must—as painful and difficult as it seems—leave reason to God.

"I know what you must be thinking: Why did God let this happen? The answer is He didn't. It is the heart of Man turned from God that allows these things to happen. Just as you have the free will to turn to God, you have the free will to turn from Him. We all possess from birth a sense of right and wrong. It is a gift of God. How we use that morality is up to us.

"So, today as we lay this dear one to rest, let us vow to remember our love for her. Let us vow to not let our hearts turn to hate for the one who took her from us. Let us vow to turn to God's love for healing in this time of sorrow.

"If you will, make this sacred vow. Please place the flower, representing the love of your dear Hanna, with the others before you. That act will claim God's vow to be with you."

The Rabbi gently laid the flower he held on top of the casket. Kelly was first, followed by Cole, to lay their flowers down. Randy was next, tears were streaming down his cheeks as he placed his carnation with the others. Leonard Chin stood looking at the Rabbi. The Rabbi smiled and nodded as if to say, "I understand." Chin bowed deeply and added his flower.

Jake Salem stood stone straight, not moving, staring at the coffin before him. The party of mourners all looked straight ahead. The Rabbi bowed his head.

After several minutes of silence, Kelly moved around to where Jake stood and took his arm in hers. He didn't respond.

"Jake, we all loved Hanna. You just recently fell under her spell. She was very special to all of us, but you, my friend, are feeling a different kind of loss. Please, Jake, know that the God the Rabbi spoke of is real. He is there through our darkest times. Do not let this terrible loss darken your heart. Take Hanna's light and love and let it give you hope in humanity, not destroy it. Can I pray with you?"

Jake didn't move. Then he gently squeezed Kelly's arm with his.

"Heavenly Father," she began, "Our hearts are broken, our thoughts are confused, and pull us from what You would have us dwell on. Please be with Jake, comfort him, and wrap him in Your loving arms, and take this pain from his heart. Go with him when we leave this place, and draw him to faith in You. In Jesus name, we pray."

Jake turned and hugged Kelly, his broad shoulders quaking, as he sobbed from the depth of his being.

After a moment, Jake kissed Kelly's cheek. "Thank you."

Jake Salem stepped up to the casket and said in a loud clear voice, "I loved you, Hanna, like I hadn't loved anyone in years. You showed me that I could love again and be happy. I will miss you always. I vow before God and these friends, I will not let your death kill what you gave me: happiness."

Jake looked from side to side at the others who loved his special lady and smiled. As tears ran down his cheeks, he kissed the flower and placed it on the casket.

Chapter Fourteen

Cole fell fathoms into his leather couch. He would meet Kelly for dinner but for now, he needed time to think, reflect, and remember. His thoughts were interrupted with the ringing of the phone.

"Cole, it's Ben."

"Well, hello."

"How you doin', Cole?" Ben asked.

"It's been a rough couple of days."

"I have some news and I wanted to tell you myself before Mom or Erin spoiled it." Both men laughed. Then Ben continued, "I've decided not to go to Houston."

"That *is* news," Cole said in disbelief. "That's a Texas-size turn of events."

"This thing with Hanna made me realize, none of us knows how much time we have in this life. I just don't want to be that far away from mom, or you for that matter. Erin hasn't made her feelings a secret either. God has brought this family together from broken pieces. I will not be the one to tear it apart."

"You're a good man, Ben. So good, in fact, I would like you to be my *best* man," Cole offered.

"I would be honored. When?" Ben was the surprised one now.

"As soon as I can get your mom to do it. We've put it off long enough. All the planning in the world can be for naught in a second. I've learned that far too well this week."

"Can I tell Erin?"

"You're the Doctor. I think it would be a blessing all around. But, let me tell your mom first. Deal?"

"You got it. Thanks, Cole," Ben said softly, then the line was silent.

* * *

Cole forced himself to go to work on Monday. The empty desk where Hanna's cheerful welcome greeted him every morning looked like a tombstone. There were no pictures. She'd had no one. The few mementos seemed forlorn, without life or purpose. Cole looked at some of them for the first time. Perhaps they meant something to Hanna, but the rest of the world wasn't in on the joke. Did he even know her, really, he thought?

He picked up the notebook she kept. The last entry was "Dinner with Jake" and she drew little hearts at each end of his name. The poor dear, Cole thought, she finally found someone. He closed the notebook and went to his desk.

The first order of business was to contact Jim Tamarance at Stanford University. The decision was made, he would accept the job if indeed they would hire Randy Callen.

Cole looked down at the yellow pad where he scribbled the number. "Let's do this," he said aloud and dialed the number.

"Dean Tamarance's office." The woman who answered sounded friendly and welcoming.

"Good morning, Cole Sage for Dr. Tamarance."

"Oh, yes, Mr. Sage, I was told to expect your call and I'll put you through right away."

Cole heard a click, a ring, and then: "Good Morning, Cole. First of all, let me say how dreadfully sorry I am to hear about Ms. Day. It must be a tremendous loss."

"More than I realized. I think it's just starting to really sink in."

"I can only imagine. Is there anything I can do to help?"

"That is very gracious, but I'm afraid she was one of a kind." Cole felt a wave of emotion come over him. He cleared his throat. "I would like to accept your offer if it is still open."

"We feel that you are one of a kind as well, and we will be thrilled to bring you into our Stanford family." Tamarance's voice betrayed his pleasure.

"Just to clarify, my assistant Randy Callen will come on board as well? That was verified?"

"Absolutely. You will have a support team of three. Mr. Callen, of course, and then it will be your decision as to whether you want an actual secretarial position filled or an administrative assistant. Academically, you will have your choice of applicant Doctoral candidates as a teaching assistant. Your tutorage and serving on their advisory committee will, of course, be credited as one of your courses. I am so pleased you've decided to come on board."

"I am humbled and honored to be accepted into such prestigious company. I am truly grateful."

"Can we meet this week sometime?"

"You name it. My calendar will be free beginning tomorrow."

"How about Wednesday morning at ten?" Tamarance asked.

"Perfect," Cole replied.

"See you then!"

"See you then," Cole agreed and hung up the phone.

"Well, isn't that something. You hear that, Mick? I'm teaching at Stanford!" Cole said looking heavenward. "Betcha didn't see that coming!"

Cole could just see Mick Brennan, his old boss, and mentor, sitting at his desk at the *Chicago Sentinel*. "Not bad, son, not bad at all." Cole wished Mick could have lived to see it.

He punched four in-house numbers into the phone.

"Research."

"Randy, this is Cole. Can you come up and see me?"

"On my way."

"Thanks." Cole set the handset in its cradle.

He pulled the bottom drawer of his desk open and took out a yellow note pad. While he waited for Randy to arrive, Cole reviewed several pages of notes, sketches, and diagrams. The pad was covered with both pencil and ink writing and scribbled-through paragraphs. Ten pages of Cole's future. To anyone else, it would be a bunch of illegible phrases, circles, asterisks, underlines, and arrows.

To Cole it was a master plan, a manifesto or thesis, to guide the rest of his working life. Near the top, written in clear, bold, black felt-tip pen, and underlined twice, was the name, Randy Callen. It was the plan Cole sketched before the Stanford offer and the changes of the last week.

"Hello," Randy said, standing in Cole's office doorway.

"Come in, please." Cole waved Randy Callen to the chair in front of his desk.

"How you doin'?" Randy said somberly.

"Kind of in a funk, to tell the truth. I miss that crazy assistant of mine. I never knew how much I cared for her...." Cole let his words drift away.

"It is going to be weird."

"Let's agree to carry on like she would want us to. We both know she would give us a good scolding if she saw us moping around."

"I can almost hear it now: 'Would you two quit sucking on lemons! We don't have time for pity parties!'" Randy laughed at his own impression of Hanna.

Cole smiled, still unable to get to a laugh. "So let's change the subject!"

"I detest the new management. Thank goodness I'm in a basement, or I might jump out the window." The remark was meant to be funny. It wasn't. "How's that?"

"How long have we known each other?" Cole asked.

"Well, I've been here five years. I think we met, I don't know, six months before?" Randy frowned wondering where this was going.

"Are you happy with where you live?"

"Not really. I have three roommates with whom I could definitely do without. Why do you ask?" Randy leaned back and pulled a crumpled packet of gum from his pocket. "Want one?"

"Not for me, thanks. If it is not too personal, how are you set, financially I mean? Could you afford to move?"

Randy shrugged. "My grandma left me a little bit. I still have all of it." Randy rubbed his face with his deformed hand. "You know something I don't know, Cole? You breaking a fall or something here?"

Cole tapped the ring on his right hand on the table twice, then raised his hand, fingers spread wide. "There are fewer than five people in the world I trust who aren't family. One, I just buried." Cole folded down his index finger. "Another is sitting in front feet of me. You, my friend, are the thumb." He snapped his hand to a thumbs up. "I can always count on you to give it to me like it is: good, bad, stop, go, insane idea or solid thinking. As a researcher, you have never let me down. Your willingness to do your Internet snooping, well, we'll keep that between us."

Randy tried to speak, but Cole stopped him with a raised palm.

"Look, I am a banana that is starting to turn brown, around here. I pretty much—no, I totally—

blew off an assignment the new editor gave me. I think down deep I wanted him to fire me. It's time for me to quit. I've been offered a teaching job at Stanford. I need to—what is it they always say about Madonna?—oh, yes, reinvent myself."

"That's what they say." Randy grinned wondering what might come next.

Cole lifted the yellow pad. "This is my parachute. This is my idea. Now, it may be as realistic as a kid in Kansas trying out for a surfing team. I may be imagining things differently than the way they work in the real world. That's where you come in."

"I'm in." Randy sat up straight, his body language left no doubt he would jump with Cole.

"You better look before you leap," Cole chuckled. "I appreciate your spirit, but the parachute might have some suspension lines missing. It might even have holes in it."

"What are you thinking?"

"This is the digital age as you're always telling me. There are websites everywhere with news and commentary. Blogs, podcasts, stuff like that, right? They all require writers. Is it possible to do one of those things of my own?"

"You could do them all on your own," Randy replied.

"But do they, can they, make money?"

"Depends on who you are. Let's take inventory here: famous, award-winning journalist, opinionated, good talker (that's for the podcast) passable looks." Randy smiled. "Seems to me you've got the bases covered."

"What does it take? Moneywise, what is the investment?"

"Time, consistency, not getting bored and quitting, and a faithful, tech-genius-sidekick, to put it all together. When do we start?"

"I already told Stanford I won't come without you," Cole said.

"Me? At Stanford? Are you kidding?" Randy was dumbstruck.

"I told them you're the best researcher I've ever worked with. I don't think that they even blinked before they said you were in," Cole reassured him.

"I don't know what to say."

"Don't say anything. Back to the other idea; could an online venture really earn us an income, a real income? Because I am willing to walk out that door right now, but I still gotta work. If this teaching thing goes south…." Cole's uncertainty was showing.

"I'm good for six months. How long can you go without a check?" Randy asked.

"A while longer than that," Cole replied. "But *you'd* still have a job."

"Not without you. We're a team. We got this, Cole. You'll have to produce a lot of copy. Weekly blog entries, podcasts, interviews, twitter feeds—there will be a lot of balls in the air. Downside: you'll have to edit and proof your own stuff. That's way above my pay grade."

"The writing isn't a problem, and I can get more interviews than we could ever print. It's an election year don't forget. But the editing and proofing—that's my Achilles' heel…make that leg!"

"So, you hire a grad student." Randy gave a confident shrug.

"I was going to ask Hanna to go with us." Cole raised his eyebrows.

"She would have loved it." Randy grinned.

"So how's tomorrow look? To walk, I mean."

"You're serious, aren't you?" Randy said. "Yeah, sure. Why not!"

Cole laughed. He needed it. "Did you ever see *Zorba the Greek*? Great old movie. There's a scene where Anthony Quinn—he plays Zorba—approaches Alan Bates, an English guy, and asks him to buy him a ticket to the next island. The Englishman is stunned by the request and says to Zorba, 'Why would I do that?' Without missing a beat, Zorba says, 'For the hell of it! Haven't you ever done anything just for the hell of it?' The Englishman buys him a ticket. That scene reminds me of us." Cole laughed again.

His analogy was lost on Randy. "How's that?"

"This, my son, is your Zorba moment!"

* * *

Cole knocked on Kelly's door. He stood waiting, a bouquet of daisies in hand, thinking how lucky she was to house sit such an incredible place. He smiled at the thought of having the woman he loved living on Lombard Street. He turned and watched a pair of cars rolling down the "crookedest street in the world."

The door opened behind him and Kelly said, "There's my sweetie!"

Cole turned, thrusting the flowers forward, and smiled.

"What a pleasant surprise. They're beautiful! You're early." Kelly threw her arms around Cole's waist and hugged him.

"Guess that means I can come in?" Cole said.

"I have been thinking about you all day. I was about to call and see if you wanted to have take-out." Kelly took him by the hand and led him inside. "Are you doing OK?"

"I'd been lying if I said I was doing fine. I really missed Hanna today. I actually called to her once. I felt so foolish," Cole said making his way to the couch.

"When someone is part of your life, and you spend so much time with them, their death doesn't just erase them from your heart and mind," Kelly said. "I remember once after Peter died, I was watching a movie on TV and asked him what the guy just said in the movie. I even looked over at his chair, expecting to see him there. It's hard. I'm so sorry you lost your friend."

"I wonder if I'll ever get over feeling somehow responsible."

"There is no way you could have known. No way. You wanted to help the girl become a writer. Hanna took her in. Big difference there. You are not responsible in any way for what happened, my darling." Kelly was seeing a crack in Cole's vulnerability, one he had never exposed before.

Hanna's death took a far greater toll on Cole than he would even admit to himself. The death of Erin's mother, Ellie, as painful as it was after their short reunion, was a kind of closure and healing for Cole. He carried her in his heart so long and so deep, no one else ever touched the memory of her love or the sorrow of his losing her. For more than twenty years, that small corner of his heart was locked and kept him from his finding happiness.

Everything Cole built in the last five years seemed to be crumbling around him: his job and the loss of Hanna. The loss seemed a monument to the mortality he felt he was immune to. The joy of Ben turning down the job in Houston, his own teaching position at Stanford, most of all his engagement and marriage to Kelly—these events should all be cause for celebration and elation.

Yet, for the first time in his life, Cole was seeing the end. The tape at the finish line seemed to be just beyond the horizon. Retirement, old age, sickness, death—things that no longer just happened to other people. If he took care of himself, he may have twenty, twenty-five more years. Then again…both his parents had passed before they turned sixty-five.

While driving to Kelly's, Cole made a vow that he would live his life differently—stop and smell the roses, as they say. He would marry Kelly, spend a few years teaching, enjoying the new media platform Randy would create, see Erin and her family more, and watch Jenny grow.

"Kelly, let's get married," Cole blurted out.

Kelly smiled and held up her right hand. She wiggled her fingers showing Cole her ring. "We are. Remember?"

"No. I mean right away. Now. Why wait? I want to, you want to, let's do it."

"What brought this on?"

"Time. It is a finite thing. I don't want to waste any more of it without you next to me. Morning and night I want to be beside you, begin and end my day for the rest of my life with the one I love."

"Oh, sweetheart," Kelly began to tear up.

"Oh, now don't start that. I asked Ben to be best man. I told him I want to do it pronto. He loved the idea."

"You thought this through, huh? This isn't just some spur-of-the-moment thing?" Kelly seemed genuinely surprised at Cole thoughtfulness.

"Of course! Look, when I start at Stanford, I won't be able to drive from where I live now. You're here temporarily, right? We need to find a place near Palo Alto. Which will be cool because we'll be closer to the kids than we are now. It will be a fresh start. A new life for both of us. What do you say?"

"Gosh, I don't know…."Kelly goaded Cole.

"Huh?"

"Well, yes of course!"

"OK. Let's plan on it. Could we have the ceremony like, on a Sunday after church?" Cole asked.

"What a wonderful idea! We could have a lunch reception in the Fellowship Hall!" "A lot of your friends will already be there. We can invite whoever."

"What about your friends?"

"I think they can both make it," Cole teased.

"I'm being serious, Olajean, and your detective friend in Chicago, Tom. Who else?"

Cole ignored the question and went on. "The morning worship band can play a song or two, or not. The pastor is already there, right. Seems easy."

"It sounds perfect! I'll call him tomorrow."

"Call him now, book a date," Cole insisted. "You two are friends, right?"

"You really want me to?"

"Yeah, why not?"

"Why not, indeed!" Kelly reached for the phone.

* * *

Cole woke ready to take on the world. He literally jumped from the bed, sang in the shower, ate a bagel and, to celebrate, he made himself *two* mochas. The mix-CD in the stereo seemed the perfect soundtrack for his drive to work. He sang and pounded out rhythms on the steering wheel, totally oblivious to the heavy traffic and the idiots who darted in and out of the lanes in front of him.

Cole got to work fifteen minutes late. Nobody noticed. He asked the janitor he passed on the way to his office to bring him a few boxes. One would be for Hanna's things. The rest he would use to pack his few belongings. When Cole left work the night before, his leather shoulder bag was bulging with all of his notebooks.

Randy volunteered to download all of his document files to a flash drive and back them up on his system at home.

"Mr. Sage, I could only find these," the janitor said from the doorway of Cole's office.

"That will be great," Cole said, giving the janitor a big smile.

"You movin' offices? Nobody put it on the work order."

"I am, but don't worry, I can take care of it myself."

"Nobody is supposed to do any moving, or switching of offices, or furniture unless the proper paperwork is turned into Building Maintenance." The janitor was showing irritation at Cole's failure to comply with procedure.

"You are absolutely right. I will take care of any paperwork that is necessary." Cole was not going to let the janitor spoil his mood.

"I just don't want to get my butt chewed out because you didn't follow the rules."

"I guarantee no one will do any chewing. I promise." Cole smiled reassuringly.

"Alright then." The janitor grumbled as he turned and walked away.

Cole worked quickly while trying not to look too closely, as he cleared Hanna's desk of anything personal. Items that seem to have no meaning went in the waste paper basket. He gave her desk and its drawers one more quick look, then he put the lid on the box. He took a thick black felt tip pen from the top drawer and wrote 'Hanna' on the lid.

It only took one box to finish clearing his office. He did, however, fill three wastepaper baskets with a collection of mail, magazines, and office memoranda.

Cole sat down and put his feet up on his desk. He would rest a few minutes and then give Faraday the news of his departure in person. He tried to think of anyone else in the building that he might like to say farewell to. There was no one.

He reached over and picked up the phone and rested it on his legs. The number he dialed was ingrained in his memory, so much, in fact, he almost didn't see the buttons he was pushing.

"Chin."

"Leonard? Cole."

"How are you doing?" Chin asked respectfully.

"I think I'm going to be OK. I just wanted to let you know not to call me here anymore."

"New rules about personal calls?" Chin asked, not quite sure of the context.

"Nope. I'm leaving."

"You get fired?"

"Have you no faith in me, sir?" Cole said in his best Dixie Colonel accent.

"When did this happen?"

"In about five minutes from now, after we hang up. I thought I better let you know in advance."

"I'll be damned. So, what's next?" Chin was reeling with the news.

"I've taken the job at Stanford, teaching journalism."

"You told them?"

"I certainly did." Cole laughed. "Don't sound so surprised. They called, asked me, I thought it over and said yes. A logical pathway to change."

"Fantastic! Good for you!"

"Thank you. The other reason I called is that I need your home address so I can send you and your wife an invitation to the wedding."

"I should have recorded this call. I would love to hear it again!" Chin chuckled merrily.

The two friends chatted a bit more and then stopped when Chin got another call.

* * *

Cole walked right past the secretary to Faraday's big walnut door.

"Hey, you can't go in there!"

"Wanna bet?" Cole replied as he opened the door and walked in.

Faraday was reading a magazine with his feet up on his desk. Seeing Cole, he threw down the magazine and jumped to his feet.

"What the hell do you think you're doing? You can't just barge in here any time you want!" Faraday shouted.

"Just did," Cole replied.

Cole walked toward the desk. The much smaller man defensively took a step back.

"What do you want? I'm busy!"

"I saw. What are the Kardashians up to these days? Getting robbed again?"

"I have had just about enough of you and your smart ass 'I-own-the-place' attitude. Contract or not, you can only push me so far!" Faraday's face was flushed with anger.

"You are standing awfully close to the window," Cole quipped.

"What?" Faraday shouted.

"Nothing," Cole chuckled.

"If it weren't so damned expensive I'd, I'd...." Faraday was literally spitting in feline fury.

"That's what I came to talk about. I really do have an ironclad hold on you. I figure with salary and benefits on the remaining two years and odd months, your firing me would not look good on your new and improved bottom line. So here's my offer, cut me a check for fifty thousand dollars, we tear up the contract, and I walk."

"Hell no! I'll fire you for insubordination!"

"You're the one screaming. Matter of fact, they probably can hear you in the lobby. Your word against mine. I just claim a hostile work environment. I'll win. There are some twenty people outside that door listening to you scream at me."

"I really hate you Sage and everything you stand for!"

"Oh, come now."

"Madeline!"

"Yes, sir." In moments the secretary was at the door glaring at Cole.

"Have a check cut for fifty thousand made out to Mister Sage. Get me his contract. Now!"

"That wasn't so hard, was it?" Cole remained calm and smiled politely at the man who just lost the battle.

Cole stepped forward and grabbed the top of one of the heavy leather chairs facing Faraday's desk and dragged it to the corner of the room.

"I'll wait." Cole smiled. "Finish your reading."

Faraday spun around and faced the windows.

It took less than ten minutes for the secretary to return, check in hand, contract at the ready. She approached her boss with the folder containing Cole's contract.

She whispered something to Faraday that Cole couldn't hear.

"Thank you, Madeline," Faraday said.

"If there's nothing else…." The secretary slipped quietly toward the door. She paused for a moment trying to decide if she should close it, after a second or two she left. The door remained open.

"This is it." Faraday held up the folder. "Void it."

"Cole approached the desk. He took one of the pens from an elaborate desk and looked down at the open folder facing him. In large double stroke letters, Cole scribbled, "void."

"Now, sign and date it."

"Not that I don't trust you." Cole put his hand out.

Faraday grudgingly handed Cole the check. Cole examined it closely. The correct amount, and bearing two signatures, it was legal. In quick bold strokes, Cole signed and dated the voided contract.

"It has been...." Cole seemed to taste his words. Then changed direction: "That's that."

Faraday snatched the signed document and spun around and faced the windows again, arms folded across his chest like a petulant child.

* * *

As he approached his office Cole felt distant and removed from any emotion or sense of belonging. It was over, he was done, finished. He picked up the box he packed with the only things he would take with him other than memories. He didn't look around, pause to reflect or have any pithy last remarks to the room he had spent so many hours in. He turned and walked out.

Hanna's box of possessions sat dutifully waiting just as she had. Cole put the box he held on top of her box. Suddenly struck with a whimsical thought, he rounded the desk and got the big felt tip pen from the top desk drawer.

A big smile crossed his face as he began to write in big thick letters, first on the top box, and then the other. He picked up the boxes and started toward the elevator. As he passed the cubicles, and open work areas, people began to stand, point, smile, and then applaud.

Cole nodded and smiled as he received comments and good wishes. He hit the "down" button with the corner of the bottom box. Inside the elevator, he had another inspired thought. He hit the button for the floor below. As the doors opened he looked out at the real workings of the paper: advertising, billing, circulation.

As he approached the first person in his path Cole smiled and said, "Can you direct me to Tim O'Malley?"

The woman pointed to an alcove along the far wall. Cole's boxes got the same reaction as upstairs except the people on this floor were even more enthusiastic, giving him thumbs up, and pats on the back as he passed by.

O'Malley was on the phone when Cole entered the alcove. Upon seeing Cole, he immediately hung up.

"Nice message."

"Thanks. I just wanted to come by and say, it *was* a sucker bet. I would have won." Cole grinned.

O'Malley laughed heartily and stood. Cole set the boxes on the corner of a desk as O'Malley extended his hand. The two men shook hands and gave each other knowing smiles."

"As we Irish are prone to say: "May the sun shine warm upon your face, and may the Good Lord hold you in the palm of His hand."

"And may you find yourself in heaven an hour before the devil knows your dead!" Cole picked up his boxes and smiled. "Be seein' ya."

The lobby was empty except for security guard Craig Simmons. As Cole approached him, Simmons said, "You leaving us Mr. Sage?"

"Yep," Cole said turning the message on the boxes so Simmons could read it.

The guard began to laugh. "Good for you!"

Cole Sage left the *Chronicle* the same way he came in, through the front doors, his head held high, and a smile on his face. As he approached the tall glass doors he paused for a moment to look at himself in the reflection. For just a second he held the boxes a little higher and nodded. As he read the message on the boxes, he knew he was doing the right thing.

NOT FIRED.

QUIT!

THE END

COLE MINE

Exclusive sample from Book 8

ONE

Kelly Mitchell found herself in a strange and wonderful new world, a world she only read about in books and magazines. She was on a mission, and for that, she was willing, even eager, to step outside the safe world of her Lombard Street apartment and venture into a place she could only find with the guidance of Google and the GPS on her phone, *Rosenberg's Kosher Deli*.

Her fiancé, Cole Sage, loves kosher food. The robust flavors of Eastern European Jewish cooking were a go-to source of gastronomic pleasure, second only to ravioli and ice cream. He often told Kelly of his love of kashe varnishkes, square potato knishes, kishke covered in paprika sauce, thick pastrami sandwiches with a dill pickle, and how he missed his favorite Chicago delis.

It was a special occasion, his birthday, and for that, she was pulling out all the stops and spread a table with all his favorites. As she pushed the door open and slipped into Rosenberg's, the smell of fresh bagels, rye bread, and steamed cabbage brought a wide smile to her face.

Cole, you're right again, Kelly thought.

"Hello, pretty lady, what can I do for you today?"

"Hi. A special birthday dinner!" Kelly said brightly.

The little man behind the counter flashed an elfish grin. The naughty twinkle in his eye didn't go unnoticed by the feisty Ms. Mitchell. He was well into his seventies and looked as if he enjoyed every year of it. His wiry salt and pepper hair was cropped much shorter than his massive white mustache.

"Any dinner with a lady as pretty as you would be special. What's on the menu?"

"I was hoping you could help me with some ideas. My fiancé likes kashe varnishkes. Do you have them?"

"Does a one-legged duck swim in circles? Of course. Next?"

"How about kishke?"

"Who is this lucky guy? What kind of sauce?"

"My fiancé, Cole Sage. I think you know him. Paprika?" Kelly asked.

"Perfect! I should have known! Cole and I have been friends since he came to San Francisco. For a Gentile, he's got an awfully Jewish palate."

The tinkle of the bell above the door sounded, and the color from the little man's face behind the counter drained. Kelly turned to see four skinheads enter the deli. Their hair was buzzed short, nearly shaved, and they all wore similar clothes: heavy black lace-up boots; jeans rolled above the boot tops; white T-shirts with various punk bands; and black, quilted cloth, waist length jackets. Various anarchy and swastika patches covered the fronts of the jackets. They were trouble, and Kelly knew it.

"Irwin! Old buddy, how ya doin'?" The greeting was less than friendly.

Kelly turned to see the man behind the counter reach for a long knife. She hoped he wouldn't be foolish enough to try and take on these thugs.

"We told you nicely we didn't want your rat-infested Jew food in our neighborhood. You don't seem to get the message. And what's with trying to call the cops? Tsk, tsk not friendly. We gave you the chance to move peacefully, but now you have hurt my feelings. If you had American food, I might order something." The young man's voice was kind and friendly, but his words and demeanor were ominous and threatening as he smiled wickedly at the old man.

"I haven't got time for your foolishness!" Irwin said boldly.

"Oooh, tough little Jew."

"Get out!" Irwin shouted.

The leader of the group pulled a foot long black object from behind his back. In the blink of an eye, the black tube turned into a nearly three-foot-long chrome baton with a marble-sized knob on the end.

"Now, that is not friendly. You act like you don't want to serve red-blooded, white Christian Americans. Is that what this is, Irwin?" the tallest of the four said, stepping forward.

A boney, pimple-faced kid of about eighteen stepped back and stood with his back to the door. Heavy boot planted firmly against the bottom corner, he crossed his arms and grinned at Kelly.

"What do you think this is?" Kelly demanded.

"We don't need any lip from a rich Jew bitch. Just shut up!" the thug with the telescopic baton shouted.

"I'm not Jewish, not that it matters; I was raised Baptist. I see no fruits of being a Christian in your behavior or insulting mouth. I think you and your buddies need to go and pick on somebody your own size."

"Look, old lady…"

"Old lady? That's it, you little punk. Go home!" Kelly's face burned with anger.

The leader bounced the baton on his shoulder as he glared at Kelly. In a swift, powerful swing he brought the baton forcefully down on the curved glass in front of the deli case. He pulled back for a second attack before the sound of exploding glass stopped echoing through the small shop.

"Stop it!" Kelly screamed, stepping in front of the raging young man.

Without hesitation, he shot his fist through the air, hitting Kelly hard just below her right eye. The blow knocked her off her feet, and she landed hard against a rack of bread and bagels, hitting the back of her head. She rolled as it toppled and lay motionless on the floor.

Blow after savage blow, the row of deli cases exploded into shards of thick glass.

"Hatichat Hara!" Irwin yelled, swinging the large butcher knife.

"You want some?" the baton-wielding thug screamed, jabbing at the old man.

"I'm not afraid of trash like you! You are not American, you Mamzer!"

"Speak English, Kike!" The thug laughed fiendishly.

As Irwin swung the butcher knife ineffectively at his attacker, the two other thugs methodically used their cupped hands and forearms to scrape the shelves in the shop bare. As they plowed through the store, they stomped and kicked cans and shattered jars in every direction.

Kelly tried to get to her feet, and the baton thug gave her rump a hard kick with the sole of his boot. "Don't even think of getting up, bitch!" he said, kicking Kelly with a crushing blow to the ribs. "Done?" Baton shouted toward the back of the store.

"Just about!" came a reply.

Reaching the back wall, the pair finished emptying the shelves, took old fashioned bottles of Cel-Ray and began throwing them across the store, watching them explode against the wall. Not satisfied with their destruction, they began smashing the fronts of the coolers.

Irwin came from behind the counter to meet his Goliath head on. In a flash of chrome, the baton came around and struck the valiant old man in the side of the head just above the ear and sent him to the ground like a hundred-pound bag of Passover cake meal.

"That should do it!" Baton shouted. "Let's go!"

The doorbell tinkled, and the first of the four exited the shop. As Baton reached the door, he took one last mighty swing and knocked the little bell off the wall.

Kelly rolled and tried to clear the fog in her head, but the pain in her side made her nearly pass out. Rising, she saw the crumpled form of the sprightly old merchant, now small, frail, and motionless. She half-crawled and half-rolled over the broken glass to where he lay. She turned him slightly and felt for a pulse. He was still alive.

"Thank God," she whispered.

Fumbling in her purse, Kelly felt for her phone. Unable to find it, she angrily dumped the bag's contents on the floor. Grabbing the phone, she pushed 911 and waited.

"There's been an attack at Rosenberg's Deli. The owner is hurt, send an ambulance."

Kelly dropped the phone. She gently raised Irwin's head enough to cradle it in her lap as she leaned against the shattered display case. Her anger brought tears of rage as they rolled down her throbbing cheek. She closed her eyes and gently stroked the old man's head as they waited for the ambulance.

About the Author

Micheal Maxwell has traveled the globe on the lookout for strange sights, sounds, and people. His adventures have taken him from the Jungles of Ecuador and the Philippines to the top of the Eiffel Tower and the Golden Gate Bridge, and from the cave dwellings of Native Americans to The Kehlsteinhaus, Hitler's Eagles Nest! He's always looking for a story to tell and interesting people to meet.

Micheal Maxwell was taught the beauty and majesty of the English language by Bob Dylan, Robertson Davies, Charles Dickens, and Leonard Cohen.

Mr. Maxwell has dined with politicians, rock stars and beggars. He has rubbed shoulders with priests and murderers, surgeons and drug dealers, each one giving him a part of themselves that will live again in the pages of his books.

Micheal Maxwell has found a niche in the mystery, suspense, genre with The Cole Sage Series that gives readers an everyman hero, short on vices, long on compassion, and a sense of fair play, and the willingness to risk everything to right wrongs. The Cole Sage Series departs from the usual, heavily sexual, profanity-laced norm and gives readers character-driven stories, with twists, turns, and page-turning plot lines.

Micheal Maxwell writes from a life of love, music, film, and literature. Along with his lovely wife and travel partner, Janet, divide their time between a small town in the Sierra Nevada Mountains of California, and their lake home in Washington State.